All I Want for Christmas is a Fake British Boyfriend

A SWEET AND STEAMY CHRISTMAS IN THE CITY ROMANCE

LILI VALENTE

All Rights Reserved

Copyright **All I Want for Christmas is a Fake British Boyfriend** © 2025 Lili Valente

All rights reserved. Without limiting the rights under copyright reserved above, no part of this publication may be reproduced, stored in or introduced into a retrieval system, or transmitted, in any form, or by any means (electronic, mechanical, photocopying, recording, or otherwise) without the prior written permission of the copyright owner. This romance is a work of fiction. Names, characters, places, brands, media, and incidents are either the product of the author's imagination or are used fictitiously. The author acknowledges the trademarked status and trademark owners of various products referenced in this work of fiction, which have been used without permission. The publication/use of these trademarks is not authorized, associated with, or sponsored by the trademark owners. This e-book is licensed for your personal use only. This e-book may not be re-sold or given away to other people. If you would like to share this book with another person, please purchase an additional copy for each person you share it with, especially if you enjoy hot, sexy, emotional novels featuring firefighting alpha males. If you are reading this book and did not purchase it, or it was not purchased for your use only, then you should return it and purchase your own copy. Thank you for respecting the author's work. Editing by Sandra Shipman and Kelly L. Cover design by Angela Haddon.

All I Want for Christmas is a Fake British Boyfriend

BY LILI VALENTE

About the Book

I came to London to plan a Christmas gala—not to end up half-naked under a streetlamp with a gorgeous stranger. And definitely not to find out, once the photos go viral, that he's a member of the royal family.

Now I'm a tabloid punchline, my client's panicking, and my perfectly planned holiday has gone straight to scandal.

The solution? Pretend we're dating until the cameras lose interest.

Simple. And nothing Emily Darling, social-media whizz, can't handle.

Except Oliver isn't the snotty aristocrat I expected. He's funny, kind, unfairly sexy—and a Christmas nerd just like me.

We're supposed to be faking it, but somewhere between the cocoa and the carols, London starts to feel like magic...and Oliver starts to feel like home.

But when a new viral headline makes me question everything, **I find myself at Heathrow with a boarding pass, a broken heart, and a question only the man shouting my name across the terminal can answer**—*Is love really all around?*

***All I Want for Christmas Is a Fake British Boyfriend** i*s a sparkling, laugh-out-loud, deep-feeling holiday rom-com full of fake dating, royal mayhem, cheeky kids, cheekier grandmothers, puppies in need of adopting, and the kind of love story that makes even a Grinch believe in miracles.

To the new year—and every soul determined to fight for what's still good and beautiful in this broken world.

Chapter One
EMILY KATHERINE DARLING

A woman determined to live out her wildest "Love Actually/Bridget Jones/The Muppet Christmas Carol" fantasies with the best Christmas in London EVER!

(If she doesn't have a nervous breakdown first...)

The businessman in 12B is glaring at me like I'm the Grinch who Stole His Peaceful Transatlantic Flight, and I've been aboard the plane all of ten seconds.

To be fair, I *did* just smack him with my giant purse while wedging my emotional support binders into the overhead compartment. But it's not my fault that Premium Economy has less than premium storage capacity.

"Sorry, so sorry," I mutter as I Jenga a Louis Vuitton

bag, a battered ukulele, and some kid's stuffed panda to make room for my roller bag.

What part of "reserve the overhead bins for rolling luggage" didn't these people understand?

Gah! If only people would follow the rules, life would be so much easier.

And I would be sweating *soooo* much less.

The plane is approximately eight thousand degrees, my wrinkle-resistant Nan Baylor blazer is already doing its best Shar-Pei impression, and the Valerian Root capsule I took in the airport bathroom to "relax me for the flight" has done nothing except make my tongue feel chalky. Meanwhile, my phone is buzzing like a swarm of bees, and the businessman is clearly not pleased to see me laying hands on his ukulele.

Or maybe that's *his* stuffed panda.

If so, he should keep it on his lap or tucked beneath the seat in front of him, where it belongs.

I finally wedge my rolling bag into place and collapse into my window seat, pulling out my phone to see a string of new texts from Maya.

> Maya: Did you remember the emergency binders?
>
> Maya: Remember, technology hates you and likes to explode when you touch it. 💀 Especially when you're nervous. If your laptop dies again, and you don't have the binders, we're screwed, Em. Seriously screwed.

Maya: If you forgot them, tell me ASAP, and I can overnight them to your hotel. Yes, it will cost a small fortune, but better safe than sorry. We have to nail this one and stick the landing.

Maya: Don't freak out, but I just found out that Willow and Stone is pitching Fletchers, too. Apparently, they pulled in a favor from Willow's godmother in Kent, who knows someone who knows the people who used to plan the Fletchers' holiday gala in the 80s. God, I hate them so much! 😡 🤢 😠 Who do they think they are? Trying to take OUR gig!?

Maya: I mean, sure, they planned a Met Gala afterparty that went viral…

Maya: But that's only because Beyoncé showed up!

Maya: BEYONCÉ, EMILY! HOW DO WE COMPETE WITH BEYONCÉ? 😩 We're going to go bankrupt, aren't we? Why did Titan have to sell to an evil global conglomerate ten days after we signed the lease on a new office? TEN DAYS! If we'd known we were losing our biggest client, I would not be sitting in this stupidly fancy office right now. I hate it here!!

Maya: Except that I love it because this view of the Brooklyn Bridge, welcoming the dawn while I sip espresso, is giving me life.

> Maya: But I also hate it because I hate uncertainty and risk. But we're still genius party planners and businesswomen, right? 😬 You'll land the Fletchers' gig, I'll lock down the Rousseau wedding in the Hamptons, and we'll be sitting pretty for another year. 🎉 Right?
>
> Maya: This will be fine.
>
> Maya: So fine!
>
> Maya: FOR THE LOVE OF MY HOLIDAY SPIRIT AND SANITY, JUST TELL ME THAT IT WILL BE FINE AND YOU DIDN'T FORGET THE BINDERS!

I type back: *Hey, just finished boarding. The binders are tucked safely into the overhead bin, and I couldn't be more prepared if I were triplets. Relax! We're going to be fine.*

I think...

The "fine" part remains to be seen—losing our biggest client to a soulless conglomerate that doesn't believe that Instagram-perfect parties are good for their bottom line has been a serious blow—but I've been preparing for this meeting with one of London's oldest, swankiest department stores for six weeks.

My PowerPoint has thirty-seven slides with embedded video montages from the viral Brighton wedding that landed me the interview in the first place. I've memorized the names of every Fletchers' executive, their assistants, and their assistants' dogs. I know that James Landford-Fletcher, the CEO of events, prefers Earl Grey to English Breakfast and that his wife collects

Royal Doulton porcelain figurines. I've studied British charity gala traditions in general (and the Fletchers' holiday gala in particular) like I'm cramming for the citizenship test.

Which, considering how much I want to live in the U.K. someday, is pretty much a matter of life or death.

I'm as ready as someone who has never had a pop star show up at one of her parties can be.

Hopefully, that will be enough...

The plane lurches into motion, and I grip my armrest, already counting the hours until I can stress-eat my weight in Cadbury Dairy Milk. Not only is the U.K. a beautiful, majestic, historically significant place I adore, it's also home to the Fruit and Nut bar, a sugary treat that heals all wounds.

When my ex-best-friend uninvited me to her wedding our senior year of college because her future husband had decided I didn't "match the aesthetic"—aka was too pudgy to look good in a lineup with the other tall, scrawny bridesmaids from our sorority—the Fruit and Nut bar was there.

When my boyfriend dumped me via WhatsApp two days before the biggest wedding of my life last summer, Cadbury held me together.

And when our contact at Titan Media wrote to deliver the devastating news that they were cancelling their six-figure contract with Darling Events, my remaining UK chocolate stash gave me the strength to keep going against all odds.

All things considered, I'm actually holding up pretty well.

Still, when we reach altitude and the flight attendant crackles over the intercom, thanking us for flying Brit Air and wishing us a "Happy Christmas season," my soul doesn't soar the way it usually would.

That familiar flutter in my chest just isn't there.

Even at twenty-eight, the word "Christmas" is usually enough to make me feel like a kid again. Growing up, the Darling family did the holidays right. Even when we were traveling for one of my little sister, Isabelle's, figure skating competitions, my parents made the season magical. December was a time for binging our favorite holiday movies, eating an obscene number of cookies, and dancing around the living room to Mariah Carey while we decorated the tree.

Once Isabelle and I were grown, the celebration had to be scaled down to a long weekend, but we still have an amazing time celebrating as a family.

This is actually our first Christmas apart…

Once I realized the Fletchers' meeting would have me in London through the holidays, Isabelle made plans to celebrate with her fiancé's family in Switzerland, skiing some large, scary mountains. (Much to the dismay of her Olympic coach, who has threatened to throw himself off a bridge if she breaks one of her perfect figure-skater legs swishing down the slopes.)

Wondering how the "not breaking a leg" is going so far, I connect to the plane's WIFI, smiling as I see the montage from *@IsabelleTheIceQueen* at the top of my social media feed.

My baby sister is the furthest thing from an "Ice Queen," but it's a great user name for a professional figure skater.

And if you don't know her personally…

Well, she certainly looks ice queenly enough online. At five nine, with naturally white-blonde hair, dazzling blue eyes, and bone structure a ballet dancer would kill for, she looks like she was born at a pricey European ski lodge. In reality, we were both born at the same hospital in suburban New Jersey. She just happened to inherit my maternal grandmother's Swedish supermodel genes, while I got the "hardy stock who survived the potato famine" DNA from my father's side.

I am the short, chubby, red-haired foil to her Nordic perfection, a fact that might have left psychological scars if Isabelle and I weren't thick as thieves. But since the day Mom laid my baby sister in my three-year-old arms, I've been her fiercest protector, and she's been my biggest fan.

It's a fact she's proven yet again by being the first to heart my "heading to London" post from earlier this morning.

I heart her post, too, even though her fiancé, Olin Nilsson the Third, is a rich, snobby dweeb who's unworthy of my adorable baby sister. Still, she seems happy with her speed skating main squeeze, and the internet worships them.

Her post is only a few hours old, but the likes have already hit the high four figures, with my mother weighing in at the top of the comments—*Have an amazing time, baby! Daddy and I miss you so much! Sending all our love and hoping we'll be together for the holidays next year.*

I blink faster, fighting a wave of guilt.

It's *my* fault the Darlings aren't together this year. Mom promised she understood, and that she and Dad were looking forward to their Caribbean Christmas cruise, but…

Well, I can't help but notice that she hasn't liked my airport post yet, let alone commented. The thought that I might have caused my favorite people pain—even teensy, tiny "first world problem" levels of pain—makes my stomach hurt.

Am I the Heartless Career Girl who Ruined Christmas, in addition to The Grinch who Wrecked 12B's flight?

Should I write my parents a conciliatory email? Send apologetic gifs to the group chat? Arrange to overnight some Cadbury to the house before they leave for their cruise, even though Dad's trying not to overdo it with the sweets this year?

*Stop being crazy and focus. The only thing worse than missing family Christmas for work would be missing family Christmas for work and **not** landing the gig.*

The Inner Voice is right—I can't afford to be emotional about the holidays right now. I have to be locked in, creatively loaded, and ready to deliver the party planning pitch of my life.

Shutting down social media, I pull out my trusty notepad and pen.

Making a list is always my favorite way to self-soothe in times of trial.

WHY THIS LONDON TRIP IS GOING TO BE GREAT!

(AND IS NOT EVEN A LITTLE BIT DOOMED)

1. You have AN ENTIRE WEEK to interview vendors, woo the celebrity florist, and finalize sample menus before the meeting with Fletchers.

That's plenty of time to recover from jet lag and be ready to wow the client in ways a client has never been wowed before.

2. British people love Americans (Source: Hugh Grant movies and that guy at the pub last summer who said he loved the way you said "aluminum.")

3. The Brighton wedding was NOT a fluke, and any imperfections were due to Fate, not personal folly. The seagull incident was beyond your control, and the groom should have known better than to wear a poorly secured toupee.

4. The Winthrop Mayberry is a fantastic hotel: v. chic, v. British, v. good WiFi. (Also v. close to favorite bakery in case emergency scones are needed in addition to emergency chocolate.)

5. Belinda Moore, AKA The Botticelli of Bloom, has agreed to squeeze a meeting into her insanely crowded holiday schedule. That's basically a yes. Otherwise, why waste her precious time? You'll see her first thing, seal the deal, and secure your ace in the hole. When Fletchers sees that you've landed THE florist, they'll have no choice but to declare you THE planner. This is basically math, and not even girl math. It's also science, as proven by the Proximity Principle. Note to self: Those psychology classes were NOT a waste of time, even though you changed your major Junior year.

6. Willow and Stone landing a pitch meeting has NOTHING to do with your talent and everything to do with nepotism. Additional Note to Self: In your next life, arrange to be born into a well-connected family. Or at least a British family, so that you won't have to worry about how you're going to secure dual citizenship. Also, arrange to have fewer sweat glands. Why are you so sweaty? Did you remember to put on deodorant?

7. You did. You smell fine. You ARE fine. This is all fine. Now, recline, relax, and try to get some rest.

Tucking my trusty notepad away, I wrap my travel pillow around my neck and close my eyes, doing my best to clear my head.

But my thoughts won't stop spinning.

After all, landing this job would only be the beginning. This gala is *the* event of the year for Fletchers and attended by the crème de la crème of London Society. It's white tie, steeped in tradition, and almost aggressively British. They've *never* let an American planner take the lead.

If I'm hired, I'll be paving the way—or poisoning the well—for my entire nation, and a year isn't *that* long in the elite party planning world.

I'll have just twelve months to transform a Georgian ballroom into a world of Dickensian elegance—where candlelit refinement meets the immersive enchantment of a midwinter fairytale forest. I've already had graphics made to match my theme, as requested by Fletchers. They want to announce the new event theme (and planner) after the holidays, while everyone's feeling festive and generous.

It's smart, locking in sponsors while they're high on Christmas spirit and looking for tax write-offs.

But what if they don't like the "gilded mirror as a portal to fairytale magic" imagery? What if they want something new at the last minute? My graphic designer is a boss, but she's also a mom to three, counting down to Christmas. What if I have to find another artist at the last minute? Yes, I have a backup, but he's not nearly as reliable, and he *also* has young children.

What if he's busy, too?

Why didn't I make sure I had a backup to the backup?

And maybe a *backup* to the backup to the backup, just in case?!

My eyes fly open, panic dumping into my bloodstream as the flight attendants push the beverage cart into Premium Economy.

"Would you like something to drink?" the taller one asks in a round, cozy English accent I'm pretty sure means she's from the north somewhere.

I force a smile. "Coffee, please. All of it? And a water, no ice?"

If I can't relax, I can at least use these hours trapped in a chair to my advantage.

As soon as the drink cart passes, I fetch my binders—earning myself another glare from 12B as I rearrange the ukulele, which has already shifted in flight. I ignore him, but silently decide that maybe ukulele players *aren't* all whimsical people who love Hawaii and cute instruments, after all.

Two hours in, I've reorganized the binders twice, practiced my pitch beneath my breath until I'm pretty sure I could recite it backwards, and eaten every bite of my bangers and mash with a small side salad.

I'm reviewing vendor contracts and their various deposit requirements with my third cup of coffee—bless the stewardess and her generous, caffeine-giving heart—when the captain's voice fills the cabin.

"Ladies and gentlemen, we're expecting some turbulence over the next few minutes. Please return to your seats and fasten your seatbelts."

Turbulence?

My gaze darts to my very full, very *uncovered* cup of coffee, which is still far too hot for me to gulp down in a prompt or efficient manner.

Pulse spiking, I begin gathering my paperwork, tucking it back into the appropriate padded, waterproof binders as quickly as possible when—

The plane drops.

I bleat like a startled sheep, watching in horror as my coffee goes airborne.

A beat later, the binders follow.

And then...

Well, then, I'm covered in coffee hot enough to make me gasp and prove the guy in 12B was right all along—I *was* a travel disaster waiting to happen.

And the waiting is now over.

Chapter Two
EMILY

As the plane continues to rattle and lurch, weeks of color-coded, cross-referenced, laminated perfection explode across Premium Economy and into the back of First Class.

"No," I mutter, stomach bottoming out as I reach for my seatbelt. "No, no, no!"

Before I can unbuckle, the plane does its best broken elevator impression, dipping down so quickly, the entire cabin lets out a collective gasp, and my bottom actually leaves my seat.

Wow! Okay.

Unbuckling is *not* the play right now.

Not unless I want to know what it feels like to be smashed against the ceiling along with that Gantt chart I spent hours perfecting...

I'm forced to stay put, clinging to my armrests as the chaos intensifies. Soon, my presentation is spreading like a Type A plague intent on infecting the entire plane, and people rows ahead are batting away airborne vendor quotes.

After the longest three minutes in the world, we stabilize—much to the relief of the woman begging the Mother Mary to spare her life somewhere behind me. The second we're permitted to unbuckle, I dive into the aisle on my hands and knees, coffee-soaked pencil skirt riding up as I hurry to rescue crumpled papers from beneath seats and shoes.

"Sorry, could you please lift your... Yes! Thank you, sorry! Yes, that's mine, so sorry." I army-crawl toward first class, where I've spotted one of my mood boards wedged under a Gucci loafer. "Oh my God, my color story," I whimper, throat tightening as I scuttle faster.

Suddenly, the first-class stewardess materializes in front of me, ready to defend her territory against incursions from the slobs in the back. "Ma'am, please return to your seat."

"I just need to grab my mood boards," I beg, still on my hands and knees. "The sunset rose fabric swatches are irreplaceable! It's a unique lot made of recycled fast fashion. Please, I'll be so quick, you'll hardly notice I'm there."

With a curl of her lip that assures me I look as disastrous as I feel, she moves aside, and I crawl on.

Five minutes later, I'm back in my seat, clutching the tattered remains of my perfectly prepared presentation. Some pages are coffee-stained. Others bear shoe prints from passengers who accidentally trampled my dreams. Still others managed to fold themselves in half sometime during the G-force attack.

And to top it all off, my favorite blue pen exploded while I was trying to make a "How to Clean Up this Mess" list.

I look like I murdered a Smurf with my bare hands and am kind of wishing someone would throw me in Smurf jail, if only to spare me the anxiety of figuring out how to put Humpty Dumpty back together again.

I spend the rest of the flight running damage control with wet wipes, my lucky Sharpie, and the fabric glue I keep in my purse for fashion emergencies. The nice flight attendant brings me extra napkins and a fresh coffee—with a lid on it, this time—and even the guy in 12B looks like he's rooting for a happy ending for me and my binders.

But by the time we prepare for landing, I've accepted that my backup plans now look like they were mauled by a T. rex with a caffeine addiction.

Then, as if the universe feels compelled to remind me that *my* career isn't the only one on the line, Maya texts during our taxi to the gate.

> Maya: How was the flight? Are you safe and sound on the ground yet? Did you get any sleep?

> Me: I didn't, but it's fine. I'll sleep when I'm dead.

And I will.

And hopefully, I'll get to carry this binder disaster to the grave with me.

I can't tell Maya the truth. At least not right now. There's nothing she can do to fix the problem, and sharing the bad news will only make her even more stressed out than she is already.

No, this is something I have to carry—and problem solve—on my own.

Inside the terminal, Heathrow Airport greets us with all the warmth of a maiden aunt who never wanted children, the passages chilly and nearly abandoned, even though it's not quite seven o'clock.

I shuffle through Passport Control, trying to look like a sane, professional human being despite the ink stains and coffee splatters.

Still, the immigration officer eyes me suspiciously. "Business or pleasure?"

"Business," I say, a little too aggressively, as if I'm trying to convince us both.

He arches a dubious brow, but eventually grants me a stamp and opens the gate. "Right then. Welcome to London."

Baggage claim is where my travel dreams often go to die, and tonight is no exception. My infamous bad luck with bags is why I always pack spare outfits in my roll-on, but still! A red sweater with dress pants, underthings, a single pair of pajamas, leggings, a sweatshirt, and the suit I'm currently wearing are not nearly enough to get me through several weeks in London!

I watch the carousel turn, willing my bag to appear. Around me, everyone else reunites with their luggage like long-lost lovers while I stand there, increasingly alone, watching the same lime-green suitcase go around seventeen times.

Finally, I have to admit that my Big Blue Baby isn't coming.

The Stella McCartney dress I couldn't afford but bought anyway. My happy Christmas holly skirt and matching sweater. My entire capsule professional wardrobe. They're all missing in action, lost to the aviation gods who hate me nearly as much as the technology ones.

The baggage attendant hands me a claim form with the pitiless gaze of someone who deals with despair so often she's grown numb to human suffering. "We'll text you as soon as we locate your bag. If you haven't heard anything in a week, feel free to call customer service." She gestures vaguely toward the bottom of the slip. "Be sure to keep your claim number handy."

A week. Great.

If they're *saying* a week, it will probably be two, and that's if it turns up at all.

Looks like I'll be doing some shopping I can't afford as soon as the stores open tomorrow.

I briefly consider popping into the airport bathroom to change before my evening meeting with Belinda, the florist, but it's looking sketchy out there—dark and blustery with plenty of snow. I don't know how backed up traffic will be in this kind of weather, and it seems best to get to where I need to be first and worry about the Smurf murder/coffee stain situation later.

Hopefully, I'll be able to change when I get to the pub, and if not...

Well, punctuality is more important than appearances.

Right?

The taxi ride is another qualifying event in the Travel Drama Olympics, as my cabbie careens wildly along the slick streets in the driving snow. London cabbies are usually the safest, classiest drivers in the world, but this man seems determined to keep my fight or flight response fully activated.

Still, I can't help admiring the view as the city streaks by.

London is even more charming in December. Every building is draped in strings of lights, and Christmas markets and tree stands seem to pop up on every corner. It's everything the movies promised—garlands wrapped around lampposts, shops full of nutcrackers and Father Christmas figurines, and the smell of roasted chestnuts somehow penetrating through the closed windows.

This is the Christmas I've dreamed about since I was a kid. All my favorite holiday movies are set in London— Bridget Jones' Diary, Love Actually, The Muppet Christmas Carol, with honorable mention to The Holiday, even though it pops back and forth between the U.S. and the U.K.

If I live through the night, I'm looking forward to wandering the streets in the daylight, soaking up the incomparably festive atmosphere.

But the way this ride is going, living isn't something I'm taking for granted.

By the time we reach the suburb where I'm meeting Belinda at a pub, I'm sweating despite the chill and have already stress-eaten half the Cadbury Dairy Milk I bought at the vending machine near the taxi station.

"First time in London, love?" the driver asks, probably because I haven't stopped gasping every time he swings around a blind corner.

"No, I've been here before. Lots of times." I sip in a breath, refusing to gasp again as he zips through an intersection, barely avoiding a man in a wool cap walking his dog.

"Aw, then you know how much fun we have at Christmas," he says cheerfully, as if he hasn't just narrowly avoided a vehicular manslaughter charge. "Grabbing a pint is a brilliant way to start your holiday."

"I'm actually here on business," I clarify, clinging to the door handle when his next right threatens to fling me across the seat. "Starting at the pub. I'm meeting a woman who's already there. Also, on business. It's an all-business night. No pints. I-I mean, probably not. Unless she wants to have one, I guess. But mostly business. Primarily."

Nailed it.

Definitely should have forced myself to take a nap on the flight.

The driver nods slowly, the way you do when you suspect a stranger might not be all there. "Right. Sounds like you've got it all sorted. Here we are, then!"

He slows in front of a Tudor-style building draped in white lights. Its wavy glass windows glow warmly on the otherwise darkened street, and a massive wreath hangs beneath a sign that reads "The Crown and Thistle" in a gorgeous gold font. It looks like a place where Christmas miracles happen all the time.

I feel my spirits lift. Surely, this is where bad travel days go to die and beautiful new beginnings are practically guaranteed! I swear, as I pay the driver and step out into the winter chill, I can *feel* my luck turning around.

My reflection in the darkened dress shop window next door assures me I still look like an electrocuted hedgehog in a wrinkled suit, but it's late, and I just got off a long flight. Belinda will understand.

Heck, we might even share a laugh over it.

Already imagining how we'll commiserate over a cup of tea as we plot floral domination, I wave the cabbie off with a smile and drag my roller bag toward the entrance. Still grinning, I push on the center of the door, right in the middle of the world's prettiest wreath.

A jolt of discomfort hits almost instantly as the heavy wood refuses to budge. I push harder, then try pulling—then pushing and pulling again—feeling increasingly silly.

And increasingly frustrated...

"This has to be it," I mutter, glancing up at the sign.

Yep, The Crown and Thistle. This is definitely the place. And I can hear muffled music—"Silent Night" in high, childlike voices—coming from inside.

I check my phone: 8:28. I'm over half an hour early for my meeting and, according to the small plaque by the pub door, it's still several hours until closing time.

I yank on the door again, putting my full weight into it.

Still nothing.

The snow is coming down harder now, already coating my hair and sneaking into the collar of my coat.

Maybe I'm at the wrong entrance?

Dragging my wheelie bag through what's becoming a proper snowdrift, I circle the side of the building, cold and damp seeping into my sensible heels. By the time I reach another door under a softly glowing lamp, my pantyhose are soaked.

This door doesn't have a sign and looks much less like a main entrance than the other, but it gives slightly when I push. Beginning to suspect both doors are swollen from the weather or something, I lean my full weight against it, shoving hard.

One more good push, and I should—

The door flies open, and I tumble inside, quickly realizing that, as I suspected, this is *not* the main entrance. I actually appear to be on a small stage at the back of the pub, where a nativity play is currently underway.

A play I am *ruining* with my terrible timing...

I try to stop myself, dropping my roller bag and digging my heels into the floor, but it's too late to halt my forward momentum. I barrel into the center of the manger scene, summoning shouts of surprise from the crowd below. My shouldered purse takes down a shepherd and clips Joseph before I trip over a stuffed animal, and my feet leave the floor. I hear one of the kids cry out in surprise seconds before I crash land in the middle of a baby Jesus made entirely of gorgeous white blooms.

I only catch a quick glimpse of the petalled Messiah as I fly through the air, but it's enough to assure me he's truly a work of art.

Or he *was*, before I crushed him.

Petals and wire explode all around me as I land flat on my back at the foot of the stage, confirming this night will go down as one of the worst nights of my life.

Bar none.

"Bloody hell! That scared me!" a little girl in a blue veil shrieks above me, before dissolving into hysterical laughter.

A female voice from the audience shouts, "Carina, don't swear," just as one of the shepherds I *didn't* knock to the ground bursts into tears. Joseph, who can't be more than seven or eight, clamps a hand over his mouth and runs off stage, muttering something about being sick.

"I'm so sorry," I tell the girl before glancing toward an audience of what seems to be London's poshest parents.

They're all holding mugs or martinis and wearing the kind of richly textured "casual" sweaters that cost more than the contents of my suitcase.

Most look stunned, a few seem to be vaguely amused, but the woman with pink-streaked hair storming toward the stage does *not* look happy.

Not happy at all.

"How could you?" she seethes, her eyes shining as she mounts the steps to the stage.

"I'm sorry, Mummy," the little girl in blue says. "I didn't mean to say a bad word."

"No, not you, darling. Her," Pink Hair says, thrusting a hand my way. "You! You destroyed it. The entire sculpture. Twenty-seven hours of labor, and we didn't even get a proper shot of it all before you barreled in and ruined everything."

"I'm s-sorrry," I sputter again as I pick myself up off the floor, brushing stray petals from my coat sleeve. "I was just trying to—" I flap a hand toward the other side of the pub. "But the door was locked, or stuck, and I couldn't—"

"And there's no time to remake it before the actual nativity tomorrow night," Pink barrels on. "This was just the rehearsal." She sniffs and wipes at her cheeks. "Now, we'll have to use a doll like every other school pageant."

"Oh no, Belinda, really?" a velvety voice sounds from the audience. "We've already told everyone that the baby Jesus would be something special this year."

Belinda?

Oh God...

Oh no, that means Pink is—

"I'm sorry, but there isn't time, Caroline. Not with all

the other holiday obligations I've already made." Belinda's voice could freeze vodka as she glares at me, still standing in the middle of the botanical crime scene. "Speaking of holiday obligations, I won't be making any with you. You're Emily Darling, aren't you? The party planner? From America?"

I nod sheepishly. "Yes, but I—"

"That's what I thought," she cuts in, her cheeks flushing pinker than her hair. "We won't be working together. Ever. Come on, Carina. We're leaving. Now."

She grabs her wide-eyed daughter and sweeps out. The rest of the parents follow suit, collecting their various biblical characters and guiding them toward the front door, which seems to be functioning perfectly for everyone else.

Within minutes, the pub has mostly emptied, leaving just the bartenders, a few old men by the fire, who are regarding me with the kind of judgment usually reserved for people who fart in church, and one well-dressed man still sitting in the corner.

Even considering the dramatic circumstances, I can't believe I didn't notice him before. He's strikingly handsome in an aristocratic sort of way, all sharp cheekbones, luminous skin, and perfectly tousled dark hair.

He looks like the kind of guy who commands a room with a word, an impression he confirms as he murmurs in a rich, slightly smug voice, "Well, you certainly know how to clear a room, don't you, Red?"

I'm trying to formulate a comeback that doesn't involve sticking out my tongue or bursting into tears when my heel catches on a string of fairy lights. I go down again, this time taking a stuffed cow posed at the edge of the stage down with me.

I thud down three stairs to the main floor of the pub, landing with a soft grunt of pain.

From my new position on the floor under the cow, I hear Slightly Smug clucking his tongue like I'm the saddest thing he's ever seen.

London—two falls and a professional fail.

Emily—zero.

Chapter Three

THE HONORABLE OLIVER DAVID DAWSON FEATHERSWALLOW

A man looking for his missing Christmas spirit and, sadly, not finding it at the bottom of a whiskey glass...

The evening started predictably enough...

Mother sends her third text about tomorrow's charity luncheon—*Please confirm for tomorrow at your earliest convenience, darling. Edward's receiving the service medal. Your presence is required, Oliver. Not suggested. REQUIRED. And they'll have Christmas pudding. You love a Christmas pudding*—which I ignore while nursing my second Macallan at my usual table.

I needed a night away from it all, and The Crown and Thistle is the perfect place.

It's quiet, charmingly dilapidated, and far enough from Mayfair that I'm simply "that odd bloke who brings a novel to the pub," not "the Featherswallow spare." The regulars are a mixture of geezers who worked at the textile mill before it closed and young professionals raising families in the outrageously expensive flats that now fill the former factories. Both are too well-bred, too drunk, or both to acknowledge that they know exactly who I am.

And my favorite bartender, Reggie, has perfected the art of shooing away the random tourist who's wandered too far from the city center and starts pestering him about the Viscount in the corner.

I'm *not* the Viscount, of course.

I'm The Honorable Oliver David Dawson Featherswallow, a title befitting a secondborn son. My older brother, Edward, is the Viscount.

He has been since last Christmas, when our father passed away...

I take another slow sip of my whisky, gaze drifting to the holiday lights strung along the stage, where a group of local children are slogging their way through a nativity play rehearsal, overseen by Belinda Moore, supermom, small business boss, and florist to the London elite. The perky piano player in the far corner transitions smoothly from one Christmas classic to another with a skill that would usually warm my cockles.

I've always adored the holidays.

Just like my father.

We were the ones who set out at dawn on the first of December each year, tromping through the woods around our country estate until we found the perfect fir for the drawing room. As a boy, I'd watch father chop down our tree and "help" carry it home by riding on his shoulders while he pulled the cart. In later years, our roles reversed. Father would watch, sipping hot tea from a thermos, regaling me with tales of how much he loved hunting these woods with *his* father as a boy, while I took my turn with the axe.

He was ten years older than my mother, seventy at the time he passed, and enjoyed a merry, meaningful life. He adored his wife, his children, his work, and his hunting dogs, and passed peacefully in his sleep the day after his last happy Christmas.

The people who loved him couldn't have asked for a better end for the sweet man who glued our quirky, sardonic, often feelings-averse family together.

I miss him like a vital organ, and strongly suspect Christmas will never be half so happy without him.

Still...

My father wouldn't want me to cringe at the sound of children's voices lifted in holiday song. He also wouldn't want me to keep my mother in suspense, even if I *have* already confirmed my attendance at the luncheon.

Twice.

Fetching my cell from my vest pocket, I tap out a quick text to the Dowager Viscountess Vivian Marie Featherswallow, a well-meaning woman who can't resist the urge to manage her grown children—*Of course, I'll be there, Mother. Promptly at noon. Wouldn't miss it. I will, however, be demanding half your pudding as tribute. The pine scent they pipe through the halls at Spencer House makes me hungry.*

A moment later, Mother types back—*Not a problem at all, dear. You know I don't have much of a sweet tooth.*

See you, then, and please shave immediately before you come. You look a bit villainous when the whiskers start to grow in, and we wouldn't want you to frighten the ladies. There will be so many nice young people in attendance. Including that lovely Kelly Campbell you went with at Oxford. What a handsome young woman she is, Oliver. And so accomplished. I heard she's a partner now at Frederick and Swan.

I sigh, beginning to rethink the wisdom of texting Mother after five p.m.

She tends to be in a matchmaking mood after dinner. And now that she has Edward happily married off, I'm the sole focus of her efforts to ensure her sons are prepared to continue the family line and fulfill our duty to God and country.

I'm sure, once Edward and Matilda produce an heir, she'll ease up a bit, but until then…

Well, until then, thanks to a string of abdications and a tragic mountain climbing accident, I am still fifth in line to the throne behind my brother's fourth. Far enough away that becoming "King Oliver" is about as likely as Swallow House sinking into the sea, but not impossible.

After all, our country estate in East Sussex isn't far from the shore, and ocean levels rise every year…

With a gentle roll of my eyes, I assure her—*Yes, I will be freshly shorn. But I will not be asking for Kelly's hand in marriage as she's currently dating Hannah, her old rowing teammate, and is no longer interested in men.*

Mother sends back a thumbs up emoji, and—*How lovely for her. There are so few men like your father on the market these days. Young women have to find happiness where they can.*

I'm briefly tempted to explain that some women

simply prefer women—whether a "man like my father" is available or not—but decide it's best to quit while I'm ahead. Mother's actually open-minded for a woman of her age and upbringing, and any text thread that ends without her setting me up on another awkward date is a good one in my book.

I've just tucked my phone away and reached for my copy of Great Expectations—a favorite holiday reread—when the children launch into an especially ear-shredding version of Silent Night.

I love a holiday carol, but good God...someone should have told the tone-deaf shepherds in back to lip sync and tiny Mother Mary to keep her volume to a more respectable level.

Fighting a wince, I scan the assembled parents, but they don't seem to care that their progeny won't be winning any talent awards.

They actually look chuffed to be here. Tired, but chuffed, which seems to be the norm for modern parents. Most of my friends with children are perpetually exhausted, even with night nannies and maids who come in several times a week to take care of the washing and housework. I can't imagine how an average family without the funds to hire help manages it all.

And due to the circumstances of my birth, I will never have to find out. Should I find my perfect match and start a family someday, the way Father assured me I would, I'll be able to afford all the nannies and diaper services London can provide. Not only do I receive a healthy income from our family holdings, but I'm also the owner of a successful architecture firm, specializing in sustainable housing solutions.

It's how I found The Crown and Thistle.

Those unreasonably expensive lofts that now fill the old textile factories? My design and the project that launched my firm to national acclaim eight years ago.

All in all, I am a very lucky man.

Very, *very* lucky.

But this holiday season still feels painfully dreary, no matter how many lights I string on my tree.

My thoughts are turning back to the morbid, back to my father's hand cold in mine, and last January, the most miserable month of my life thus far, when it happens...

Suddenly, the door at the back of the stage flies open, and a woman catapults into the pub like she's been shot out of a circus cannon.

In a blur of red curls and flying luggage, she barrels into the nativity scene. Her wheeled bag catches on a wiseman's cane, sending the poor boy sprawling, and her oversized purse swings wide, taking down a shepherd on her way to center stage. There she trips over her own feet and takes a tumble...

Directly into the manger.

The baby Jesus, a Belinda Moore floral masterpiece, I was just thinking looked silly surrounded by children with leaking noses dressed in sheets, explodes on impact. Petals burst upward like glitter in a snow globe, wire springs leaping in every direction as the woman lands flat on her back in the hay.

Slowly, the floral rain settles atop her, making the poor thing look like she's been attacked by a wedding bouquet. Her hair—that profusion of red—fans out around her like a Pre-Raphaelite painting. She seems to have broken a shoe, and her skirt has twisted up to reveal ripped tights and the start of an ugly bruise.

For a moment, everything freezes.

The audience stares.

The wise men and shepherds gape.

Even the stuffed cow looks vaguely offended.

Then the child playing Mary starts giggling maniacally while shouting "bloody hell," Joseph makes a break for the loo, and Belinda—poor, perfectionist Belinda who did the flowers for Edward's engagement party and still hasn't forgiven me for being forty minutes late—looks ready to commit justifiable homicide.

Red scrambles to her feet, babbling apologies in an accent that I peg as Manhattan by way of New Jersey. I recently finished staffing my New York office, and that clipped, "no time for niceties" cadence is still fresh in my memory. A scan of her wrinkled clothing reveals an ink stain, brown patches on the pale gray wool, and stray tufts of cotton, possibly from a wise man's beard.

All in all, she looks like she's been through a war.

One she lost.

Still, her smile is warm and appropriately apologetic. She doesn't seem to be completely mad, but you wouldn't know it from the way Belinda snatches her daughter away, like Red's carrying a virus she suspects is catching.

After announcing that she won't be working with Red—*ever*—she sweeps out of the pub, little Mary in tow. Within moments, the other parents follow suit, fetching their semi-traumatized offspring, bundling them into coats and wellies, and guiding them out into the storm.

Soon, the pub has emptied of respectable society, leaving just me, Reggie, and his busboy, and the old fogeys by the fire who haven't moved from their spots since 1987.

And, of course, the American disaster standing in the wreckage of baby Jesus, blushing such a bright, fetching pink, I can't resist teasing, "Well, you certainly know how to clear a room, don't you, Red?"

Her head snaps toward me, and I get my first proper look at her face. Green eyes flash with indignation, freckles dust her upturned nose, and the stubborn jut of her chin makes it clear that she's prepared to do battle. She's beautiful and fierce and still blushing in a way that makes her eyes seem to glow in the dark.

And, God help me, I'm suddenly more excited to be out of my apartment than I've been in months.

I'm waiting with baited breath, eager for the dressing down this curvy firebrand is poised to deliver, when Misfortune strikes again. Red opens her mouth, preparing to unleash what I'm sure would have been a scathing retort. But before she can speak, her foot catches on a string of fairy lights.

The universe, it seems, isn't finished with her just yet...

Down she goes again, arms windmilling, taking out the stuffed cow as she thuds down the stairs. She lands flat on her back with a grunt that might have been concerning if she didn't immediately stomp her foot into the floor and exhale an outraged huff, proving she's still in one piece.

Once again, I can't seem to help myself...

"But your commitment to destruction is admirable." I cluck my tongue in only slightly mocking sympathy. "And thorough."

She surges to her feet with surprising grace for someone who's fallen twice in five minutes. One heel is definitely broken, her skirt is twisted so badly the back zipper is in the front, and there's straw mixed with the petals in her hair.

Still, she faces me with the dignity of a queen as she breathes, "Thank you, sir. I try to be thorough in all things. And who are you exactly? The pub peanut gallery?" She glances around, her eyes widening theatrically. "Don't you have a child to fetch home? Or are you drinking alone on a Monday with no one to talk to except down-on-their-luck strangers who have already been humiliated several times tonight?"

"Touché." I raise my glass in acknowledgement of her point. "Yes, I was drinking alone, but only while I waited for the entertainment to arrive. And I must say, you've exceeded expectations. Do you do birthday parties? Or do you specialize exclusively in terrorizing nativity plays?"

"I'm not sure, yet," she mutters, hitching her purse back on her shoulder as she tugs at her skirt. "Seeing as I've just torpedoed my shot at hiring the best florist in London, I might need to explore other career options." She sniffs, her gaze still fixed on her rumpled clothing as she adds, "Why? Are you about to have a birthday? Fiftieth just around the corner?"

"Sixtieth, actually," I say, loving her spirit. "I'm quite aged and decrepit, a fact I'm sure would be more apparent if it weren't so dark in here."

She looks up, arching a wry brow. "Right. Decrepit. That's the first word that came to mind when I saw you smirking in the corner."

Was that a hint of flirtation? A grudging acknowledgement that I'm not bad to look at?

Perhaps, but she truly doesn't seem to have recognized me.

That isn't all that strange, of course. She's American,

and aside from the current monarch and his or her offspring, the average American has little knowledge of who's in the British peerage, let alone what we look like.

Especially a secondborn son like me.

Relishing the chance to flirt with a beautiful woman who has no clue I'll be rubbing elbows with the highest of high society tomorrow afternoon, I decide it's time to extend an olive branch. "You're right, I *was* smirking, and that was poorly done of me. You've had a rough go of it this evening without being smirked at on top of it. Please accept my most humble apologies."

She blinks at me, obviously suspect.

"I'm truly sorry, Red," I maintain, motioning to the empty chair across from mine. "Please, take a seat. Let me buy you a drink."

For a moment, I think she's going to accept, but then her chin goes up again.

"No, thank you," she says, her voice chillier than it was before. "I'm not interested in drinking with a man who thinks it's funny to kick a girl while she's down."

My lips turn down hard at the edges. "Oh, come on. It was all in good fun. And I *have* apologized. Most sincerely, I might add. I'm frightfully sorry."

She shakes her head, her eyes narrowing. "Nope, don't even try it. I've been a victim of British manners before. You're all—'Oh, terribly sorry, old chap, frightfully bad form, pip pip, cheerio!'—but you don't really mean it." Her attempt at an English accent is horrifically bad. "What you really mean is that you want to be exonerated without making yourself vulnerable or fully acknowledging your wrongdoing. And that way is the coward's way. Therefore, I will be buying my own pint and drinking it by myself."

Just like that, I'm even more thoroughly charmed.

When was the last time someone rejected my apology?

Possibly...never.

It's exhilarating.

She spins on her broken heel, nearly goes down again, and catches herself on a chair before announcing, "Or maybe I'll just get a taxi and leave. Right now. Before I can break anything else." To Reggie, behind the bar, she adds in a softer voice, "I'm really sorry about the mess. Do you have a broom and a dustpan? I'm happy to sweep up before I go."

Reggie, who's unloading the washer behind the bar, offers her a kind smile. "Don't worry about it, love. Knowing Belinda, she's already got someone scheduled to come in tomorrow morning. But you might want that pint, after all. I doubt you'll find a taxi. Not until the storm passes. It's getting ugly out there."

Red pulls in a breath, shoulders sagging as she exhales, silently admitting defeat.

Through the windows, we can all see he's right. The snow that was pretty an hour ago is coming down in sheets, already piling up against the door. We're all here for the duration.

Which is just fine with me.

We wrapped up our last big project before the holiday this morning, and I gave the entire office three weeks off. Aside from our holiday party next Monday night, my responsibilities at the office are on hold until the new year, and I don't have to be at the luncheon tomorrow until noon.

I'm free to burn the midnight oil with Red, who I'm now *determined* to win over. Edward is the prize-winning polo player in the family, but we're both wickedly competitive.

I never back down from a challenge or a dare, and Red's quickly becoming both.

"You're right," she says, nodding toward Reggie. "I'll take a pint of whatever's best for a case of wounded pride then, please."

Reggie nods. "Pint of Guinness. Coming right up."

As she limps to the bar with as much grace as one can manage with a broken heel, I consider my options.

Put a song on the ancient jukebox and ask her to dance? Offer my vintage copy of Great Expectations for her entertainment by way of further apology? See if I can find an open shoe store willing to deliver a new pair of heels at this hour?

Not likely in a storm, but worth a try.

As I open a search window on my cell, Red pulls a pen and paper from her purse. She begins furiously scribbling, muttering something about a "career obituary" and "death by poinsettia" beneath her breath.

Death...

Death is not funny.

If she's *that* upset, I owe her more than a new pair of shoes.

I stand, crossing to the bar. When I slide onto the stool two down from hers, she doesn't look up, but her pen stops moving.

"I am deeply and honestly sorry," I say, in my most conciliatory tone. "Please, don't commit death by poinsettia. You seem like a lovely girl, and that sounds like an awful way to go." I wait until she glances my way before adding, "You'd have to eat an obscene amount of it, as well, since it isn't actually all that poisonous. And that's far too much work for someone who's already down on her luck. So…"

"I was kidding. But thank you. I'll mark death by poinsettia off my list."

"May I?" I ask, gesturing at the paper.

After a brief hesitation, she slides it over with a shrug. "Sure, why not? It's not like tonight can get any more embarrassing."

Her handwriting is surprisingly tidy for a woman who looks like she's never met an iron, a hairbrush, or a cup of coffee she wouldn't spill on her skirt.

Post-Worst-Day-Ever Action Items

1. Track down Belinda Moore and beg her forgiveness on your hands and knees. On your belly, if necessary. Offer to de-thorn roses in her shop until you pay her back for the damage you've caused.

2. Find a new career, a gig you can work alone in shame-free isolation. (Librarian? Lighthouse tender? Dog walker? Dogs don't judge nearly as much as rich people. Especially rich British people)

3. Change name. Get new nose. Possibly new face.

4. Give Maya your share of the business while apologizing profusely for being a failure who fails.

5. Move to a remote island where no one plans parties or has social media.

6. Become hermit.

7. Learn to make furniture from coconuts.

8. Drown sorrows in the ocean.

9. Drown sorrows in island rum.

10. If sorrows refuse to be drowned, consider poetic method of death. Possibly by poinsettia.

"Well, this won't do at all," I mutter, brow furrowing as I scan it again. "Your nose is perfect the way it is. Your face is quite nice, as well. And I've heard that coconuts are notoriously difficult to work with."

She arches a wry brow. "Oh? Is that right?"

"It is," I assure her seriously. "Far more difficult than rich people. Even rich British people. Coconuts are all attitude, wrapped in a spitefully hard exterior. And strangely hairy. No fruit or nut should be that hairy. It's bizarre. And unpleasant."

She huffs. "Noted. I'll cross that line out, then. Think of something else."

"I think that's best," I agree. "And can I suggest one more modification?" When she nods her permission, I push the list back across the bar. "New number one: Let annoying British man buy you drinks, food, and songs on the jukebox until the storm passes. Put off all life-changing decisions until tomorrow."

Her lips twitch. It's not quite a smile, but it's progress. Definite progress. "I don't know. That many changes might violate the integrity of the list."

I frown. "List integrity? I thought you Americans were all about breaking the rules and rewriting the lists?"

"Maybe most Americans, but I've always felt more comfortable in other cultures," she says. "Especially ones that like rules and don't rush to change them."

I hum beneath my breath. "Well, you'd love where I grew up, then. The village council has been fighting to keep a parking lot from going in by a popular local farm stand for years. They intend to stand in the way of progress and fun at any cost." I shrug. "But mostly at the cost of the poor farmer looking for a way to keep his head above water after another shite harvest. There are times when rules and lists simply must be changed, Red." I spin my nearly empty whiskey on the bar before adding in a more pointed tone, "Especially when it comes to death of any kind, but especially by poinsettia."

When I glance her way again, her gaze is softer, less guarded.

I shoot her my most winning "please have pity on me, I didn't mean to be an ass" forehead wrinkle. "So...about that drink?"

To my delight, she laughs. "Fine. You can buy the next round. But fair warning, I'm playing exclusively carols on the jukebox. I'm determined to get back in the Christmas spirit."

"Here, here!" I clink my glass against hers before downing the last of my drink, signaling Reg for another round as I add, "I love the holidays. The more carols, the better. And throw in some Mariah Carey while you're at it."

She blinks, looking surprised. "Really?"

"Really."

"Most people I know hate that song. Even my mother's sick of it."

I shake my head. "Not I, not sick at all. Let's get in the spirit, Red. Just let me find some coins." As I dig in my pockets with one hand, I extend the other. "I'm Olly, by the way."

She clasps my palm, and I can't help but notice how soft her skin feels against mine. "Emily. Emily Darling."

"Darling," I murmur. "Any relation to the family from Peter Pan?"

"No, but my grandmother did have a Saint Bernard when I was growing up. She let me call her Nana even though her real name was Eleanor," she says with a self-conscious roll of her eyes that makes her look younger, vulnerable, and very sweet.

Sweet is…problematic.

I don't usually mix casual and sweet.

Feisty and casual? Yes.

Fiery and casual? Always.

But sweet is a good way to wade into deeper waters than would be wise in this situation.

I strongly suspect Emily Darling isn't here to stay.

"As you should have," I agree. "Nana is the perfect name for a Saint Bernard. So, you're here for business? Business with some sort of floral, party planning component, judging from the context clues?"

"Yes." Her fingers tighten around her beer. "I'm pitching a gala concept to a high-profile client in a few days. I was hoping to have Belinda on lock as the floral designer before that happened, but..." She sighs. "I'll start reaching out to my backup florists tomorrow. I'm hoping I can make amends and convince Belinda to give me another chance, but just in case..."

"Always good to have a backup," I agree, silently thinking I might be able to help her out with Belinda.

But that's a thing we can both worry about later. Before we go our separate ways, I'll offer to intervene with Belinda as a balm to my swift goodbye.

Because I *will* have to say goodbye.

And swiftly.

I can already tell that more than one night with Emily Darling would have me feeling things that could become painful, considering there's usually an ocean between us.

I don't do long-distance relationships. I'm not the kind of person who can pull off that sort of thing without a pitiful amount of pining. I don't fall often, but when I do, I fall hard.

But one night is fine.

Assuming Emily is interested in letting me make further amends in private...

I try my vest pocket and finally produce a handful of coins. "Here we go. Let's give this place some proper holiday atmosphere, darling Darling. But please, do try not to injure yourself on the way to the jukebox."

She winks. "I'll try, but no promises." She slides off her stool, hips swaying temptingly beneath her rumpled skirt as she crosses the pub.

I watch her lean over the machine, auburn curls falling forward as she studies the selections, wishing we were alone so I wouldn't have to limit my admiration of her curves to a quick, cursory glance. A moment later, the first triumphant notes of "All I Want for Christmas" boom through the pub's surprisingly fabulous speakers, and she turns back to me with a grin that's a direct hit.

Damn, that smile…

And that's it.

The moment I should have known that I was in trouble.

Bloody serious trouble…

Chapter Four

EMILY

I'm not this girl.

I'm really not.

I haven't been on a date—not even a casual one—since Stephen broke up with me over WhatsApp last summer. I can't remember the last time I stayed up past ten for anything but work, rarely drink, and have never, repeat *never*, picked a man up at a bar.

I'm a "meet through friends" or on a dating app person. I like a guy who's been vetted—either by mutual acquaintances or by me, via several days of intense texting and stalking of his social media.

But here I am, two beers in with a sexy British stranger with mischievous blue eyes and a panty-melting accent even better than Colin Firth's. And not only am I allowing him to buy me a third beer before I beat him at another game of rummy, I'm pressing my knee against his under the table and hardly thinking about the nativity fiasco at all.

I'm even considering asking Olly back to my hotel for

a nightcap when the pub closes, and I don't even know his last name.

That therapist who thought I was too uptight and controlling would be so proud.

Or concerned.

Maybe both!

But for some reason, that suddenly feels exciting instead of terrifying.

"Gin," I purr, laying my cards down with a flourish.

"Again?" Olly groans, but he's smiling as he adds, "You've hustled me, haven't you?"

"I don't hustle," I inform him primly. "I strategically withhold information about my card-playing abilities until it's too late for my hapless opponent." I grin as I scoop the small pile of coins into my hand. "Now, all your ten pence pieces are mine."

"Diabolical," he mutters. "How did you become such a beastly little card shark?"

"I could tell you…" I shrug. "But then I'd have to kill you."

The truth is, I learned gin rummy from my grandmother during Isabelle's endless skating practices, back when I was too young to stay home alone and mom and dad were still at work. It was either that or watch Isabelle do the same leapy, turny thing eight hundred times in a row.

But Olly doesn't need to know that I spent my formative years in ice rink waiting rooms, making the best of being the "less interesting and talented" sister. He also doesn't need to know that this is the longest I've gone without checking my email in months. Or that I eat lunch at my desk every day to squeeze more work in.

Or that, lately, my list-making habit is inching past "cute coping mechanism" into "pathological" territory.

No, all he needs to know is that I'm a wild and fabulous redhead who crashes nativity plays, picks all the best Christmas songs, and can drink him under the table.

At least, I think I can...

I don't drink that often, but when I do, I'm usually the last girl standing at the bachelorette party. I never lose a shoe on the dance floor or ask the male stripper if I can take a picture of the "junk in his front trunk." (That last one was Maya, who still has an impressive collection of "front trunk" shots on her phone from our friend Georgia's bachelorette party in Atlantic City last year.)

Still, by the time we're on our fourth—fifth?—drink, my lips are starting to tingle and my words slur a little as I say, "Yes, the seagull stealing the toupee was bad, but nothing compared to what happened in Florida. It was a destination wedding at the Everglades Botanical Gardens. We were halfway through the toasts when suddenly the swans turned feral. They just started honking and snapping at people, and one chased the mother-of-the-bride into the lagoon." I gesture Olly's way with my pint glass. "Which might not have been so bad, but there were also alligators in the lagoon. Because of the Florida of it all."

His jaw drops. "Christ. I forget how terrifying America can be."

"So terrifying," I agree. "I'm never going to Florida again. A place with killer dinosaurs in the water is not a place where I belong. And the humidity is horrible. My hair was a giant frizzy fuzzball the entire time." I sip my beer, willing myself to take this one slower than the last.

"So?" he prods after a beat.

I blink. "So what?"

"So did the mother-of-the-bride die a horrible, bloody death by swan and/or alligator?" he demands, giving my thigh a teasing squeeze beneath the table. "You can't leave a man hanging like that, Red."

I giggle. "Oh, sorry. No, she didn't. But she *did* have to fight off two giant male swans with her high heel before the garden staff were able to fetch her out of the lagoon. Apparently, she'd crashed through their nest while she was running from the other swans, and they were angry that she'd bothered their babies. Even though they'd obviously stolen the babies from some poor mama swan while her back was turned." I take a quick drink to wet my parched throat before adding, "Did you know that twenty-five percent of male swans are gay?"

Olly throws his head back and laughs, a rich sound that makes dangerous warmth pulse through my veins.

God, he's sexy. And gorgeous. And has the best laugh.

But I can't have a one-night stand with a complete stranger.

Can I?

I *can* invite him back to the hotel lobby for one last drink and get his number and maybe kiss him on the sidewalk before he gets in his cab, but that's it.

After all, I've *never* had a one-night stand.

Ever.

Not even in college, when one-night-standing was all a girl on scholarship at an Ivy League business school, who was also secretary of her sorority, had time for.

No, I'm not that type of person.

I'm not impulsive, especially not in a sexual way.

But maybe it's time to start, a wicked voice whispers in my head.

I'm still blushing when Olly squeezes my thigh again and declares, "You're making that up."

I shake my head. "No, I'm not. One in four male swans are full-blown gay."

His lips twitch. "As opposed to just a wee bit gay? The way I get when I watch too much Outlander."

Now, it's my turn to snort-laugh. He grins wider in response, clearly pleased with himself for getting a snort out of me. And damn, I think I might be falling in lust with his chin dimple. Who knew a chin dimple could be so delicious?

"Understandable," I say, once I can breathe again. "Jamie Fraser is insanely hot."

"You're not too shabby yourself, Darling," he murmurs, making my cheeks heat as he leans closer.

I lean in, too, my pulse fluttering wildly in my throat.

I've never kissed a man in a bar, either, but our lips are about to meet over our forgotten cards when a creaky voice behind me calls out, "Oi, young people! Come settle a bet."

Olly and I startle apart, turning to face a man in a plaid vest standing beside the jukebox, flanked by two shorter gentlemen, both with magnificently thick gray moustaches. "You've obviously got decent taste in music, but can either of you do the Lambeth Walk?"

"Excuse me?" I start, but Olly's already standing, offering me his hand.

"Dance from the 1930s. Bernard forces it upon the bar at least once a year," he says with mock annoyance. "He forgets we're not all older than Father Christmas."

"Aw, you love it, Oliver," Plaid Vest—Bernard—says, waving us over before hollering at the other men still camped out by the fire. "Come on, you lot. Get off your asses and join the fun. Lord knows you could use the exercise, and it's Christmas dammit."

I abandoned my broken shoe an hour ago, so I pad over in my stocking feet, already grinning as Bernard and his friend Albert—shorter moustache man— demonstrate what looks like a cross between the hokey pokey and someone having a seizure.

"It's all in the hips, love," Albert insists, demonstrating with an impressive amount of flexibility for a man his age. "Then you shout 'Oi!' and slap your knees. It's great fun."

"Looks like it." I giggle as Olly gets in on the tutorial, hips swiveling right along with Bernard.

What follows is the silliest fun I've had in a long time. Olly and I follow their increasingly elaborate instructions while a bizarre song called "A Lovely Bunch of Coconuts" plays on repeat on the jukebox. We stomp and swivel and "oi!" until we're all laughing so hard, we can barely breathe.

Then we switch partners and go for another promenade around the bar.

"Brilliant work," Bernard cheers as he hands me off to Olly again, "but you're meant to turn left, love, not right."

"I did turn left!" I protest with a laugh.

"Your other left," Olly says in my ear, spinning me back in the correct direction.

His hands are warm on my waist, and he smells like expensive whiskey and woodsy cologne. He's also smiling down at me like he thinks I'm the best thing since figgy pudding, and suddenly, I can't think of a single reason why I *shouldn't* take him back to my room.

After all, you only live once, and so far, in my life, I've

managed to make it twenty-eight years without ever meeting a man who made me want to jump straight into bed with him.

Who knows how long it might be before I meet another?

At this rate, I'll be fifty-two by the time lightning strikes a second time, and I don't imagine getting naked with strangers is something that gets easier with age.

By the time the coconut song finally gives way to an instrumental of "Good King Wenceslas," the old men are beaming like they've just taught their grandchildren to ride bicycles, and I'm blushing bright red.

But it's a determined blush, not an embarrassed one.

Now, I just have to figure out how one asks a man if he'd like to get naked together in a low-key, temporary sort of way…

"Right then, I'm off," Albert says, bundling into his coat. "Got an early boxing class tomorrow. Mind how you go in this snow, ladies and gents."

"Us, too," Bernard agrees, holding his friend's coat. "Best get tucked into bed before the drifts are too deep. Happy Christmas, Olly and Emily. It was a delight." He shoots us a knowing wink as he joins the old man posse shuffling toward the door.

In a few moments, they're gone, the jukebox shifts into another light instrumental, and the pub feels very peaceful.

Intimate…

"Fancy a glass of water by the fire?" Olly suggests.

"Sounds good," I agree, grateful for a few more minutes to gather my one-night-stand courage.

We claim a cozy spot on a worn leather sofa, and Reggie appears with waters and two steaming mugs.

"Mulled wine on the house," he announces. "The least I could do for the entertainment you two have provided tonight." He nods over his shoulder as he backs away. "We're starting closing duties, but you're welcome to stay until we head for the door."

"Thanks, Reg," Olly says. "Appreciate it."

I take a sip of the wine and moan. It tastes like Christmas in a cup—cinnamon and cloves and a citrus explosion. "Oh my God, this is so good. Where has this been all my life?"

"You don't do mulled wine in New York?" he asks, scooting closer.

"Not really, no." We're still not touching, not quite, but he's close enough that I'm keenly aware of the centimeters between his thigh and mine.

"What do you poor Yanks drink at Christmas?"

"Eggnog mostly. Which now seems completely inferior." I take another sip, sighing as the warmth spreads through my chest. "Though honestly, I don't do much holiday drinking. I'm too busy with work. I did ten parties in six days last December."

"That's criminal."

"That's business." I tuck my stocking feet underneath me, wondering if I have the guts to pull off a Sarah from Love Actually and make Olly stand by the entrance to my room while I quickly change into something sexier.

I'd really rather not face my first one-night stand in a wrinkly, coffee-stained suit and my everyday underwear.

"This year was supposed to be different," I continue. "I was going to take a week off for the holidays, then head down to New Jersey to spend time with family. But then this opportunity to pitch Fletchers came up, and..."

"And you couldn't say no," he finishes.

"Couldn't afford to say no," I counter. "My business partner and I just lost our biggest client, right after signing the lease on a fancy new office space we can now no longer afford. Money is tight, and if I don't land this contract..." I sigh. "If I let Maya down after I promised I could handle this..." I trail off again. "Sorry, I didn't mean to bring down the vibes."

I really didn't. Ugh. So far, I suck at transitioning from flirting at the bar to sealing the deal.

"You didn't," Olly assures me gently.

I glance over to see a serious expression on his face for once.

"I get it," he says. "I work a lot, too. And there's nothing worse than feeling you've let a friend down. Or family." He glances toward the fire as he adds, "My father used to say that as long as you're trying your best, with integrity, there's no need to worry about things like that, but..." He turns back to me with a wry smile. "He wasn't a man who often made mistakes. He always seemed to know exactly what to say, what to do. Navigating a position of great responsibility and public scrutiny came easily to him."

"He sounds like a wonderful man," I say, sensing there's a reason for the grief lingering beneath Olly's words.

It's a hunch he confirms when he adds, "He was. And very wise. I miss his wisdom the most, I think. And his laugh. This is our first Christmas without him."

I cover his hand, giving it a squeeze. "I'm so sorry. I can't imagine how hard that must be."

"Thank you." He turns his hand over, threading his fingers through mine, sending a fresh tingle of awareness across my skin. "Now who's harshing the vibes? Can you forgive me?"

I nod, my gaze locked on his, trying to pin down the exact color of his oh-so-magnetic eyes. They're not purely blue or purely gray, but a mixture of the two, like the River Thames in winter.

It's a romantic thought, not a sexy one, but I can't help it. Sometime in the past hour, a part of me has started to wonder what it might be like to have more than a one-night stand with this man.

"Can I escort you to your hotel on the subway, Emily Darling?" he asks. "Not to be a cad, of course. I'll behave myself. I just want to make sure you get home safely. The subway's likely the only form of transport still operational in this mess, and it can be a little tricky if you're new to the tube and had a few."

"That's very kind of you," I murmur, knowing it's now or never. I gather my courage, suck in a bracing breath, and add, "But what if I don't want you to behave yourself?"

"No?" His eyes darken. "You don't?"

I shake my head slowly back and forth, hyperaware of every point where we touch—hands, knees, the side of my thigh pressed against his. "No. I don't."

"Well, in that case, I—"

Reggie clears his throat nearby, making us both flinch. I glance up, shocked to see the bartender standing just a few feet away.

I was so locked in on Olly, I didn't hear him coming...

"Sorry, folks," he says, looking nearly as embarrassed as I feel. "Hate to interrupt, but I've got to lock up. Wife'll have my head if I'm any later. We're getting up at the crack of dawn to finish the holiday shopping, and her mum's coming by to watch the kids. You know how it is."

"Of course, thank you so much for letting us stay," I say, bolting to my feet, wondering where my shoes have gotten off to.

"Absolutely, Reg, no trouble at all," Olly says. Then, as if reading my mind, he points beneath our card table. "I think your shoes are under there, Em. If you want to fetch those, your purse, and your coat, I'll rescue your suitcase from the manger, and we'll be off. You said you're in Mayfair?"

I nod. "Yes. At the Winthrop Mayberry."

"That's quite a jaunt," Reggie says, concern in his voice. "And I haven't seen a cab in hours."

"I'll get her home safe on the subway," Olly assures him, the protective note in his voice melting the last of my hesitation.

Yes, he was a sarcastic ass at first, but only for like five minutes. Then, he apologized and has been completely lovely and funny and charming for…two hours? Three?

I suddenly realize I have no idea what time it is.

I fetch my cell from my purse as I stuff my feet into my ruined shoes.

Midnight.

The witching hour.

Not a good time to make big decisions of any kind, but as we bid Reggie farewell outside and toddle off in the direction of the closest tube station, I can't help looping my arm through Olly's.

The last thing I want is to say goodbye.

The storm has gentled into a dreamy, cinematic snow. Fat, lazy flakes drift down from the gray sky, catching the light from the street lamps. The city is covered in a pristine coat of white, the streets are empty, and it feels like we're the only two people in London.

"God, it's beautiful," I breathe, lifting my face to the sky.

"You're beautiful," Olly murmurs, summoning a fresh flush to my cheeks. "Very beautiful, but there's no pressure. If you've changed your mind about me behaving myself, I can see you home and take my leave."

As we stop at the corner, I glance his way, deciding he's even sexier in the snow. "No," I whisper, heart galloping in my chest. "I haven't changed my mind. Unless...you've changed yours."

"No, I haven't. Not at all." He clears his throat, looking almost as nervous—and exhilarated—as I feel, making a foolish part of me hope this isn't something he does every weekend, either.

Yes, he's a gorgeous, classy, funny, likely-wealthy man if his leather Crockett and Jones Oxfords are anything to judge by.

But he's also been grieving his father.

And he said he works a lot, too.

In the name of bolstering my confidence, I let myself believe we're in the same boat as he threads his fingers back through mine. "So, the tube station is about a ten-minute walk this way." He nods in the direction we've been going. "And then we'll have a transfer to get to Mayfair. Or...we could go to my guest place."

He turns, pointing across the street. There, on the other side of a small, open square, is one of those beautifully redesigned structures they're turning into luxury apartments all over the city.

"I keep a flat in the building for family and friends when they're visiting," he continues. "All the comforts of home and, best of all, we could be warm and dry in two minutes flat."

Two minutes...

I could be alone with Olly in two minutes.

I mean, I'm already alone with him, but we could be *alone* alone. In a place with a door, we can close to shut out the world.

A place with a bed...

I should say no. I shouldn't go home with a man I barely know, who I haven't even kissed yet. I should tell him I would be more comfortable if he came to my hotel, where there will be plenty of people around to hear me scream for help, on the off chance I need it.

Even better, I should march my frozen feet to the tube all by myself, go back to my sensible hotel room where I can make sensible lists and stay focused on salvaging my professional reputation.

That's what Responsible Emily would do.

But Responsible Emily would have left hours ago and missed out on the best night she's had in years. And then I wouldn't be standing in the snow with a beautiful man looking at me like I'm the only thing he wants under his Christmas tree.

So, really, there's only one thing left to do.

One obstacle left between me and a steamy night with the sexiest man I've ever met in real life.

"I think the guest place is a no-brainer, but there's one thing I need first," I say, my voice wobbling as I step closer, bringing my hands to his chest.

"What's that, love?" he asks, the huskiness in the words giving me the confidence to slide my arms around his neck.

"A kiss, silly," I whisper.

His lips curve as he cups my face in one big hand. "Of course. You're right, how silly of me."

Then his lips are on mine, and I instantly know that the world will never be the same.

My world, anyway...

I've been kissed before, obviously. And in my share of romantic places. I've been kissed at a swanky rooftop party on New Year's Eve and on the Brooklyn Bridge at the end of a hazy summer night. I was once even kissed at the top of the Empire State Building by a man who'd just said he loved me for the first time.

But I've never been kissed like I'm something worth stopping time for.

Like I'm a treasure a man can't bear to think of sharing...

Olly's teeth graze my bottom lip, and I gasp, my fingers tangling in his hair as the kiss grows hotter, deeper.

All of a sudden, something inside me cracks. All the grind of the past year, all the nights choosing working over living, all the times I've watched other people heading out for fun on the weekend, only to feel I didn't deserve fun until I levelled up. Until I proved that I could be as exceptional as the rest of my family. As exceptional as Dad is as a history professor and Mom is at selling real estate, and Isabelle is on the ice.

But right now, I don't care about *being* exceptional; I just want to feel.

Exceptionally.

I want to drown in this man's kiss, melt beneath his touch, get lost and found in the electrical field we create together, and finally feel what it's like to throw caution to the wind and burn.

I've never burned before, but tonight...

I'm already on fire, and we're still completely clothed in the middle of a snowstorm.

When we finally break apart, we're both breathing hard.

Then, I grin.

And he grins.

And then we're kissing again with even more wild abandon than before, giggling and moaning and exhaling eager, can't-wait-to-touch-you sighs as we stumble back the way we've come.

Back toward his guest flat.

Where we're going to be alone.

Finally, *alone*.

A very happy Christmas to me...

Chapter Five
OLIVER

The snow doesn't slow us down.

If anything, it helps blast through the last of our guardrails.

In this white, hushed world, we're the only people on earth. There's no one to stare or judge or whisper secrets to HELLO! Magazine. It's just Emily and me and a hunger—a freedom—unlike anything I've felt in ages.

She tastes like mulled wine, salt from our pretzel snack, and a sweet surprise I wasn't expecting on this cold winter's night. She's a fucking delight, and I can't seem to stop kissing her.

Not even long enough to watch where I'm going, apparently...

I grunt, cursing as the back of my head knocks against something cold and metallic.

"Watch out for the lamppost," she mumbles against my lips.

"Thanks," I murmur back. "You delivered that warning in the nick of time."

I spin us around, pressing her against the post, swallowing her laugh with another kiss that's hot enough to make my wool coat feel like overkill. We proceed to claw at each other, tongues stroking deep as Emily wraps a leg around my hips, and I grab eager handfuls of her fantastic ass.

I haven't been this desperate to get a woman alone in...

Christ, I can't even remember, and it's been an eternity since I've had such authentic, unguarded fun.

As a member of the peerage, one never fully drops one's guard in the city. Hell, these days, it's not entirely safe in the country, either. Since my father passed, and Edward and I each moved one step closer to the throne, it feels like there's a paparazzo hiding behind every mailbox and teapot.

The Honorable Oliver David Dawson Featherswallow is not a normal man. He has to keep his impulsive side on a tight leash so as not to mortify his mother, reflect poorly on the aristocracy, or draw the disapproving eye of the crown. The spare to the Viscount isn't allowed to kiss women in the snow like a lovesick uni student.

But Olly is.

Fuck, I love being Olly.

Just Olly.

Especially with Emily...

We kiss-stumble-laugh our way across the street, tripping over her suitcase and our own feet, but having a damned good time doing it. When we finally reach the entrance to the lofts, I smash my key fob against the sensor without coming up for air.

We trip again on our way across the lobby, and Emily starts giggling, that wicked, mischievous giggle that's already one of my favorites. While we wait for the lift, I nibble her earlobe, she nips at my neck, and suddenly things aren't nearly as funny.

I want her.

Desperately.

I'm already hard, my erection straining the front of my suit pants.

I'm in trouble with this woman. Deep trouble, and getting deeper with every passing minute. Saying goodbye tomorrow morning is going to be torture.

Which is why I'm not going to think about tomorrow.

All I'm going to think about is her lips and her curves and the way her tongue spars perfectly with mine.

The lift ride is torture and bliss. I press her against the wall, and she presses against my cock, making me groan as she grinds closer.

"I love a woman who knows what she wants," I murmur.

"And I love feeling how much you want me," she whispers back.

"I want you a rather alarming amount, Darling," I confess, fingers digging into her hips. "I can't wait to make you come, Red. Can't wait to hear the loud, American sounds you're going to make."

She laughs again, but it's a breathier sound this time, and soon becomes a moan as I cup her breast through her shirt. She's the perfect, overflowing handful, and getting her nipples in my mouth is quickly becoming my new mission in life.

Before I can confess that or any of my other wicked thoughts, the elevator door opens and we kiss our way down the hall.

At the flat door, I wrench my lips from hers long

enough to do battle with the lock, and then we're inside, finally alone in the cool, citrus-scented darkness. I just had the flat serviced in preparation for family coming down to do some Boxing Day shopping after the holiday, which means clean sheets for us to dirty.

And dirty them we will...

"I should shower first," she says. "And put on something less—"

"Don't even think about it, Red," I say, stripping her blazer down her arms. "I can't wait that long to have you naked in my bed, and I've been dreaming about getting you out of this suit for hours. I want to unwrap you like a business-casual Christmas present."

She laughs against my lips as we kiss our way through the minimalist living room. "A rumpled, coffee-scented Christmas present. I'm pretty sure Albert spilled beer on me, too, while we were dancing."

"Hot," I say, tossing the blazer to the rug by the couch as we move into the darker hallway.

"You like it dirty then, do you, Mr..." She pauses, pulling back to gaze up at me, wide-eyed in the shadows. "Jesus, Olly, I still don't know your last name."

"But you know that I'm devoted to your safety and pleasure," I say, kicking open the door to the primary bedroom behind me. "Or you will know, very soon. Permission to undo the rest of your buttons with my teeth, Emily? My lips and tongue would very much like to pay tribute to your gorgeous, coffee-scented breasts."

She sighs, her head falling back as I kiss my way down her throat. "Permission granted, you very bad man."

"No, not bad," I promise as I tangle my fingers in the chaos of her fabulous hair. "I'm going to be a very good man tonight, darling Darling." I open her top three buttons with my teeth before pausing to press my lips to the constellation of freckles dusting the tops of her breasts. "So beautiful... And your nipples hard for me through the wrinkles? Poetry." I move lower, capturing one tight peak in my mouth, sucking it through the fabric of her blouse and bra, pulse pounding faster when she moans and arches closer.

"God, Olly," she pants, confirming that being Olly is far better than Oliver any day of the week.

"Good?" I murmur, dispensing with the rest of the buttons with my fingers, too eager for party tricks at this stage.

"Perfect," she says, her breath catching as I curl my fingers around the cups of her bra, dragging them down until her breasts spill free.

Bloody hell, her pale, peachy nipples are a revelation.

And all the inspiration I need to resume my worship...

The first taste of her bare skin—salty and hot against my tongue—makes my erection test the integrity of my zipper. The way she clings to me as I lick and suck her soon has me so hard, I have no choice but to ask, "Is it all right if I take off my trousers? Things are getting tight."

"No," she says, dropping the temperature a good five degrees as she pulls away.

Before I can apologize for rushing things, her fingers are busy with my belt, one hand dragging the leather through the clasp as the other rubs me through my pants. "That's *my* job," she adds. "I like to unwrap things, too, you know."

"I love that about you," I say, my cock twitching as she drags my zipper down and resumes stroking me through just my boxer briefs.

"I love this..." She rubs her thumb across my swollen head, where the fabric is already damp.

"That I'm so turned on, I'm already leaking for you?" I ask, the dirty words emerging without my conscious permission.

But she doesn't seem to mind.

In fact, she rather likes them, if the way she bites her bottom lip is anything to judge by. "Yes. Is that filthy of me?"

"Utterly." I reach for the zipper at the back of her skirt, bringing my lips to her forehead as I confess, "But like I said, Emily, I love a dirty girl. Now let's get you out of this skirt so I can see if your pussy tastes as lovely as your tits."

We tear at the rest of each other's clothes, quickly disposing of the rest of the barriers keeping skin from skin. And then this magnificent, winter storm of a woman is naked on my bed, save for a pair of little cotton briefs, and bloody hell...

She's stunning, all curves and flushed skin, pure temptation as she crooks her finger. "Come here, Olly. Right now. I have something I want to tell you."

"What's that, love?" I ask, lengthening myself on top of her.

We both exhale a soft groan at the first, full-body contact. She's so soft and hot, her curves heaven against me as she wraps her legs around my waist.

And fuck, she's wet.

So wet I can feel her through her panties.

"I want to tell you that I'm on the pill," she whispers in my ear, making me groan as I grind closer, rubbing my cock against her clit. She shudders, a hungry sound wrenching from the back of her throat. "But I still want to use a condom. Is that okay?"

"Anything you want is okay," I assure her in a husky voice. "I'll grab a condom from my wallet in just a second. As soon as I work up the strength to stop humping you through these filthy little panties."

"My panties are not filthy," she teases, dragging her nails down my back in a way that makes it even harder to imagine leaving the paradise of her arms, even for a moment. "My panties may, in fact, be the only item of clothing that escaped both coffee and beer."

"Really?" I nibble her dainty lobe before whispering into the pink shell of her ear, "Then why are they so wet, Ms. Darling?"

"I don't know, Mr. Olly," she counters. "Why don't you do some investigating and find out?"

Investigate, I do.

Most thoroughly.

Until her equally dainty pussy lips are swollen beneath my mouth and she's soaking my tongue as she moans and writhes on the mattress.

"Fuck, you're sweet," I say, my jaw clenching as I glide two fingers inside her. "And so soaked for me. God, Em, I really need to go fetch a condom. This drenched little fanny isn't going to fuck herself."

"Yes, condom. Yes," she chants, even as she reaches down to grip my face in her trembling hands. "But not yet. Just do that thing again first. The thing with your... Oh, God. Oh God, yes, Olly. Oh God!"

Then, she's coming for me, arching off the bed as she grinds her delicious pussy into my mouth, and I'm embarrassed to say that I go completely out of my head. I lose time, lose my mind, lose something necessary to continuing cognition because the next thing I know, Emily's on top of me, and I'm watching her spread those pink, swollen lips to make way for my cock.

My cock, which is mercifully already sheathed in latex, though I have no memory of grabbing the condom from my wallet.

But I must have done.

Or maybe Em fetched it for me. She's clearly a brilliant, beautiful girl who has no trouble taking charge when needed.

"Fuck, yes, darling," I murmur, gaze locked on her gorgeous curves as she fits me to her entrance. "God, could you be more beautiful?"

She leans forward, and I surge up to meet her, needing her nipples in my mouth as she seats herself on my cock. She gasps as I suck her deep, arms shaking as she braces them on either side of my face.

"Yes, just like that." I groan as she starts to move, rocking against me with an urgency that makes it clear she's already close again. "Take what you need, Em. Ride me until you come because all I want is you." I flick my tongue across her nipple. "Coming." Flick, flick. "On my cock."

"Yes, God, yes," she pants, the words trailing into a moan as I continue to lavish attention on both her gorgeous breasts.

Soon, she's grinding on me with an enthusiasm that has me fighting the need to explode with every fiber of my being. But I refuse to let her down by going off this early in the game, and I'm nowhere near ready for this to be over.

I want to watch her breasts bouncing above me, her

face twisting as she chases her pleasure, for as long as humanly possible.

"Stunning," I murmur, urging her on with my hips, my hands gripping her ass. "You're stunning when you're about to soak my cock. Fuck, yes, Emily. Yes, darling, come for me. Come for me, love."

She comes with that loud, unabashed American scream I was hoping for, her nails digging into my shoulders, her pussy gripping me with a ferocity that banishes all hope of switching positions before I lose the battle against the release bearing down upon me.

The best I can do is thrust up—hard and deep—lifting her into the air as I follow her over the edge. I cry out, the orgasm so intense it rearranges things inside me as my cock jerks and pulses, drenching my every cell in bliss.

For a moment, we just cling, sweat-slick and shaking, her breath hot against my neck, mine ragged in her hair. I realize I would very much like to stay buried inside her, potentially forever, but—

"Let me get rid of this condom, Em," I whisper against the top of her head. "And I'll be right back."

"Oh, right, sorry," she says, sounding dazed as she rolls onto the sheets beside me.

I dash to the loo, chucking the condom and giving my hands a quick wash, before I'm back beside her, pulling her against me as I flip the duvet atop our rapidly cooling bodies. She curls into my chest and I hold her there, not surprised to find that she fits just right.

"Excellent work," I murmur, kissing the top of her head.

"Thank you. Not too shabby yourself."

"No, seriously, that was a banger of a start, Em, but

I..." I fake a moment of awkward hesitation before I add, "Well, I think you could scream a little louder, don't you? Really do your homeland proud?"

She giggles. "I don't know. That was pretty loud for me, but I'm open to trying again if you are."

"Oh, I am," I say. "I really am. I want you under me as soon as I can get Wee Willy Winky down there to cooperate."

She lifts her head, arching a brow as she purrs, "Darling, there's nothing wee about your winky. Nothing wee at all."

"Damn." I bite my bottom lip. "I like it when you call me darling."

"Yeah?" she asks, grinning.

I nod. "Yeah. Now try 'love.' I think hearing you call me 'love' will get my willy winking again in no time."

"Of course," she says in that sexy, just been fucked voice that's already working magic on my cock. "Happy to oblige, love."

"Oh, yeah, that's it," I say, playing it up as I surge up and over her, rolling us across the rumpled sheets.

We laugh and kiss, then laugh some more, then moan and swear and agree it's past time for round two. And then she's under me, bucking into my cock, and I'm cursing myself for only carrying two condoms and not stocking any in the apartment.

After all, my friends and family might enjoy a responsible shag from time to time.

God knows I do...

As Emily comes for me again, crying out my name as I rub her clit in slow, determined circles while pumping deep, I'm the happiest I've been in ages.

Not just since last January. Since long before my

father's death. Since before I became a business owner, with the fate of a few dozen employees resting on my shoulders. Since before all those bloody abdications during my time at Oxford, which brought our family unexpectedly close to the throne.

As I come buried in her sweetness, I'm nineteen again. Nineteen and carefree, with nothing on my mind except a gorgeous girl and how much I love being naked and in her arms.

Afterward, I finally allow Emily a shower while I whip up some cheddar cream puffs, the only thing in the freezer that's remotely edible. We eat them on the couch in the darkened living room, while watching the city lights twinkle in a blanket of white.

"This has been so wonderful," she says with a sigh, leaning her damp head against my shoulder. "Thank you for a fantastic night, Olly. I'll never forget you." She yawns. "But I should get some sleep. I need to get up early. I'll try not to wake you when I go."

And then, she's up and off the couch, on her way to the bedroom without me, before I can respond to any piece of that word bomb she just dropped.

Try not to wake me when she goes?

Wake me when she *goes*?!

No, "we should get breakfast," no, "let me type my number into your phone," not even an "I'll jump on your cock again in the morning, one last time for the road?"

And sure, I was originally thinking a one-night situation would be best too, but now...

Well, now, I just want her screaming my name as many times as possible before she flies back to America.

How can she *not* want that, too?

How can she be okay with one and done after a night like this?

I have half a mind to ask her, but when I get to the bedroom, she's already curled under the covers, sleeping like the dead.

It makes sense, I suppose—she's just off a transatlantic flight, and has been awake for God only knows how long—but still...

I find myself feeling a little miffed.

Hell, more than a little miffed.

I'm flat out pouty. So pouty that I snag her phone off the bedside table and pop back into the kitchen, setting it to silent before sliding it atop the refrigerator.

I push it back far enough to ensure she won't be reaching it without my help and head to bed, satisfied we'll have the chance to talk things through in the morning. She's not about to make a break for it without her phone, no matter how eager she is to put our fantastic night of passion in her rearview.

It *was* fantastic. I refuse to believe a second of our time in bed together was forced or fake.

There has to be some other reason she's decided to bolt.

But what?

I lie on the mattress beside her, staring a broody hole through her sleeping head, wondering how she manages to be so transparent and completely unpredictable at the same time?

I don't know, but it makes me irritable.

And excited.

And frustrated.

And fascinated.

A terrible combination that feels an awful lot like the first flush of falling in love...

Chapter Six

EMILY

I wake to that kind of pink, December morning light that makes everything look romantic.

Even epic mistakes.

But damn, what a gorgeous mistake...

For exactly five seconds, I let myself enjoy the warm weight of Olly's arm draped across my waist, the way his dark hair falls across his forehead, the calligraphy of his swoop of an upper lip.

His mouth is a thing of beauty.

And so skilled at delivering orgasms, it should come with a warning label: Caution—May Cause Pleasure so Intense You'll Wake up Hoarse from Screaming this Man's Name.

His name...which I still only know *half* of.

The thought chills the warmth kindling between my thighs.

I still have no idea who Olly really is. Or how he pays for this luxury flat. For all I know, he could be a drug dealer who rules the London suburbs with a rakish smile and a switchblade. Or a wickedly charming City solicitor who's priced out every family-run shop on the high street.

Or—even worse—a crypto bro with a podcast.

The thought makes me shudder. I have to get out of this bed and pull myself together. Make a plan. Get my business trip back on track.

Figure out what time it is…

I glance toward the bedside table, but my phone isn't there.

My stomach knots. Did I leave it at the pub? Or, even worse, somewhere outside in the snow? The chances it could have fallen out of my coat pocket while Olly and I were vigorously making out against that lamppost are greater than zero.

Far greater.

Shit!

This is bad. Very bad!

What the hell were you thinking, Emily Katherine Darling?

The answer is, I wasn't. For one glorious night, I stopped making lists and analyzing consequences and threw caution—and my panties—to the wind.

But morning always comes, and with it, the resurrection of all the real-life problems that didn't magically vanish in the heat Olly and I generated between the sheets last night.

Anxiety continuing to creep in on stabby needle feet, I ease out from under his arm and slip from between the covers. My bare feet hit the cold floor, the chill helping to banish the last of the morning-after glow. Yesterday's clothes are scattered around the room and out into the hall like evidence at a crime scene, looking even more rumpled and pathetic in the light of day.

I gather everything quietly and tiptoe out to the living room with its breathtaking views of snow-covered London. There, between the couches and the gleaming modern kitchen, my roller case waits by the door, miraculously intact despite our chaotic entrance last night.

Thank God for small favors and sturdy luggage.

The guest bathroom is decorated in a tasteful mix of bamboo and recycled glass tiles that's giving Luxury Spa, but my Zen remains thoroughly out of reach. I quickly change into fresh clothes—cream-colored wool pants and my lucky red sweater, the one I was wearing when I landed two high society weddings in one day last fall. My hair is a disaster from going to bed with it wet, the curls flat on one side and coiled into ringlets on the other. I dig through my toiletry bag, making do with a small bottle of sea spray curl refresher. I would wet my hair and try again, but all my full-sized curl products are missing in action, along with my checked baggage.

Stupid London airport.
Stupid lost luggage.
Stupid sex hair.

Still, I can't fully regret the sex hair, even as I tie my curls back with a poinsettia print silk scarf that looks more "fussy old lady" around a ponytail than it does when knotted at my neck. Last night was, without a doubt, the best sex of my life. No contest.

I mean, it's not like I've had all that much sex, especially recently, but my college boyfriends were both very committed to leaving it all on the field in the bedroom. They tried, bless them, though their efforts often had little effect until my vibrator joined the fun.

I'd just assumed I wasn't a particularly orgasmic person. That maybe I was too uptight to fully relax into the experience. Or that perhaps I'd ruined my clitoris for human hands and tongues with too much mechanical stimulation and would be dependent on a vibrator to "get there" for the rest of my life.

But no.

I just needed an Olly between my legs.

Olly's fingers, Olly's tongue, Olly's...

"No, you're not going to think about *that*," I mutter to my reflection.

Thinking about Olly's penis is a good way to end up back in bed with it again, and I can't afford distractions right now. Not even a fabulously sexy one so perfectly shaped and highly skilled that I might never meet its match again.

My entire professional future is on the line. Maya's counting on me. The catering company and florists we keep busy in New York are counting on me. And how will my family feel if they learn I bailed on our Darling Family Christmas only to fly home an embarrassment and a failure?

Nope. That's *not* going to happen.

I refuse to let it.

I hustle out of the bathroom, stuff my old clothes into my dirty linen bag, and zip up my roller. A few minutes later, I find my giant purse on the floor by the couch, my laptop still tucked safely inside its protective sleeve.

But a thorough paw through the rest of the contents turns up no sign of my cell.

I open my suitcase again to check my blazer and skirt pockets—nothing—then empty my purse onto the floor. But aside from a roll of mints I missed the first time, my purse holds nothing of interest. Popping a mint into my mouth, I check the cushions on the couch, every inch of the carpet—including in the bedroom, where Olly is still fast asleep—and the hallway leading to the elevator outside.

Fifteen minutes later, I've checked everywhere, including inside the mostly-empty kitchen cupboards and the fridge, and I'm starting to panic.

I can't leave without my phone!

My entire life is in there—my calendar, my contacts, my notebook app full of lists, my color-coded crisis management apps.

But it's also synced with my laptop, I remember, a whisper of hope filtering through my increasingly anxious thoughts. And my laptop has a "find my device" app I've used before, back when my ex-boyfriend and I had the same phone case, and he kept taking my cell to work by mistake.

The tightness in my chest easing a bit, I pull out my laptop and settle onto the couch. I connect to the building's thankfully password-free WIFI, but before I can navigate to the app, the notifications hit like an avalanche.

> Maya: OMG EMILY ARE YOU OKAY? 🙉 HAVE YOU SEEN IT? YOU HAVE TO HAVE SEEN IT, RIGHT? Ugh, I'm so sorry. Journalists are awful. I hate them! I mean, not all journalists, but the tabloid ones. They deserve to be drawn and quartered. Or at least have every embarrassing picture anyone has ever taken of them leaked online.

Maya: Shit, it's not even six a.m. over there. You might not have seen it. You probably aren't awake yet, are you? Or you might be DEAD! 😾 😨 💀 🪦 Are you dead? Please text me as soon as you get this and let me know that you're not dead, okay?

Maya: UPDATE: You are probably not dead. 😅 I just googled this guy, and he seems harmless. I mean, not harmless to your reputation as you are currently TRENDING ON UK TWITTER in a very unpleasant way. And I'm pretty sure this is the kind of thing that proves not ALL publicity is good publicity. But harmless as far as the chances that you are lying dead in a ditch with your guts spilling out onto the blood-splattered snow. 💧 ⛄ God, I've watched way too many crime documentaries. I'm going to stop that in the New Year. Or start watching even more if we go bankrupt, and I have nothing to do with my time except move back into my childhood bedroom and binge Netflix with my parents. Please know that I'm not blaming you for this—you have every right to go home with a hot British guy—but this could be the nail in the coffin for Darling Events. We have to get out ahead of this and make it better somehow. Rewrite the narrative. Take control of the story. Something! There has to be a way.

Maya: I have an idea! 💡 A brilliant idea. Call me as soon as you get this. I'm not going to bed until we run damage control.

> Maya: I mean it. Call me the second you wake up.

> Maya: ✋ DO NOT PASS GO, DO NOT LOOK AT TWITTER. 😃 IT WILL MAKE YOU SAD, AND I NEED YOU FOCUSED, NOT SAD!

"What is happening?" I mutter, rising to pace in front of the couch, laptop balanced in one hand.

I could try Facetiming Maya on my computer—that should work until I can find my phone—but I have to know what's happening first.

And why half my contacts in New York are texting me, too…

A quick scroll through the rest of the messages reveals a mixture of friends congratulating me on my hot date, apologizing for how cruel people can be, and asking me to text them all the hot gossip ASAP.

There's also a text from my mother— *Sweetheart, Isabelle just sent me a concerning update about your London trip. Please call when you get a chance. Love you.*— and several from Isabelle.

Though my little sister doesn't seem "concerned."

Elated is more the word I would use…

> Isabelle: OMG EM, you're famous!!!! 😱 💐💚

> Isabelle: And you look GORGEOUS! Don't listen to what those pathetic basement dwellers are saying in the comments. 🍪 They're just stupid, woman-hating jerks. Your curves are gorgeous, and clearly Oliver was a BIG FAN. 😏

> Isabelle: So, how serious is this? How long have you two been dating? And why didn't you tell me that you have a BRITISH BOYFRIEND?!?! 🇬🇧 😍

> Isabelle: I hope it's not because I've been too caught up in wedding planning stuff. No matter how busy I am, I always have time for my big sissy. 🥺 You know that, right? And I am SO HAPPY for you!!!

> Isabelle: I mean, could this be more perfect? 🤩 💖 😍 The girl who made me watch Sense and Sensibility ten thousand times as a kid is now living out her very own Colonel Brandon fantasy with a gorgeous British guy with a country estate!! Have you been there? Is it swanky as fork? 👀 A Viscount is a pretty big deal, right? I bet it's super swanky.

Viscount?

What the...

I switch tabs so fast I almost drop the laptop. My fingers tap frantically at the keyboard, typing—Oliver, Viscount, mid-thirties, United Kingdom—into the search bar.

As the results load, I slowly forget how to breathe...
Because they aren't all about Oliver.
Half of them are about Oliver and...*me*.

The Honorable Oliver David Dawson Featherswallow Spotted in Passionate Embrace with Mystery Woman.

Featherswallow Spare Finally Settling Down? Fifth in Line to Throne Gets Cozy with Plush Redhead

EXCLUSIVE PHOTOS: *Lord Oliver's Late Night Lamppost Liaison with Plump Pin-up*

The pictures are grainy but unmistakable. There's me, pressed against a lamppost, kissing Oliver like the world is ending. There's Oliver's hand in my hair, then cupping my breast through my shirt. There's my leg doing something that felt natural at the time, but in photos reminds me of that woman who encourages women to get out in the forest and rub their "minge" on trees.

"Minge" is the British word for pussy, and mine is about two inches from being out for show and tell in the last shot.

And the comments.

Oh God, the comments...

Who's the tubby mess in the cheap suit?

She has to be American. They have no class. None

at all. He should have stayed with Aisling. 🙄
Why did they break up!?

Poor thing looks like she's been dragged through a hedge backward after a donut binge. If I'd known the spare loved thighs that thick, I could have set him up with my sister. At least she knows how to use a hairbrush.

Ew. 😱 What exactly is going on here? Is she kissing him or eating his face? Has anyone checked on the spare's face? Does he still have a face? 🙊

A man this good-looking could do so much better. SO much. SO SAD.

Ignoring the shame swelling in my chest and heating my cheeks, I click through to Oliver's Wikipedia page with numb fingers.

The Honorable Oliver David Dawson Featherswallow. Thirty-four. Second son of Viscountess Vivian Marie Featherswallow, née Plimpton, and the late Viscount Harry Herbert Featherswallow, which tracks with what Olly was saying last night about his father.

Fifth in line to the throne.

That part is enough to blow my mind—and explains why he has paparazzi following him around.

Graduated top of his class at Oxford. Owns an architecture firm. Considered one of Britain's most eligible bachelors...

Apparently, he once dated an earl's daughter who

looks like a supermodel. And an actual supermodel. And an Irish soap star with hair as red as mine, but thighs half the size, who has something of a cult following

Her fans are already in the comments, insisting I'm the poor man's Aisling Grey and clearly a stand-in for a man regretting breaking up with his gorgeous Irish actress lady love.

Shit!

I'm going to throw up.

I really might.

I'm about to shut my laptop and make a run for the guest bathroom, just in case, when Maya texts again:

> Maya: WHY AREN'T YOU CALLING ME? CALL ME!! 😫 I've tried calling you, but it just rings and rings before going to voicemail.
>
> Maya: It's 7:10 over there. I know you're up by now. You never sleep past 7.
>
> Maya: Emily, please, just call me. I promise, I'm not mad.
>
> Maya: But we need to get ahead of this.
>
> Maya: Take a deep breath and call me, and we can start sorting this out together.

Before I can Facetime her, two more texts pop through, within seconds of each other—

. . .

> Bounty and Bloom: Good morning, Ms. Darling. Unfortunately, I won't be able to consider working with you on the Fletchers' gala. A trusted colleague has advised me against doing so. Wishing you the best.

> Sunday Best Florists: Please remove us from your potential vendor list, Ms. Darling. I don't work with careless people. And your behavior last night at the nativity play—and afterwards, if that's really you in the pictures with the Viscount's brother—proves you are careless in the extreme. Kindly lose our number.

Oh God, no.

Belinda is still pissed and up early making calls. It's the only explanation.

Maya's going to kill me. *I'm* going to kill me. How could I—

"Morning, darling."

I yip in surprise, nearly jumping out of my skin and sending the laptop flying. I manage to catch it—thank God for small miracles—and clutch it to my chest as I spin to see Oliver standing in the hall. He's wearing boxer briefs and nothing else and, unlike yours truly, looks even better naked in the daylight. He's all muscles and the perfect dusting of dark hair and dancing blue eyes so warm and happy to see me, I almost forget he's a dirty liar who lies.

Almost.

"How could you do this?" I demand, the words emerging shakier than expected. But then, I'm pretty darned "shook" right now.

His smile falters. "Do what?"

"Lie to me. Trick me. You said your name was Olly," I say, rolling my shoulders back in hopes it will help me feel less small. "Not Oliver with some other names in the middle, *Featherswallow*. I'm no fan of the peerage, but even I know that name."

"Because it's ridiculous," he supplies with a charmingly self-effacing smile, I refuse to fall for.

"Exactly," I agree. "If you'd said *Featherswallow*, I would have known who you were and had at least some idea of what I was getting into. But you didn't say it, because you didn't want me to know. You wanted to keep me in the dark until it was too late, and I was a national laughing stock."

He frowns. "What? Emily, I—"

"More like an *international* laughing stock," I cut in, my voice cracking. "Everyone in New York and New Jersey has seen the pictures, too. As well as my sister in Switzerland and God knows who else."

He drags a hand through his hair. "Fuck. How did this happen? We were completely alone!"

"Except that we weren't," I say, fighting tears. "And now our lamppost erotica is all over the internet. Hell, the entire world probably has an opinion about the pudgy disaster you were making out with in the snow last night by now."

His gaze hardens. "Has someone said that about you? If so, I'll—"

"You'll do nothing," I say, shaking my head. "You

can't do anything. You're *fifth in line to the throne*, for God's sake. You have to behave yourself and be a good little Viscount's baby brother. I know how the royal stuff works." I sniff. "And you'll be fine anyway." I stuff my laptop back into its sleeve with shaking hands. "You're a hot single guy. It's the rest of us who are cannon fodder for the monsters of the internet."

"I'm so sorry, Emily. Truly," he says, the pleading note in his voice making it harder to fight the tears stinging into my eyes. "Let's just calm down, take a beat, and then—"

"It's not fair, Olly," I force out, blinking faster as I turn to meet his gaze. "You let me think you were just a guy drinking at a bar. A nice guy, who was kind of a sarcastic shit at first, but then turned out to be...pretty great." His handsome face swims as I add in a whisper, "You lied to me."

He exhales a rush of breath, his forehead furrows deepening as he says, "I didn't, Em. I wasn't lying, I promise. I was just...withholding."

"Withholding," I echo with a sharp laugh. "Well, the next time you decide to *withhold*, be decent enough to be discreet about it. That way, the next woman who's dumb enough to go home with you won't have to wake up to internet abuse and the possible end of her career."

"It's not going to be the end of your career. I won't allow it." He steps closer and I back away, nearly tripping over my roller bag. "Listen, I have connections in high places, I can—"

"I bet you do," I say, hating the tears now streaming down my cheeks. "But I don't. And I have to go."

My laptop pings in my purse.

I gulp and swipe at my eyes. "That's probably another

florist, texting to let me know that they don't work with people Belinda Moore hates. She's turned the entire London floral industry against me, and it's not even eight o'clock."

"Emily, please, I can help," he insists. "I promise I can."

"You've helped enough," I say, stuffing my feet into my ruined shoes. "I just need to find my phone, get out of here, and call my business partner before she has a nervous breakdown." I bite my lip, fighting a fresh wave of tears. "But I've already looked everywhere, and I can't find my phone, so it's probably lost to a snow drift somewhere and—"

"No, it's not," he cuts in. "It's on top of the fridge."

I blink. "Wh-what?"

"It's on the fridge," he says, a sheepish expression on his face. "I may have put it there last night after you said you were leaving first thing in the morning."

My jaw drops. "You hid my phone?"

"I didn't *hide* it. I relocated it." He crosses to the kitchen and reaches up—way up, to a place I never could have seen without a stepladder—and retrieves my phone. When he turns back, seeing my no doubt stunned expression, he adds, "Okay, fine, I hid it, but I didn't do it to upset you. I just... I didn't want you to leave without saying goodbye. And perhaps giving me your number..."

The admission makes my chest ache in a way that can't be totally chalked up to anger or betrayal.

Which only makes me angrier. I can't afford to have soft feelings for Oliver Featherswallow right now. Or ever again.

I snatch the phone from his hand, noting the twenty-something missed calls.

Probably Maya.

Or my mother.

Or Isabelle.

Or more florists calling to assure me I'll never secure a floral arrangement in this town again. I might as well tuck tail and waddle back across the pond.

"Goodbye, Oliver," I mutter, ignoring the stab of regret in my gut as I shove the phone into my purse. "Good luck with everything. I'm sure you have a P.R. person, but just in case they're at a loss for ideas, I'd suggest getting back together with Aisling." I grab my roller and start for the door, tossing over my shoulder, "The people in the comments really liked you two together."

"Don't do this, Emily," he calls after me. "Last night was special. You know it was."

I pause in the doorway, glancing back at him. He's still in his underwear, looking gorgeous and genuinely distressed, and for a split second, I'm tempted to close the door. Go back into the gorgeous flat. Let him hug me and "help."

But he can't help, not really.

It would be like a seagull trying to help a fish. Or a tubby chunk of kelp growing on the ocean floor. We live in two completely different worlds, and the sooner I face that reality, the better. Olly and I don't work.

Heck, there is no Olly.

There's only Oliver Featherswallow, an obscenely wealthy man in line for the throne who has no idea what life is like for the rest of us.

And no, he can't really help that.

But he could have helped what he did last night. He didn't have to lie and play me for a fool, leaving me defenseless against an onslaught of the kind of attention I've never wanted. I make other people's parties go viral; I have no urge to be the focus of the spotlight myself.

Especially this kind of spotlight.

So, I just shake my head and close the door softly behind me. Then, I hobble down the hall in my broken heels.

The elevator arrives with a cheerful ding that feels like another stab in the back. As the doors close, I catch my reflection in the polished steel. Yesterday's eye makeup is smeared under my eyes. My ponytail looks like I've been electrocuted by Christmas lights. And what might be a hickey is peeking out of the top of my cowl neck sweater.

The British tabloids were right.

I am a disaster.

A tubby, American, nativity-destroying, career-imploding agent of pandemonium who's just walked away from the first man to make her "Big O" without help from a battery-operated boyfriend. The first man to make her laugh and feel carefree in longer than she can remember.

A man who did seem genuinely sorry for the mistakes he'd made...

"And he seemed to like you," I whisper. "As much as you liked him."

As the elevator descends, I allow myself two floors of regret.

Then I pull out my phone and start typing a list into my notes app:

Operation: Fix Everything

1. Call Maya. Apologize Profusely. Tell her about

florist blackballing. Assure her you will not rest until you make this better.

2. Run damage control with remaining florists.

3. Find wizard/time machine to undo last 12 hours

4. Stop thinking about Oliver's hands

5. And all his other parts.

6. And his smile and the fact that no man has ever been so desperate for your phone number.

7. Do NOT cry in the Uber.

8. Remember: You're a strong, independent, entrepreneurial woman. You fix things. You don't need a prince (or fifth-in-line-to-the-throne) to save you.

The elevator opens to the lobby, and I square my shoulders, marching out into the snowy London morning like a general heading to war.
A war I'm probably going to lose, but still...
At least I'll go down fighting in sensible shoes.
As soon as I find time to buy some.

Chapter Seven
OLIVER

Three hours.

Just three bloody hours since Emily walked out of my flat, and I've already seen enough vile internet commentary to make me consider hunting down every keyboard warrior in Britain and introducing them to the business end of my great-grandfather's cavalry saber.

What is *wrong* with these people?

Don't they have something better to do than spew hate at a total stranger?

Apparently not...

> @BurmingFam: America called. They want their portion sizes back.

> @LiamInLondon: She's giving 'lost tourist asking for the loo at Buckingham Palace' vibes. 🤣

> @Daisy553: American abroad starter pack: bad

suit, bad shoes, bad decisions. God, if polyester could cry, that suit would be sobbing into a pint.

@Irish4Fabs: I can't believe he went from Aisling to THAT?! 🤢 😩 Please, someone, make it make sense. MAKE IT MAKE SENSE!

I scroll through the latest batch of poison on the train, my jaw clenching harder with each swipe of my thumb.

"Maybe because Aisling loved fame more than anything on God's green earth?" I mutter beneath my breath. "Including food, laughter, fun, and me? And on the rare occasions that she did laugh, she sounded like a constipated horse having an asthma attack."

The old woman in the big blue muffler beside me shoots a narrow glance my way, clearly wondering if I'm a serious threat or simply a sociopath who doesn't know how to keep my mouth shut on the tube.

Pressing my lips together, I tuck my chin tighter to my chest.

This isn't the day to attract attention.

I've already done enough of that for one news cycle, a fact proven by the Twitter poll that pops up next on my feed:

@GlitterAndScandal: Emergency poll ladies: Who styled our randy American? 🌍 👗

A) Paddington Bear's dry cleaner
B) An angry Primark mannequin
C) The lost & found bin at Heathrow

D) Her worst enemy (mission accomplished)

14,002 votes · Final results in 3h

She'd just gotten off a seven-hour flight, lugged her bags through a snowstorm, and crashed through a manger. Don't these people have any empathy? Or capacity for reason?

And yes, the suit was bad, but the woman herself...

Well, she's magnificent, truly one of the most beautiful women I've met in years. I seriously can't understand the comments attacking her physical appearance. Are they fucking blind? I mean, Christ, those curves, that glorious Viking goddess hair, those eyes that threaten annihilation when she's angry and set your soul on fire when she pulls you down for a kiss and—

I cut the thought off at the pass as I exit the train, refusing to let my brain start flipping through images from last night.

There's no time for that. Not until I make this better. Because Emily isn't just a sexy redhead who destroyed me in bed; she's the whole brilliant, authentic, quick-witted package.

She deserves better than this.

And I'm going to make sure she gets it.

Up top, I pocket my phone and stride quickly through the busy streets before cutting through the Hyde Park Winter Wonderland crowd. The massive Christmas market is in full festive assault mode. Carousel music competes with carols piped through the speakers, and the scent of hot chocolate, cinnamon rolls, candy nuts, and gingerbread is thick in the crisp morning air.

And clearly, the children are already thoroughly sugar-infused and ready to rumble.

Just past the puppet theater, a small girl in a reindeer jumper crashes into my legs while chasing her brother, both of them shrieking with joy.

"Sorry, mister! Sorry!" she calls, waving over her shoulder as they race toward the hot chocolate stand.

I lift a hand in acknowledgement of her apology, holiday nostalgia tightening my chest as I watch them go.

Twenty-something years ago, that would have been Edward and me, running wild while Father pretended to be cross, but secretly egged us on with extra sticky buns and a promise to stay for the sweary puppet show they put on for the adults after the sun went down.

He loved a sweary puppet show. And a Christmas market and mulled wine and spoiling his boys with sweets and stealing kisses under the mistletoe until Mother laughed, threw her arms around his neck, and called him "simply awful."

But he wasn't awful.

He was so good and all love.

"Best time of the year, Olly. It really is," he used to say, beaming at everyone we passed like they were long lost friends. *"We should always be like this. So full of joy and kindness and hope. Never lose hope, son. There's so much good in the world. Love is going to win, one day. I just know it."*

It's almost as if he knew his youngest son would grow up to be a man prone to a touch of nihilism. To seeing the evil in the world and deciding we might all be better off if a meteor sent humanity the way of the dinosaur.

The events of this morning certainly haven't given me much reason for hope...

I shake off the melancholy before it can settle in. I have to keep moving.

There's a lovely girl's reputation to salvage.

Belinda Moore's shop occupies a prim corner in Marylebone, between an organic deli and a children's clothing store full of tiny hand-knitted jumpers. Her look is earnest-meets-expensive—a little rustic, a lot luxe. The window is a showstopper packed with white roses, silver branches, and cream-flower stags arranged like guardians protecting the realm. It's equal parts "Claridge's winter wedding" and "you're paying for the story."

It's beautiful, a touch smug, and the subtext is clear. Belinda has staked her claim on this particular corner of the kingdom.

And if you cross her?

Well, she'll rearrange your life into something less than pretty...

The bell chimes as I enter, and Belinda looks up from where she's fussing over an elaborate white poinsettia and twig bouquet behind the counter.

When she spots me, her expression goes from professional welcome to Arctic tundra in record time.

"Well. Oliver." She doesn't quite seethe my name, but it's close. "You're up and about awfully early this morning. Considering the evening you had after you left the pub..."

Well, there goes any doubt that she's seen the pictures...

"Morning, Belinda. Lovely display. Very festive." I flash my most charming smile. Never let them see you sweat or cave to so much as a hint of shame. "And yes, about last night... That's why I'm here, actually. I think we should talk."

"If you're here to apologize for your *friend*, I'm afraid that would be a waste of time." She turns back to her flowers, dismissing me with the efficiency of someone who's dealt with her share of aristocrats. "The woman demolished a very expensive, very time-intensive-to-create floral arrangement, made poor little Timothy Blake cry, and ruined the tableau before I got a single shareable photo." She clucks her tongue before adding beneath her breath, "Not to mention flashing her knickers in a room full of children."

"Knickers? She didn't flash her knickers. I think I would have noticed if—" I catch myself before I make things worse, forcing another smile as Belinda shifts slitted brown eyes my way. "Right. Yes. Well, of course, you're correct. It was an unfortunate outcome, all around. Though in her defense, the door *was* quite stuck, and she was dead on her feet. She'd just flown in from New York on a miserable flight."

"I don't care if she'd just flown in from Mars." Belinda jams a stem into the arrangement with unnecessary force. "She's reckless and unprofessional. And clearly has no respect for the care and skill that goes into creating a piece of art. If she did, she would have done a better job of apologizing."

"Oh, come on, Bel," I murmur as I lean against the counter. "She *did* apologize. Several times. I heard her."

But Belinda only flicks her pink-streaked hair from her forehead and hitches her nose higher in the air.

"She was clearly devastated after you left," I add. "The moment you were out the door, she sat right down and started making a list of ways to get back in your good graces. Action item number one was begging for your forgiveness on her hands and knees. Then, on her belly, if necessary."

Belinda pauses, one wrinkly twig poised above her vase. "Seriously?"

"As the grave," I assure her. "There was also something on there about offering to de-thorn roses for you until she'd worked off her debt. I'm not sure if that's a thing florists actually do, but she really was quite sorry." I exhale a meaningful sigh. "Though not as sorry as she was this morning, when the bullying from the Who's Who of the London floral community hit her inbox full force." I arch a brow her way. "Your doing, I presume?"

Belinda has the grace to look slightly abashed. "I made a few calls. As a gesture of professional courtesy. We look out for each other in our industry. We have to. You wouldn't believe the way people try to take advantage of vendors in the hospitality field, Oliver."

"Well, no, I can't, but I imagine it's awful. So many entitled people making unhinged demands." I cock my head and furrow my brow, begging for a scrap of empathy like a homeless puppy. I'm not too proud to beg, especially if there's even a chance I can get Belinda to give Em the benefit of the doubt. "But Emily isn't one of those people, Bel. She's a party planner. In the hospitality field trenches, just like you. She's a comrade in arms, not your enemy."

"I'm not so sure about *that*," she mutters, but there's a hint of doubt in her tone that wasn't there before. "Though I *do* have sympathy for anyone trying to pull together a pitch for an event like the Fletchers' gala. That's nearly as much pressure as a royal engagement."

"I'm sure you're right," I say, before adding idly, "Speaking of society functions, my mother's looking for someone to do the floral design for our New Year's Eve party at Swallow House." She isn't, actually. We never do flowers for the New Year's event, not since Edward and I both grew quite serious about sustainable holiday decorating in our teens. Shipping a massive load of blooms in the dead of winter isn't environmentally responsible. But we can make an exception. Just this once... "It isn't a massive event, but the royal family always stops by for dinner before they're off to their other engagements. And when they do, I'd be happy to mention who did the centerpieces for the table. I hear they haven't decided who's doing the flowers for the princess's wedding summer after next, so..."

Belinda's hands go completely still, and I'm sure dreams of being the lucky florist who lands the next royal wedding dance behind her eyes.

"I mean, if you would have time to fit in a few centerpieces and something for the entry hall." I examine my nails with studied casualness. "I know you're very busy. What with all the holiday parties and events and crushing the dreams of accident-prone, but very hardworking, very *apologetic* Americans..."

She wrinkles her nose. "Subtle, Featherswallow."

"No, just hopeful, darling," I counter. "I've never seen a woman so broken up about tripping over her own feet. And that's all it was, Bel. Just a silly accident."

Belinda sighs, setting down her stem as she turns to face me fully for the first time. Then, with the air of someone making a great and noble sacrifice, she pulls out her phone.

"Fine. One last chance. *One*. I'll shoot her an email, offering her another opportunity for a consultation." She types quickly, her thumbs flying with impressive speed. "But if she destroys anything else, I'm billing you personally."

I grin, some of the tension easing from my chest as I thank her.

Profusely.

"I'm serious," she adds as she finishes the email and sends it on its way with a final tap to her screen. She sets the phone down before pinning me with a stern finger, "If she's late or pushy or shows the slightest sign that she'll be difficult to work with, I'm done."

I nod, sobering. "Understood. But I'm sure she won't be. Emily's delightful. Completely delightful. Once you get to know her, of course."

"Clearly, you think so." Her lips hook up in a knowing smirk. "But try and keep your enjoyment of her 'delights' indoors from now on, all right, Oliver? I don't know about you, but if shots of me snogging by a lamp-post were all over social media, my mother would be having a meltdown."

"My mother doesn't pay much attention to social media. Or any media at all, really," I say, before adding with a dry smile, "But my grandmother *has* texted a dozen times." I lift my cell as I back toward the door. "Speaking of, I should get back to her before she sends the mounted police to fetch me. As for the New Year's Eve party, I—"

"I'll have sketches to you by early next week, and you can forward them to your mother." She waves me off.

"Go on. Call your grandmother and beg forgiveness for being a slag."

She softens the words with a laugh, which I appreciate.

I have no shame about being a slag, but I'm grateful that I'm no longer on Belinda's shit list. She really *is* the best florist in London.

As I step outside, the cold hits me afresh.

The sight of another text and two missed calls from my grandmother increases the chill. Her meddling makes my mother's attempts at matchmaking seem quaint by comparison. Her mother, the Dowager Baroness Plimpton, is a shameless bully who steamrolls through her grandchildren's lives with zero apology. When you're on her good side, she can be an invaluable ally and fantastic, silly fun.

But get on her bad side…

Bracing myself for another charm offensive, I tap her contact, booming a warm, "Grandmother! Happy Christmas, how are you?" when she answers.

"Oliver. Good gracious! Finally!" Her voice carries the kind of authority that once commanded diplomatic missions and now leads the Corgi Appreciation Society with zero tolerance for shirking or shenanigans. "I was beginning to think you'd been kidnapped. Or worse, were avoiding me…"

"Never, Grandmother. Simply had some business to attend to."

"I imagine you did." Her tone shifts to barely contained delight. "I've seen the photographs, darling. Everyone has. Lady Prescott called to ask if you were having some sort of breakdown, and the duke next door is convinced you should join his support group for wastrels who can't handle their liquor."

I close my eyes with a wince. "I'm so sorry, Grandmother. Truly, I never—"

"What on earth are you apologizing for, child? Honestly, I couldn't be more delighted." She lets out a musical laugh that stops me in my tracks. "What a gorgeous creature. She's absolutely stunning, Oliver. And so refreshing! None of that skin-and-bones-lugging-a-designer-handbag nonsense you usually parade about. This is a real woman with real appetites and a genuine passion for my grandson. And I, for one, think that's fantastic. When do I meet her?"

"Oh, well, I—" I clear my throat as I duck into a small pocket garden for privacy. The snow is already melting, but still deep enough that I'm alone on this crystal-clear morning. "She's in town on business, so I'm not—"

"Business is well and good, but a woman has to eat," Grandmother cuts in. "Bring her to dinner. Tonight. I'll have Deirdre make that lamb with mint that you like."

"I'd love to, but things are a bit more complicated than that, I'm afraid."

She sighs. "Everything's complicated with your generation. In my day, when a man was photographed ravishing a woman against a lamppost, he proposed, and we set about planning the wedding. Oh, your girl would be a lovely winter bride! Redheads pop so beautifully against freshly fallen snow. Though, of course, you'd have to plan the ceremony for farther north to be sure you—"

"Different times, Grandmother," I cut in before she can book the venue.

"Better times, if you ask me." She sighs dramatically.

"Certainly, simpler ones. Oh, all right. She's working, fine. But she'll be at the party with you on Saturday, of course. There's no way you can show up alone or with another woman." She sniffs. "If you did, I might be forced to assume the duke has a point. If you're kissing one woman like that on Monday night and out with another by Saturday... Well, it wouldn't reflect well on your character, Oliver."

"No, it wouldn't," I agree, properly chastised.

My grandmother's no fool—she knows that modern dating culture, even for the aristocracy, is the furthest thing from classy or refined—but she expects her grandsons to keep their scandalous behavior out of the gossip rags.

I've let her down, and must do my best to make amends.

Luckily, our agendas are aligned this time around. She wants Emily at her party; I want Emily back by my side, enjoying the holidays.

I just need to find a way to make both our Christmas wishes come true...

"And I'm not getting any younger, darling," Grandmother continues, her voice suddenly trembly and thin. "This could be my last Christmas, and I so desperately want it to be a good one."

I shake my head, a wry smile twisting my lips. "You're terrible."

"I am not!" she objects, her words once again steady and strong.

"Yes, you are. You're nowhere near your deathbed bed and manipulation is beneath you. I'll issue the invitation for Emily to join me as my plus one right away. And if she isn't able to make it, I'll come alone. I promise."

"Oh, she'll be able to make it! Of course, she will.

What else is there to do in London this time of year except go to parties? Though I will still expect you to wear your punishment sweater. You lost a bet, and rules are rules." She makes a puckering sound. "Kiss, kiss, darling. And don't worry about the beastly people on the internet or the rest of the tongue waggers. They don't know you like I do. You're clearly smitten with this woman, and I think it's lovely. High time you found a lady who could match your spark and fire. See you soon."

She rings off before I can respond, leaving me standing in the melting snow by the garden's silent fountain, pondering her words of wisdom.

Emily *does* match my fire.

And I *am* smitten with her after a single night.

If the world knew just how smitten, I'm guessing a lot of this ugliness would go away. The certainty that Emily's just another notch on a randy aristocrat's bedpost seems to be driving the bulk of the cruelty. And the British tabloids love any excuse to pile on a random American tart in a tight skirt.

But what if she wasn't random?

What if we made it clear we're together? A proper couple?

The press would likely report the news that the Viscount's little brother has an American girlfriend with their usual disdain for anyone they deem "unsuitable," then quickly grow bored, once Emily and I proved to be as yawn-inducing as every other aristocratic pairing. They'd get sick of snapping photos of us at high society events or volunteering to serve food at my mother's charity, and move on to the next scandal.

Emily's reputation would be saved, and I'd be back in

Grandmother's good graces. Not to mention I'd have the perfect excuse to spend more time with a certain redhead.

Surely, once the internet heat is turned down, Emily would relish the chance to spend more time together. Her laughter last night was real, and I can't help feeling she could use more happy, carefree nights in her life.

Yes! This is it. The brilliant plan I should have known would come to me, sooner or later.

And there's no time like the present for putting it into motion...

I pull out my phone, pulse picking up as I see how quickly the morning has flown by. I have less than an hour before the charity luncheon, but this can't wait. Every minute we delay is another minute Emily spends marinating in nasty internet bile. If I delay too long, she'll have convinced herself I'm the worst thing that ever happened to her, and I can't let that come to pass.

Even if we never spend another night together, I don't want the online annihilation of an innocent woman on my conscience. Especially at Christmastime.

Especially *this* Christmas, when it would already be so easy to give up, crawl under the covers, and pronounce the world a miserable place, barren of joy, basic human decency, or holiday spirit.

But I can't give in that easily.

I have to fight. For Emily. For myself. And for a reason to believe that there's actually something worth celebrating in a world without my father in it.

The walk to Mayfair passes in a determined blur, my thoughts racing as I compose my arguments and counter-arguments. By the time I reach the hotel, I have my strategy sorted.

Catching my reflection in the golden elevator doors at

the back of the lobby, I straighten my collar. I look like what I am: a man of privilege on his way to a charity luncheon.

I can't help that.

I *am* a man of privilege, but it's what I do with that privilege that counts. Hopefully, today, I can employ it to ease the suffering of a lovely young woman.

Of course, Emily might not want saving. She made it pretty clear this morning that she wanted nothing more to do with me or my lying, lamp-snogging, fifth-in-line-to-the-throne face.

But people don't always know what's best for them. Sometimes they need a nudge in the right direction from someone with a clearer perspective.

I exit the lift with the confidence of a man on a mission of righteousness.

Emily Darling doesn't know it yet, but she's about to become my girlfriend.

I simply refuse to take no for an answer.

Chapter Eight

EMILY

It's just after eleven, and so far, this day is proving that old adage that things can always get worse.

And worse and worse...

"Okay, so two more florists blacklisted you," Maya calculates on the other end of the line, her voice surprisingly calm for someone doing catastrophic math. "That only makes five total. That's not so bad! There are dozens of amazing florists in London."

"Six," I correct, pacing the length of my hotel room in bare feet, while I wait for my new shoes to be delivered. "The Rose Tattoo sent a 'take your dumb face and go home,' email while you were refilling your wine."

"Oh, God," she says, with another gulping noise. "I'm so glad it's still night my time. If I couldn't wine the pain away, I'd be having a panic attack right now. How are you holding up? I can't imagine Earl Grey is taking the edge off."

"I'm fine," I assure her, wincing as I stub my toe on the desk leg.

My room is "very chic" as promised by the online

reviews, but my standard is barely big enough for a proper panic pace. Every lap, I have to dodge the room service tray I ordered an hour ago—stress-eating scrambled eggs and blood sausage seemed like a good idea at the time, but now the congealing grease is making me nauseous—the desk, and a plush chair I refuse to sit in.

I don't deserve comfort, not after the mess I've made.

"Seriously, this doesn't make any sense," Maya says. "You said the whole thing was an accident, right?"

"Yes, but I destroyed baby Jesus." I spin at the window, turning away from the normal people living normal lives on the street below. People who aren't watching their careers implode in real-time... "A floral baby Jesus constructed of outrageously expensive orchids that took twenty-something hours to make."

"Sounds creepy if you ask me."

"It was kind of creepy," I admit, "but it was clearly very important to her. And I'm clearly now the devil who crushed the Messiah in his manger and must be vanquished at all costs."

"And you apologized profusely?"

"Profusely," I assure her. "I did everything but get down on the floor and beg, and that's only because I was already on the floor when I started apologizing."

Maya sighs. Curses. Then sighs again. "All right, well... We'll just have to hope there are a few solid florists in London who don't bend the knee to Queen Belinda. Looks like the Rousseau wedding is off the table for this summer, too, so we need to lock Fletchers down more than ever."

"What?" I stop mid-pace, nearly tripping over my exploded roller bag. Apparently, stress brings out my messy side. "But we've been courting them for months! I sent them a custom proposal with hand-painted watercolors!"

"I know, they suck. I hate them. Whatever, though. Moving on."

Smelling a rat, I demand, "What really happened, Maya? Tell me."

She heaves a tortured sigh. "Fine. They just texted. Said they're going with someone with a 'more refined social media presence.' Apparently, having a planner who's trending for being a sexy minx whose milkshake brings all the English lords to the yard isn't the vibe they want for their 'elegant Southampton soirée.' Which is ridiculous. Those pictures were hot. You were hot! And have they been alive lately? The gossip cycle moves so fast, you'll be old news months before they send the final invitations. By January, no one will remember you were ever in London."

"I hope you're right," I mutter, fighting to swallow past the lump forming in my throat.

My laptop pings with a new email, making me flinch.

I shouldn't look. I really shouldn't.

But hell, I'm already spiraling, might as well keep swirling down the despair drain.

Ms. Darling: After careful consideration, we've decided our firm wouldn't be a good match for what you have in mind for the Fletchers' event. But we wish you the best in your future endeavors. Nathan Smythe, Chelsea Botanicals

"Make that seven florists," I mutter, sinking onto the bed with my laptop on my trembling knees.

"Seven? How is that even possible? It's not even noon!"

"Belinda Moore rides at dawn." I refresh my email,

watching two more rejections pop up in real-time. "Eight. Nine." I scroll, throat growing tighter as I scan the messages. "The last one includes a personal note advising me to leave the country as soon as possible. Apparently, once the British tabloids have someone in their crosshairs, they're like a dog with a bone."

"Well, at least that's kind? Sort of?"

"Sort of," I agree. "But they also included a link to a meme of me crushing the manger. Apparently, one of the parents was filming when I fell." I click over to Instagram, unable to stop myself from looking. "Nearly a million views, Maya! Already." My stomach pitches as I realize it's set to 'All I Want for Christmas,' and that they've timed it so I land on baby Jesus right when Mariah hits the high note. My breath comes faster, and my ribs squeeze tight. Tighter. Tightest. "I'm a meme. A horrible, embarrassing meme. And once you're a meme, there's no escape, Maya. Once you're a meme, the internet will haunt you forever. This is now my own personal, hellish Ghost of Christmas Present! And Future! And—"

"Emily, breathe," she cuts in. "This isn't helping. We have to calm down and strategize."

"I think we're beyond strategy, Maya." I scroll through other social feeds, each one bringing fresh horror. "This is it. *I'm* over. Finished. I'll have to change careers. Move away from people who have access to the internet. Maybe I can get work on an insect farm in rural Kenya. They speak English *and* Swahili, so maybe I could—"

"Stop it, woman. Right now. And listen to me." Maya's voice takes on her no-nonsense boss babe tone, the one that usually means she's locked in on a solution against all odds. "I've been scrolling, too, and a pattern has emerged."

I frown. "A pattern that I am a hideous, klutzy sow with a leg that does weird things when I'm kissing?"

"A pattern of assumption," Maya counters. "The pictures actually aren't that steamy, Em. And you don't look silly at all."

"The comment section would beg to differ."

"Well, I beg to differ with the trolls, and so should you. You look like a cute woman, fresh off a long flight, having a steamy night with a hot guy," she says. "The problem is that the tabloids and the gossip accounts and everyone else are assuming you're some rumpled nobody who threw herself at a drunk aristocrat who kicked you to the curb as soon as he sobered up."

"Thanks," I say. "You're making me feel so much better."

"Let me finish. You're only a scandal because you're an outsider. A nobody. Some spicy stranger who popped up in connection with this usually well-behaved guy they're assuming you led astray with your big American boobs."

"Don't remind me." I squeeze my eyes shut, but the shot of Olly cupping my breast through my shirt is burned into my brain.

"What I'm saying is they're assuming you're fair game. But what if you weren't? What if you weren't a stranger or a nobody? What if you were something far more banal?"

I exhale, my eyes flying open. "I don't understand."

"Emily, what's the most boring story in the world?"

I shake my head. "I don't know. Watching paint dry?

British parliamentary procedure? My love life before last night?"

"An established couple getting drunk and handsy after date night," Maya says, victory in her voice. I don't understand. "Nobody cares about a man kissing his girlfriend outside a pub. I'm sure it happens literally every night. It's normal. It's boring. The press would move on in forty-eight hours, guaranteed."

My stomach drops as I realize where she's going. "Maya, no."

"Listen, you said he apologized this morning and wanted to see you again. I'm sure he'd be open to bending the truth a bit in the name of making this up to you."

"Absolutely not."

"Oh, come on. All you have to do is pretend you've been dating for a while, and this whole thing becomes a non-story. You're not some random hookup. You're his girlfriend who missed him so much she couldn't help making out with him in the snow."

"I can't fake date a Viscount's little brother!" I stand up too fast, laptop sliding dangerously. I catch it, setting it back on the bureau, before I add, "He's fifth in line to the throne. That's like being a Kennedy. But with actual crowns and probably a castle or giant manor home somewhere."

"And he clearly likes you, so stop inventing problems," she says. "We're in the problem-*solving* business here. You could even say you guys were celebrating something special last night. Something that would explain why you both got carried away. The point is, you're legitimate. You belong in his world. And as someone who belongs, you are granted a certain amount of protection from the worst of this. Not to mention the fact that more people will be inclined to stick up for you if you aren't a one-night stand. Slut-shaming is real, Em. As much as we'd like to believe that we've left all that nonsense behind and a woman can get her bang on as freely as a man, we both know that's not true. Women still face consequences for embracing their sexuality that men don't."

"I understand what you're trying to do, but it's too late for a reframe, Maya," I say as I resume my pacing. "I'm already a meme."

"Which is exactly why you need to act now, before it gets any worse. Change the narrative and you'll stop the social media bleeding. Then, you spend a few weeks playing the boring, dutiful girlfriend. Go for lunch at a stuffy restaurant, buy a Christmas tree, do some holiday shopping for his—"

"I can't, Maya. Even if I wanted to." I bite my lip hard enough to send pain flashing through my jaw. "I completely shut him down. Hard. Gave him the Big Goodbye. Practically slammed the door in his face."

"So? Men are forgiving when they're horny, and he's clearly horny for you."

"I'm not so sure about that," I say, cheeks flushing hot as I imagine Oliver reading all the terrible things the internet's had to say about me. He's probably decided I'm repulsive by now. "And even if you're right, I didn't get his number."

"What?!" she bleats loud enough to make me pull my cell away from my ear. "You didn't get his number?"

"Nope. And I refused to give him mine. I was too busy being outraged that he'd lied about being famous. Or infamous. Or whatever it is that royal-adjacent people are."

"Okay, fine, then we find another way," Maya says, clearly not ready to let this go. "What about social media? Does he have any? You could slip into his DMs."

"His Instagram has a blue check and two million followers. I'm not sliding into those DMs."

"Then leave a message at his office. You said he owns an architecture—"

She's interrupted by a sharp knock.

"Hold on, that's my shoes," I say, heading for the door. "The lady at Selfridges said they would be here by noon."

"Your shoes?"

"I broke a heel during the nativity disaster." I navigate around the room service cart, avoiding the judgmental gaze of my soggy eggs. "It's probably one of the reasons I looked so weird in those pictures, one of my heels was..." I reach for the door, words trailing off as I swing it open.

My jaw drops and my eyes widen.

It's my shoes all right, a sensible pair of nude pumps in a Selfridges box.

But that's no delivery boy.

That's Oliver Featherswallow, in a charcoal suit that's giving major designer vibes and a sapphire tie that makes his eyes look even more dangerously blue-gray. His hair is perfectly styled, his shave is fresh, and he's studying me with a determined expression.

So determined, it's bordering on confrontational, in fact, but that doesn't stop my stupid body from tingling at the sight of him.

"Hello, love," he says with a brisk, but warm, familiarity, as if I didn't give him the "big goodbye" just a few hours ago. "I have it all sorted. The answer to both our problems. It's brilliant, so am I, and you're welcome." He lifts the shoe box between us. "Now, where do you want these?"

He pushes past me, summoning a startled huff from my lips.

Before I can speak, Olly adds, "And don't even think of putting up a fuss, Darling. Pretending we're an established couple to throw the bloody press off our scent is the perfect solution. I won't take 'no' for an answer. I simply won't. You would be wasting your breath and my time. And considering I have to be at a luncheon in less than an hour, that would be ill-advised."

"Did you hear all that?" I mutter into my cell.

"Sure did." Maya's laugh is loud and delighted. "What a clever man with fantastic ideas! I like him a lot."

"I'm sure you do," I say through gritted teeth.

"Who's that?" Oliver nods toward my cell.

"Maya, my business partner," I grit again.

He brightens as he sets my heels on the bureau. "Lovely! Hello, Maya, delighted to meet you. I'm Oliver, Emily's new fake boyfriend. Though I'd appreciate it if you'd keep the fake part between us."

"Will do," Maya shouts, loud enough to make me wince. "Goodbye, Em. Sounds like you're in excellent hands."

Then she hangs up.

Just...hangs up.

Leaving me alone with the wickedly handsome man currently stretching out on my still-made hotel bed. He parks his hands behind his head with a grin, before asking, "So, how do you want to play this, Em? Personally, I think we have to have been seeing each other for a while. A lengthier connection makes everything far less scandalous. So, assuming you haven't been dating anyone Stateside…"

"I haven't," I say before I've given my lips permission to move. "But that doesn't mean I'm agreeing to any of this," I hurry to add. "I don't like lying. I'm not a liar."

"Well, neither am I, love, but sometimes a little truth-bending is necessary in the name of the greater good." His brows lift. "Speaking of the greater good, have you checked your email recently?"

Frowning harder, I nod. "Yes, why?"

"You should have received something hopeful from Belinda, yes?"

"No, I—" I cut a glance toward my laptop. "I don't think so, but I guess I could have missed it in all the… excitement."

"Check and see," he encourages. "I stopped by her shop this morning for a little heart-to-heart. Once I explained how sorry you were, she agreed to give you another shot at a consultation."

I stand up straighter, hope flooding through my chest. "What? Really?"

He nods toward my computer again. "Really. See for yourself. I'm not sure what times she's offered, but I would recommend rearranging your schedule to accommodate her."

"Oh my God, of course, obviously." I lean over the bureau, scrolling through my email with shaking fingers, breath rushing out when I see a message I apparently missed. "You're right. She reached out about half an hour ago. She said she can do Thursday morning! Right before she opens. Which is perfect, I—" I break off with another relieved exhale as I spin to face him. "Thank you, Olly. Seriously. You have no idea how much I appreciate this."

He beams. A little smugly.

But hell, a little smugness is completely deserved.

And I *do* really appreciate his help.

But that doesn't mean I think it's a good idea to lie to the entire world…

I'm about to tell him so—and do my best to explain why even casual lies are against my moral code and better judgment—when a message pops through on my phone.

It's my contact at Fletchers, Christoph, asking if I'm the woman in the tabloid photos that are all over the U.K. this morning.

"Damnit." I knead at the stress knot forming in my neck.

"Bad news?" Olly asks.

"It's all bad news this morning," I mutter.

Now, I'm going to have to explain myself to my client. And I'm sure that explanation will be a lot less damning if I tell Christoph that my "boyfriend" and I got carried away with our reunion after months apart instead of confessing to a sloppy one-night stand with a stranger I didn't realize was a paparazzi target.

"Okay. Fine," I mutter, shutting my phone off with a jab of my thumb and tossing it onto the bureau by my shoes. I'll get back to Christoph later, after Olly and I have everything worked out. "A fake relationship it is." His expression lifts, but before he can speak, I warn, "But we'll need rules. Iron-clad ones. And a backstory to match"

He nods. "Of course. I would expect nothing less. I know how much you like rules. And lists." His eyes glitter as he adds, "I'm assuming there will be lists? I admit, I'll be disappointed if I don't get a least a list or two of my very own."

"I'm serious," I say, refusing to be drawn in by his charm. Not again. "We'll need to be smart about this. And careful. Very careful. If we get caught in a lie, it would make an already bad thing a hundred times worse."

Sobering, he says in a softer voice, "Yes, Emily. I understand. And I won't let you down, I promise."

My stomach flutters at the sincerity in his gaze, that same gaze that penetrated my soul last night as other parts of him penetrated...*other* parts of me.

The flutter prompts me to whisper, "And it's going to be fake, Olly. It has to be. I don't have the bandwidth for anything more. I didn't before the tabloid disaster this morning, and I certainly don't now."

"I understand," he says with only the slightest hint of disappointment, and he's already smiling again as he adds, "But that doesn't mean we can't have a little fun along the way. It's Christmas, after all. The time for joy and good cheer." He bounds off the bed. "Get dressed."

I blink. "I am dressed."

"I mean *dressed* dressed," he says, adding in response to my no doubt perplexed expression, "In something you can wear to a society luncheon. It's an old-school crowd, so best if it's a dress that hits below the knee. With tights of some kind. Mother has a thing about people showing up to functions with bare legs, even in the misery of summer."

He claps his hands before making a little shooing motion my way. "Spit spot, off you go. I can step outside if you don't want to change in the loo, but we need to be quick." He glances at his watch. "We'll need to leave in twenty minutes to make it on time, and that's assuming traffic isn't beastly on the way to Spencer House. My mother has zero patience for tardiness, and we'll want a few minutes to spare for the introductions."

My eyes go wide. "Oh, no, Oliver. I can't. I couldn't possibly." I claw at the neck of my sweater, the cowl neck suddenly feeling too snug. "I can't meet your mother. Not now, not today, right after—"

"Of course, you can," he says. "Best to rip the bandage off and get the wound to healing."

I frown. "That doesn't make any sense."

"My metaphors aren't the best after a night at the pub," he says. "I just meant, it's best to get last night behind us and set off again on the right foot. The luncheon will be the perfect place to start. My brother is the star of the day, the speakers will keep us from being forced into too much small talk, and we'll show the world we're a united front right away in..." He glances at his watch again. "Less than six hours from when the pictures dropped." He shifts his focus back to me with a grin. "Pretty damned good, if I do say so myself."

"B-but I don't have anything to wear," I say, instead of the dozen other anxious thoughts racing through my mind. "The airline lost my big suitcase, and I only have—"

"Right," he cuts in. "Then, we'd best be off. There's a dress shop at the end of the block. I'm sure they'll have something in your size." He grabs the box with my shoes inside and heads for the door. "Grab your coat, love. We have a dress to buy and a backstory to concoct before we feast on cold sandwiches and Christmas pudding."

He pauses at the door, shooting a firm glance over his shoulder. "Come on, Em. No time to dilly-dally." His voice gentles as he adds, "You can do this. I know you can."

"Yes, I can," I shoot back, suddenly irritated by his assumption that I'm a lily-livered coward. (Even though I'm still feeling plenty lily-livered at the thought of meeting his family mere hours after shots of me humping his leg hit the internet.) "But I can't do it without shoes."

He glances down at the box under his arm, then back at me with a grin. "Oh, right. Sorry about that, Darling."

"Not a problem, Featherswallow," I say, lips twitching despite myself as I take the box he sheepishly hands over. "Your name really is ridiculous. No offense."

"None taken," he says. "According to the family lore, it originated in the eleventh century, with an ancestor who rather unfortunately resembled a bird."

I squint up at him as I perch on the bed to pull on my new pumps. "Yes...I think I see it now. A bit of pigeon around the eyes..."

He smiles, one of his wicked grins, the one that first imperiled my panties last night at the bar. "Flattery will get you nowhere, Darling. This relationship is fake. I will *not* be tempted back into your bed, no matter how many compliments you hurl at my feet. Or my pigeon eyes."

Fighting a laugh, I nod. "Understood. I'll try to control myself in the future."

And I will.

But I'm not naïve enough to think it will be easy.

We're less than two minutes into this, and I'm already having a hard time suppressing a fresh tingle as my fake boyfriend tucks my arm through his and aims us toward the hotel lobby.

Chapter Nine

OLIVER

I thrive on a sense of urgency, but this is *really* cutting things close...

Seventeen minutes. That's all we have to find Emily a dress suitable for meeting the crème de la crème of London society, then dash over to Spencer House before the salad course is served.

But at least there's no overzealous member of the sales staff hovering about, slowing our progress.

Once I explained the situation, the shop assistant—a severe-looking woman who introduced herself as Claudette—deposited us in the largest fitting room with an armful of options before discreetly withdrawing, seeming to recognize that panic purchases require focus and privacy. Or perhaps she recognized us from the gossip sites and assumed we might want to be alone for other reasons.

Either way, her absence is a blessing given the delicate nature of the things we need to discuss.

"How's the first one coming along?" I call through the velvet curtain.

"It's doing weird things to my chest," Emily calls back.

"Well, Christ, can't have that. That's my job," I joke without thinking, then catch myself.

Fake relationship, Featherswallow.

Boundaries. Etcetera.

"Sorry," I add, "I was just—"

"Just joking, I know," she cuts in. "Don't worry about it. That was my fault. I set you up too perfectly. But here, you can see what I mean."

The curtain swishes open, and Emily emerges in what can only be described as a catastrophe in beige. The dress appears to be attacking her from all angles—crushing her chest while simultaneously adding volume to her hips, with sleeves that could double as shriveled bat wings.

"Oh, dear, Darling," I mutter, making her laugh. "How tragic."

"I know," she agrees. "I look like an accountant on my way to the ball."

"No, you look like my Year Three headmistress," I counter. "Mrs. Broombottom. She dressed exclusively in beige and smelled of cold turkey. Which is a very beige smell, if you think about it."

Emily laughs. "It is."

"She loathed me. Made me write 'I will not put frogs in the fountain' three hundred times after class on multiple occasions. Very unfair."

She arches a brow. "*Did* you put the frogs in the fountain?"

"Well, yes, of course. Repeatedly," I confess without hesitation. "In the fountain, in the gymnasium, in the cook's pantry by the flour bins. I was quite committed to amphibian relocation as a boy." I wave at the dress. "Point is, we can't have you going about looking like a Broombottom and giving me flashbacks. Next, please. We're scandalously short on time."

"Right." Emily retreats behind the curtain.

The rustling of fabric fills the small space as she changes, and I try very hard not to think about the fact that she's naked just a few feet away.

Try and fail, but hell, at least I tried.

"Speaking of being short on time," she says, her voice muffled by the velvet, "We should get our story straight. At least the basics, so we're not scrambling to answer questions on the fly. So, how did we meet, how long have we been dating, etc?"

"We met at a cocktail party while I was in New York in September," I say, having already thought this through on the walk to her hotel. "I was in the city for three weeks, so that provides the perfect time frame. We met my first weekend there, clicked instantly, and spent every spare moment together. Things were going so swimmingly, we decided to give a long-distance relationship a go."

"But we decided not to tell our parents or friends because...we were worried it might not last?" she poses.

"Yes," I agree. "We were absolutely made for each other, of course, but neither of us had ever pulled off a long-distance relationship before. Does that track for you?"

"Absolutely," she confirms. "I'm not a long-distance girl. I have a hard enough time keeping a relationship going when we're in the same time zone."

"Right. Same," I agree, my stomach sinking at the reminder that more than pretend likely isn't in the cards for us.

But she's in London now, and I *was* in NYC in September...

Seems like two savvy travelers might be able to manage long-distance without too many headaches if properly motivated by good times and hot sex.

"All right, that was easy. On to the rules of fake dating engagement, I guess," she adds, pulling me from my hopeful reverie.

"Ah, yes, the parameters of our deception." I lean against the wall. "What did you have in mind?"

"Well, obviously, we keep the fact that it's pretend a secret. Only Maya knows the truth. I hate lying to my family, but if my mother or sister knows that I'm fibbing, they'll accidentally spill the beans. They're wonderful people, but very bad at keeping secrets."

"My family is the same," I agree. "And my grandmother's rather invested in this being the real deal. I'd hate to spoil her fun right off the bat."

The rustling behind the curtain stops. "What do you mean, invested?"

"Well, she rang earlier," I confess. "I thought she was going to haul me over the coals, but turns out she's a big fan of lamppost kissing. And of yours, actually. She gave her stamp of approval right away and ordered me to bring you round to her holiday party Saturday night. Assuming you're free, of course."

A muffled groan fills the air. "Oh, Oliver, I hate that. I don't want to lie to some sweet old woman."

"Oh, she's not sweet," I assure her quickly, though lying to someone I admire as much as Grandmother isn't particularly high on my list, either. "She's a feisty old broad and only has patience for meddling in her grandchildren's love lives November through March. Come spring, when her garden's back in bloom, she'll be distracted by more important things. She just gets bored in winter. Last January, she tried to set Edward up with her dental hygienist and a woman who teaches exotic dancing to seniors at her social club."

Emily snorts. "How did that go?"

"Awkwardly. Edward was already engaged and living with his fiancée at the time. Matilda didn't appreciate the interference. Or the reminder that Grandmother finds her so forgettable for some reason." I check my watch again. Fourteen minutes. "Speaking of living arrangements, you'll need to move into my flat."

"Excuse me?"

"The press will be watching," I explain, pretending the thought of shacking up with Emily isn't making me slightly giddy. "It would be strange if you weren't staying with me, considering the long-standing nature of our relationship and all. It would lead to more questions instead of putting curiosity to bed. And my flat is walking distance from Fletchers, Belinda's shop, and half the restaurants in London. It'll be a fantastic home base for you while you're here."

"All right," she agrees after a pause, though she doesn't sound happy about it. "But we'll sleep in separate rooms. Every night. No exceptions."

"Emily, you wound me. When have I been anything less than a perfect gentleman?"

"Last night," she says, her voice huskier than it was before. "Multiple times."

The memory of just how ungentlemanly I was hits hard, sending scandalous images flashing on my mental screen. Her hands in my hair, her legs around my waist, the sounds she made when I had my mouth between her legs, devouring that gorgeous fanny of hers...

Before I fully regain control, the curtain opens again, revealing dress number two, a safe navy number that lands just below the knee.

It's modest. Adequate. Completely forgettable.

But the way it molds to her backside is enough to ensure I'm still a little hard when I murmur, "Good enough, but try number three. Let's see if we can find something a bit more fun. If not, we'll come back to this one and be on our way."

"Okay." She holds my gaze a beat longer than necessary, making me suspect she feels it, too.

The electricity sizzling in the air between us...

As she disappears behind the curtain again, I silently talk my cock down from his ridiculous state, before asking, "Speaking of future plans, would you be up for an excursion Thursday afternoon? I thought we could do a museum trip tomorrow, to prove how snoringly boring we are, but I'd like to show you some London holiday fun, too."

"Sounds good," she says. "I have most afternoons free. I scheduled all my meetings early in the day, so I'd have time to explore the city before it got dark. What did you have in mind?"

"Let me surprise you," I say. "It'll be easier to fake delight for the cameras if you *don't* have to fake it. And you'll be delighted, I promise, even as the gossip hounds grow increasingly bored by how banal we are."

"Okay." She pauses before adding in a more anxious tone, "But what if they don't get bored? Even after I fly home? What if being on different continents isn't enough to make them stop sniffing around?"

The question hangs in the air, and it isn't hard to understand the worry beneath it—what if this follows her home?

What if it affects her business in New York?

"Then we'll issue a respectful statement in March or April," I say, finding the thought strangely sad. "The distance was too difficult, but we remain the best of friends, wish each other well, et cetera. The standard high-profile breakup script. Very dignified, very final."

"All right. So, I guess you should arrange to see me off on the 5th?"

"Of course," I assure her. "I'll drive you to the airport myself. We'll stage a romantic goodbye for any lingering photographers, complete with longing looks, a passionate kiss, and some sniffling on my part." I glance at my watch. "How's it going in there, Darling? We're down to eight minutes to pay and zoom out the door."

"I know! Sorry. I'm almost ready! The zipper's a little tricky on this one."

The sound of her buzzing zipper—the same sound from last night when I buzzed her out of her skirt— threatens to hit me below the belt all over again.

I pinch the bridge of my nose, reminding myself that *I'm* the one who suggested this arrangement. I have no one to blame but myself for this zipper-induced torture.

The curtain opens one more time, and my jaw hits the floor.

The deep emerald dress skims her curves like water, hitting near the middle of her shins, the modest length somehow making it even sexier. The neckline is appropriate for a charity luncheon, but showcases the elegant line of her throat. Her shoulders are bare except for small cap sleeves, and the color makes her cheeks pink and her hair glow like copper in firelight.

Damn...

She's breathtaking.

I've seen Emily in coffee-stained business casual (quite fetching despite the smell) and nothing at all (perfection), but this...

This is something else entirely.

Suddenly, the madwoman who crash-landed in my life last night looks like a society darling, capable of holding her own at any upper-crust event. She's poised, elegant, exactly the type of woman my mother's been after me to find.

And if my mother and grandmother join forces to push this agenda?

Well, I might be disowned if I fail to seal the deal.

"What do you think? I thought it was perfect, but..." Emily cocks her head, a frown line forming between her brows. "I liked that the green complemented your tie, but...maybe it's too much?"

I still can't speak.

My brain appears to have short-circuited somewhere between realizing just how beautiful she is and how *dangerous* she is.

Maybe this isn't such a brilliant plan, after all...

I'm seriously in for a world of pain if my nearest and dearest form an attachment, and then I appear to have let this lovely girl slip through my fingers. Unlike many noble families, they won't care that she's American. They'll just care that she made me feel free to be my truest self, and that I didn't appear to treasure that as much as I should have.

I'll have to take the blame for the end of the relationship, after all, it's the only way to protect Em from further cyber harassment.

Yes, mistakes may have been made, but…it's too late to turn back now.

Forcing a smile, I shake my head. "No, it's not too much. It's perfect." Our gazes lock, hold. "*You're* perfect, and we should be on our way."

Like a retail specter eerily attuned to her customers' vibrations, Claudette suddenly materializes beside me. "Yes, that's the dress. It's incredible on you," she announces, with a definitive nod. "The color is divine, and the cut couldn't be more flattering."

"Agreed, we'll take it," I say, still having a hard time pulling my gaze from Emily's. "But as we mentioned, we're in quite a rush."

"Of course! Let me just snip the tags, and you'll be ready to go." Claudette flutters around Emily, wielding a pair of tiny scissors, before bustling out with practiced efficiency. As she goes, she calls over her shoulder, "I'll meet you at the register."

And yes, I *do* stand there gaping at Emily for nearly another full minute before pulling myself together.

So far, this fake boyfriend nonsense is off to one hell of a start.

"Right, then, do you want to gather your things, and I'll meet you up front?" I ask as I back away. "I'm sure Claudette will give you a bag for your other clothes. This is my treat, by the way."

"Thank you," Emily says, "but I'm happy to pay you back for—"

"Stop," I cut her off. "What kind of fake boyfriend would I be if I didn't buy my fake girlfriend a proper 'meet the parent' dress? Speaking of, I should fill you in on the things that irritate Mother. There are only three cardinal sins in the World of Vivian, the Dowager Viscountess, but commit any of them, and she'll be cranky."

Emily gulps, her eyes going wide. "Shit, Olly, you should have led with that! Now I'm going to be a nervous wreck."

"Never, you're gorgeous," I assure her. "And we'll have a full five minutes to prepare in the cab."

"Five minutes!" she squeaks.

"Don't worry! You'll be great!" I duck out of the fitting room, congratulating myself on maintaining my composure and keeping my hands to myself.

But how long will I be able to keep up the farce?

I have no idea.

I only know that I'm looking forward to an excuse to perform "pretend affection" for Emily before an audience of my family, friends, and peers far too much....

Chapter Ten
EMILY

I've forgotten how to breathe, and it has nothing to do with the shapewear beneath my dress.

Okay, maybe it has a *little bit* to do with the shapewear, but I'm not about to complain. Claudette was a genius who picked out the perfect thigh minimizer and waist-cinching bustier.

No, it has much more to do with this "meet the parents at first sight" thing Olly somehow talked me into. Meeting someone's mother is terrifying enough when your boyfriend is from a normal family and you've had time to prepare. But meeting a Dowager Viscountess? Moments before a very important ceremony honoring her eldest child, the Viscount?

Without time to do anything to my hair except coil it into a low bun with tendrils in the dressing room and hope for the best?

Well, needless to say, I'm spiraling.

And gasping.

Maybe even hyperventilating?

"Deep breath," Oliver murmurs as we hurry up the

stone steps of Spencer House, past topiary trees wrapped in white lights that twinkle like champagne bubbles. "You've got this."

The December wind smells like it might snow again soon, and somewhere nearby, carol singers are working their way through "God Rest Ye Merry Gentlemen." London at Christmas is aggressively festive, even at midday. Normally, I'd be enchanted, but right now, all I can think about are the three rules Oliver drilled into me during our four-minute cab ride.

Rule number one: Don't talk with your mouth full.

I mean, it *sounds* easy. I'm pretty sure I mastered that particular aspect of table manners around ten, when my mother threatened to make me eat dinner in the trash can with the raccoons if I didn't stop spraying breadcrumbs at dinner. But knowing my luck since I landed in London, I'll probably forget Rule One and give our table a "see food" exhibit during the salad course.

Baby Jesus in the manger, I'm not ready for this kind of trial by high-society fire. Not even close...

We push through heavy doors into sudden warmth and grandeur that takes what's left of my breath away. Crystal chandeliers cast the large entryway in a warm, golden glow, and massive wreaths hang between oil paintings of stern-looking dead people. The air smells like pine, expensive perfume, and a hint of wood rot.

Or maybe mothballs?

Something in here reeks of humans fighting to hold back the tides of time. It's a smell I find both delightful and sad, but I know better than to mention that aloud.

That would be a clear violation of Rule Two: Don't discuss anything personal in public—or at all, really, until you've known someone at least six to twelve months.

That one's trickier.

What counts as personal? I obviously shouldn't share that smells give me feelings or confess that I cry every time I watch any version of Little Women, especially around the holidays. But what about "I run my own business?"

Is my job too personal? I mean, considering that I started the company? Personally?

How about my favorite color?

The fact that my new shoes aren't proving nearly as comfortable as I'd hoped?

I wince as we stop in front of the coat check, wishing I'd thought to grab bandages for my heels on the way out the door.

"Just this and two coats, my good man." Oliver hands the bag containing my other clothes to the elderly fellow behind the desk before turning to help me with my coat. As he slides it off my shoulders, revealing my new frock, the old man's bushy white eyebrows shoot up in approval.

Well, at least the coat check guy thinks I've nailed the assignment.

Hopefully, Oliver's mother and the rest of the high-society set will agree.

Though, of course, I'm sure they won't comment directly on the dress, as that would be a violation of Rule Three: Don't offer compliments. Aristocrats, especially those of previous generations, find compliments gauche and embarrassing.

Not to mention overly personal, which could be considered a *double* violation of both rules two *and* three.

Rule three is the one that's really going to kill me.

I love a compliment! I'm a bit of a compulsive complementarian, in fact, but I've never worried about it too much before. A sincere compliment, discreetly delivered, is the ultimate social lubricant, and genuine praise always brightens someone's day.

Or, at least it does in New York.

In London, apparently, a compliment is considered an act of aggression, one that obligates the receiver to waste precious energy rebuffing the compliment in order to reaffirm their own modesty.

Therefore, I will have to remember to suppress my "love your dress" habit, while simultaneously meeting my fake boyfriend's Dowager Viscountess of a mother in a room full of fancy strangers who have all seen photos of me humping Oliver against a lamppost like a horny cat.

Brilliant.

The thought is enough to make my pulse spike with panic as we sweep into a ballroom filled with tables draped in fine linen and topped with elegantly festive centerpieces.

I suppose there's always a chance that these people haven't seen the pictures.

Maybe they're too important or rich or old to be online as much as the rest of us…

That hope is quashed three steps in when a woman at a nearby table squawks, "Oh my, is that her? The American by the street lamp?" I glance over to see an old woman wearing enough diamonds to feed a small country clutching her bejeweled neck with a delightfully scandalized expression.

Her companion, an even more ancient woman wearing nearly as many baubles, leans forward, squinting at my dress. "Oh, that's her, all right," she says, not even bothering to lower her voice as she adds, "But she's prettier in person than in the pictures. Much less busty."

My face burns as we move deeper into the room.

Busty?

I was wearing a jacket in those pictures. A Nan Baylor suit jacket, no less! One of the many *modest* Nan Baylor jackets Maya enjoys teasing me about because they're so "middle-aged, middle management" coded.

Why so much hate and judgment for my poor suit set?

And why aren't the old biddies in here obeying rules two and three?!

By the time we reach table nine—front and center, where everyone can stare at the horny young people on display—I've caught several whispers about my hair (fabulous, frizzy, and "obviously from a bottle") and my chances of "landing a Featherswallow."

All parties agreed my chances aren't good. Even if he *has* brought me to a family event and pulled out the seat next to his mother.

By the time I've settled into my chair beside the Dowager Viscountess Vivian Featherswallow, I'm certain my cheeks are Jolly Saint Nick on a Bender red.

"Mother," Oliver says, leaning past me to press a kiss to her pale cheek. "I'd like you to meet Emily Darling from New York. Emily, this is my mother, Vivian."

"Oh, call me Viv," the elegant blonde says as she warmly clasps my hand. "All Oliver's friends from his school days do. How lovely to meet you, Emily."

She's not at all what I expected. After all Oliver's talk of "cardinal sins" and "making her cranky," I'd expected a fussy, Lady Grantham sort. Honestly, she reminds me more of the "hippies" in the Hamptons. The ones who are obscenely wealthy, but do their best to hide it, and are much more concerned with feeding their family organic food than wearing the latest fashions.

Vivian's pale blue dress is gorgeous, but clearly far from brand new, and she's wearing mismatched earrings—one pearl stud and one dangly Art Nouveau silver swirl. Whether that's on purpose or simply because she forgot to choose between the two when she was getting dressed, I instantly decide she might be a kindred spirit, after all.

"Lovely to meet you, Viv," I say, smiling as she releases my palm with a light squeeze. Fighting the urge to compliment her on her dress or her excellent work raising a very charming, so far very *decent* man, I add, "Thank you so much for making room at the last minute. It's so nice to be a part of honoring Edward's accomplishments. I was so pleased when Oliver invited me."

Vivian beams. "Oh, I was, too! Oliver so rarely brings a plus one, and we're thrilled to have you." She introduces me to the rest of the table—two Ladies and an Honorable, I greet with full titles, as expected at a first introduction—before motioning to a formidable-looking woman with deep smile lines around her brown eyes. "And of course, Lady Agnes Thornfield-Rowe, a dear family friend."

"So nice to meet you, Lady Thornfield-Rowe," I say.

"Agnes, please. The other's too much of a mouthful." Agnes chuckles in a way that makes me suspect she knows all my dirty, Oliver-humping secrets. "And I'm charmed, Ms. Darling. It's always fascinating to meet one of Oliver's friends from the real world."

"Partner, actually," Oliver corrects with a winning grin. "We've been dating for a few months now, and have decided to make things official."

Vivian's blond brows lift, and a flash of something—disapproval? Irritation?—flashes behind her eyes before her expression smooths into another warm smile. "Why, what lovely news! Love makes the holidays even more special."

"It really does," Oliver murmurs, gazing at me with a smitten expression that makes me want to kick him beneath the table.

Pretending to be a couple to get the press to leave us alone is one thing; faking some kind of deep, romantic attachment is another.

The first feels like an acceptable falsehood; the second feels...wrong. And the superstitious part of me is pretty sure faking true love is a good way to ensure the universe never gives you a shot at the real thing.

And I want the real thing someday.

I want it more than I realized before last night, when a certain charming Brit reminded me how good it can feel to share a night out with someone who makes you laugh and think and come your brains out.

Making a mental note to have another boundaries talk with Olly—and to stop thinking about coming my brains out while seated inches from his mother—I turn my attention to eating the freshly delivered salad.

Thankfully, it's a finely chopped salad, and I'm able to chew and fully swallow each small bite in between small talk.

We discuss mine and Oliver's plans for the holidays—merrymaking and celebrating in between my business obligations. Vivian insists I attend the family's annual New Year's Eve party, offering a formal invitation just in case Oliver hasn't already, and Lady Thornfield-Rowe delights the table at large with a story about last year's celebration. The under forty set decided to "chilly dip" before midnight, and the *over forty* set stole their towels from the shore as a prank.

"They all came dashing into the great hall shivering and cursing, with icicles hanging off their noses. Best party I've been to in ages," Agnes finishes, as the other ladies, whose names I can't remember, chuckle behind their hands. "Can't wait to see what trouble you get up to this year, Oliver."

"Me? Trouble? I would never." Oliver casts a faux innocent look around the table before turning to me with a wink. "Isn't that right, Emily?"

Realizing what he's up to, I play along, rolling my eyes as I mutter, "Of course not, darling. You're as pure as the driven snow. We both are, really. A very proper pair."

"Very demure," Oliver adds.

"And discreet," I supply.

By the time we're done with our routine, the entire table is tittering and we've obviously won over Agnes, who, when I glance her way, offers an approving nod. Clearly, she's the type of woman who believes in looking the elephant in the room in the eye and giving it a cheeky wink.

As the lights dim and the first speaker mounts the stage, Oliver captures my hand, giving it a tight squeeze. I squeeze his back, the first genuine smile of the afternoon curving my lips.

So far, we're navigating our first time out and about as a recently disgraced couple pretty darned well, if I do say so myself!

Now, all that's left is to sit politely during the ceremonies, tuck into dessert, and make a graceful exit.

Surely, we can manage that.

Grateful that the hardest part is over, I relax into my chair, nibbling on finger sandwiches as the awards are handed out.

The first honoree runs a program teaching sustainable farming to at-risk youth. The second has spent thirty years protecting wetlands from development. And the third runs a "retirement home" for elderly dogs. The small, gray-haired woman practically weeps with gratitude as she thanks the committee for the honor and the audience for their generous donations.

By the time they announce Viscount Edward Featherswallow, I'm genuinely moved.

But then, I'm a sucker for anything to do with helping animals, especially dogs. They really are the best of us. I look forward to working less in the future for many reasons, but a big one is finally having time to spoil a puppy of my very own.

Oliver's brother looks like an older, slightly thinner, more serious version of Oliver. Same sharp cheekbones, same devastating jaw, but where Oliver has mischief in his eyes, Edward has gravitas.

He takes the stage with such quiet confidence, even the gossipy old ladies in the back stop whispering to pay attention.

"Failure is never an easy thing to admit to, but not long ago, the Swallow House Fishery was failing," Edward begins without preamble. "It had been for years. But not because the good people who worked there weren't giving it their all. Sadly, our previous manager refused to see that new farming methods were needed to meet the moment, and I was too distracted with other projects to realize how dire the situation was until it was nearly too late. When I took the reins five years ago, almost everyone I consulted said it would be best to shut it down."

He pauses, scanning the room, his gaze softening as it lands on his mother, who's beaming up at him with love and pride.

"But my mother and father reminded me that the fishery employed forty-three people," Edward continues. "Families who'd worked those waters for generations, and who deserved better from us. So instead of shutting down, we innovated."

Edward briefly explains how they converted to "wildish raised" fishing—a hybrid model that protects wild populations while maintaining jobs. How they eliminated hormones and chemicals to make their harvests more attractive to buyers, and how, in time, employment at the fishery actually increased.

"But none of that would have been possible without my parents' care for our community, or my brother's help and inspiration," Edward says.

I feel Oliver tense beside me as he continues, "Oliver, a gifted architect, designed our new processing facilities to be carbon neutral. But more than that, growing up, Olly was the kind of boy an older brother could be proud of. He made me think and question the status quo, and once stayed up all night helping clean a flock of oil-damaged birds that had washed up by our home. Even though he was only ten years old at the time." His voice roughens slightly as he adds, "We both cried when all but two of them passed away, but Olly was the one with fire in his eyes when he said we had to make things better when we were grown. He made me promise I would never stop fighting to fix all the broken things in the world, and I'm so glad he did. Everything I've become, all the good I've done, has grown from that night, and that moment of clarity." He lifts his award into the air above the podium. "So, I must insist on sharing this lovely medal with my parents and Oliver, incredible people who I'm so honored to call family."

The room erupts in applause and a few teary sighs as Edward cedes the microphone to the master of ceremonies to conclude the presentation.

I glance Oliver's way, seeing him with new eyes, this mischief maker with a heart of gold. I squeeze his hand again, and he shoots an almost shy smile my way that makes my throat a little tighter.

I lean in, whispering, "I know compliments are terrible things, but I think that maybe you're an excellent brother. And maybe it's okay to be proud of that."

He laughs, his cheeks flushing as he glances down at our joined hands. "Never, Darling," he whispers back. "Pride goeth before the fall and all that."

I hum beneath my breath. "Well, then, I guess I'll have to be proud for you. Good job, Olly." I kiss his cheek before murmuring for his ears only, "I'm very proud to be the fake girlfriend on your arm."

As I sit back in my chair, he catches my gaze with an intensity that's probably inappropriate for a charity luncheon. His lips part again, but before he can speak, the lights flicker on and Edward joins us at the table.

Claiming the last empty chair on Vivian's other side, he leans in for a kiss on both cheeks. "Oh, well done, darling. Well done," she says, her gushing restrained but heartfelt. "Your father would be so proud, and so am I."

"I hope I didn't embarrass you too terribly, Olly," Edward says, glancing his way.

"Oh, a little," Oliver says, reaching out to clasp his

brother's hand. "But I love you, so I suppose it's all right."

"I love you, too," Edward says simply.

The dessert arrives just then—Christmas pudding, dark and rich and smelling of brandy—but I'm too busy fighting tears to thank the server who delivers mine.

Gah! They really are the *sweetest* family, so close and open and down to earth, despite their Britishness and proximity to the throne. It isn't what I would have expected from nobility, and I confess I'm very pleasantly surprised.

"Wonderful speech, Edward," Agnes says. "Very moving."

"Thank you so much, Agnes." Edward's voice is polite, but he's clearly uncomfortable in the face of so much attention. That probably explains why he suddenly makes a point of motioning my way. "And who is this charming addition to the table? I don't believe we've been introduced."

"Edward, meet Miss Emily Darling, an incredible woman I met during my last trip to New York, who has mercifully decided to date me," Oliver says, summoning a wider smile from his brother. "Emily, my brother, the best man I know, who is, as you've just learned, also very handy with fish."

"So good to meet you, Edward," I say, grinning as I take his offered hand.

"Oh, the pleasure is all mine, Emily, I assure you." Edward gives my fingers a friendly pump. "Anyone who makes Olly smile like that is someone special, no doubt about it. So, how long are you in London?"

"Until January 5th," I say, instantly feeling terrible again.

Edward is so nice! And he seems genuinely excited that his brother's found a partner. Lying to him is upsetting, so upsetting that I quickly scoop up a large

bite of Christmas pudding to ensure that I won't have to lie to anyone again for at least the next minute.

Thank goodness for Rule One.

And thank goodness to whoever baked this treat…

The rich, spiced cake practically melts on my tongue, and I can't help the soft moan of appreciation that escapes my lips.

"Good?" Oliver murmurs, his fingers curling around my thigh beneath the table.

The touch makes me suck in a turned-on breath, pulling something far too hard to be cake into the back of my throat. I try to move it discreetly to the front with my tongue, already panicking about how to spit something out in present company without looking like a feral gutter snipe with no table manners.

But it turns out I shouldn't have bothered.

I *can't* spit it out.

I also can't swallow it.

Heck, it's so far back there, I can barely breathe.

I try to sip in oxygen. Fail. Try again, and—

Shit, I can't breathe!

I really can't.

I can't breathe!

My hands fly to my neck in the universal sign for choking, panic flooding through me as my vision starts to blur.

This can't be it. This can't be how I die! I'm too young to choke to death on Christmas pudding in front of London society and my sexy fake boyfriend, who is now looking like a very *worried* fake boyfriend.

"Emily?" Oliver's panicked voice assures me I must look as terrified as I feel. "Emily!"

Suddenly, his arms are around me from behind, hands positioned below my ribs. He lifts me out of my seat and into the air, performing the Heimlich with surprising competence. He heaves me up once, twice, and then—*pop!*—the object comes flying from my mouth.

I gasp and cough, air flooding back into my lungs as my heart hammers with gratitude. I'm alive! I'm still alive.

And Oliver's still holding me, his body trembling against my back.

"Christ, Emily, are you alright?"

I pat his arm with what I hope is a reassuring hand. "Yes, fine. Sorry. I was choking."

"You sure as hell were." He lowers me to my feet before gently turning me around. Leaning down, he squeezes my shoulders, searching my face with wide, worried eyes. "And now? Is everything all right? Are you—"

"I'm fine," I say, my cheeks heating. "Just mortified that I almost choked to death and ruined the celebration."

The table erupts into reassuring murmurs that I "didn't ruin anything" and "we're just so glad that you're all right, dear!"

But it's Oliver who commands my full attention as he pulls me close, kissing my forehead with a shaky sigh. "Thank God, love. You scared me."

And for a moment, I *feel* loved.

I feel like *his* love, before Agnes pipes up with a laugh, "Well, at least it looks like all the gagging was for a good cause."

Oliver and I glance over to see Lady Thornfield-Rowe

holding up her fork, a slightly cakey ring dangling from the tines. My cheeks start to burn again as I realize that must be what I horked across the table.

Her brown eyes dance as she adds, "Looks like we might be hearing wedding bells again sooner than later, Vivian."

"Oh, the ring!" The matronly woman in the brown dress, whose name I *think* is Lady Maybeth, breathes, "Oh, my goodness, you found the wedding ring! Good show, Emily!"

"Thank you?" I say, my voice still a little wheezy as I glance Oliver's way.

"It's a holiday tradition," he explains, looking slightly embarrassed. "Christmas puddings sometimes have treasures baked inside. Coins for wealth, silver wishbones for luck, rings for—"

"Marriage within the year," Agnes finishes triumphantly. "Looks like you might not be escaping London so easily, Ms. Darling. So, let's hope the press goes a little easier on you from here on out."

"Whatever do you mean, Agnes?" Vivian asks, sounding so genuinely confused, it's clear that she *hasn't* seen the pictures.

But judging from the range of expressions at the table —horrified, amused, knowing, second-hand-embarrassed, and even more amused—she's the only one who hasn't.

Soon, they're all staring at us, waiting to see how we're going to explain ourselves to Olly's mother, and my cheeks feel like they've been set on fire.

Thankfully, Oliver recovers more quickly than I do, offering in a placating tone, "We'll discuss that later, Mother. I should get Emily outside. She still looks pale. I think a walk in the winter air would do her good."

I nod quickly. "Yes, thank you, Olly. It would. It really would."

"Most welcome, but no need to thank me, darling. Your health is my top priority, today and every day," Oliver says, helping me to my feet. His arm stays firmly around my waist as he addresses the table. "If you'll excuse us?"

"Of course, dear." Vivian still looks concerned, but willing to let the moment pass. For now. "But please call me later. I want to know you're both all right."

"Of course, Mother," Oliver says.

"And don't forget this," Agnes pipes up as we turn to go.

She holds out the silver ring, now sitting in the center of a crisp dessert napkin. "A souvenir of your holiday," she says with a smirk.

"Thank you," I say, collecting the napkin with shaking fingers.

Oliver shoves it into his pant pocket, and we finally make our escape, hustling through the room with a smattering of applause rising in our wake.

Looks like just about everyone saw Oliver's heroic efforts to help me cough up my pudding.

"Quick thinking, lad," a male voice calls out. "Good work."

"And so romantic," a quivery female voice adds.

"Yes," another agrees, "such a lucky girl!"

I remind myself that I *am* lucky and grateful to be alive, even though I'm currently so mortified that I have to make a concerted effort not to sprint for the door.

But by the time we visit the coat check, retrieve our things, and make our way onto the street, my cheeks are nearly back to their normal temperature. The cold

December air helps, and I gulp it gratefully as Oliver and I head down the stairs.

"Well, *that* was terrifying," I say, clinging to the stone railing. "But honestly? Not as bad as I expected."

"Agreed." Oliver keeps a steadying hand parked at the small of my back that I appreciate. "I mean, you almost died, but you didn't. I'd call that a win any day."

"Agreed." I laugh. "And the speeches were great."

"Nearly as good as the Christmas pudding," he quips, making me giggle again.

At the base of the stairs, I turn to face him, chest filling with a mixture of happiness, relief, and a tightness I can't fully explain. All I know for sure is that I'm glad Oliver was there when I was in trouble, and I'm just as glad that he's here now, when I'm not.

"What?" He reaches up, brushing a wayward lock of hair from my forehead. "What's going through that busy head of yours, Red? A list of all the reasons British holiday traditions are hazardous to your health?"

Before I can confess that I like British holiday traditions nearly as much as I'm starting to like *him*, my phone buzzes.

Then buzzes again.

And again.

"Uh oh," I mutter, stomach dropping as I pull it from my purse. "Maya never texts more than once unless it's something really..."

The words shrivel and die in my mouth as I scan the list of notifications.

These aren't texts from Maya. They're Google alerts from various socials. News feeds. And a British tabloid site promising a "scandalous new scoop."

Looks like a fresh batch of mortifying photos just hit the internet...

"Featherswallow Heir Saves Choking American" is the kindest headline.

The others focus on how repulsive I look—feet dangling, face red, arms flailing as I convulse mid-retch.

But the worst one, the one that makes me groan aloud, is a shot of the exact moment the ring flew out of my mouth. My eyes are bulging, my mouth is open in an O of surprise, and Oliver's arms are so tight around me, my breasts seem to be attempting to launch themselves out onto the table, as well.

The caption reads: "Proposal or attempted murder? Featherswallow has some explaining to do..."

"Oh no, Olly," I moan, as I turn the screen to face him.

Oliver takes one look at the photo and bursts out laughing. Not a polite chuckle, either, but a full bodied guffaw that makes his eyes crinkle at the edges.

"It's not funny!" I protest, but his laughter is infectious. "They're accusing you of attempted murder! And I look like a hideous green sausage monster."

"You look like a gorgeous woman who's still alive after being rudely attacked by holiday pudding," he corrects, still grinning. "The rest is just noise, though I'm afraid our plan to be boring isn't off to the best start."

"You think?" I ask dryly, as I scroll through more headlines. "Here's a great one—American spits on British Tradition. They make it sound like I did it on purpose." I shift my narrowed gaze to his. "When really it was all *your* fault."

His eyes go wide as he presses a hand to his chest. "Me? How so?"

"You put your hand on my thigh," I say, remembering how it all started now. "You fondled me under the table, which made me pull in a breath, which made me suck a Christmas pudding toy into my throat!"

His lips twist, but he has the grace to look apologetic as he says, "Well, now, Emily, I was simply performing the part of the besotted boyfriend as promised. You can hardly blame me for that."

"Can't I?" I ask, arching a brow.

But I'm not about to tell him to keep his hands to himself from now on. A part of me likes the thought of his hands on me far too much.

Which is a problem. Nearly as much of a problem as the way my chest went tight during Edward's speech, highlighting his brother's fantastic heart.

It *does* seem to be fantastic, but it isn't mine, and it never will be.

As wonderful as Olly is, we would never last. We're from two different worlds, and I can't handle this level of scrutiny from the press. It's already making me twitchy, and we're less than twenty-four hours into this mess.

So, I force myself to take a step back and banish the flirtation from my tone as I ask, "So, where to next? I need a quiet place to call my Fletchers' rep and explain myself." I sigh. "Or attempt to explain myself. What do you think? Do fresh pictures and rumors that you tried to kill me with pudding make things less scandalous or more scandalous?"

"Less scandalous, for sure," Oliver says with an unconcerned scoff. "You were at a luncheon with my mother when the attempted murder went down. That's the opposite of scandalous. And there are just as many headlines claiming I was trying to propose as there are accusing me of plotting your demise. Your contact will be confused by the warring reports and *desperate* for the real story. You'll give him the scoop, he'll feel important, and you'll be in the clear."

He takes my arm, threading it through his as he starts down the sidewalk. "Then, we'll spend the rest of the evening safely tucked away in my apartment, eating curry takeout and prepping you to shine at your meeting with Belinda on Thursday."

I smile up at him. "Sounds like a great night."

"To my place, then?" he asks. "And I'll have a courier fetch your things from the hotel?"

I nod. "To your place."

Curry, takeout, and a night at Oliver's flat.

Totally innocent. Utterly safe.

Except for the tiny, inconvenient fact that I'm catching feelings for my fake boyfriend...

Chapter Eleven

OLIVER

Two days later...

It happens every year.

I get caught up in the holiday spirit, excited about hot chocolate in the great outdoors, and forget that I'm a horror show on skates and the Somerset House ice rink is a battleground where I've been vanquished time and again.

It sure is festive, though...

The courtyard-turned-ice-rink teems with families, couples, and gangs of ruddy-cheeked kids, all gliding about like they were born with blades strapped to their feet. Giant Christmas trees ring the space, twinkling lights stretch overhead, and "Winter Wonderland" blares from speakers big enough to power the raves I used to sneak into as a pre-teen.

But this isn't a rave or a pub or any other place where

my serviceable dance moves might spare me shame and ridicule.

No, this is the ice rink, a place where I have always done the opposite of shine.

What *is* the opposite of shine?

"Dull" doesn't make much sense...

Wither isn't quite right either.

Spasm and flop, while accurate, aren't logical antonyms.

I lean against the barrier, continuing to ponder the issue as a toddler in a puffy pink coat streaks by—backwards—while her father films. The little rascal can't be more than three.

This is going to be humiliating.

I suppose I could text Emily and arrange to meet for a hot toddy at the pub near my place, instead. But when I told her where we were headed last night, she seemed so excited about skating. Turns out her sister is an Olympic figure skater, and some of her best Christmas memories involve strapping on their "granny skates" and taking to the frozen pond by their grandparents' house in Maine.

The way her eyes lit up as she talked about the thermoses of hot chocolate they'd hang around their necks and the portable karaoke machine they'd drag out onto the ice to sing Christmas carols made me wish I'd been there.

"Maybe American Christmas isn't total rubbish," I'd said last night, feeling the opposite of "rubbish" after another fantastic day with my fake girlfriend.

We had a blast at the British Museum, nerding out over the mummies, before lingering at a two-hour lunch while Em snuck in some work on her laptop. We finished with a stroll through the park before heading back to mine for leftover curry and a movie.

We watched Bridget Jones's Diary in our pajamas, and I'm not ashamed to say I loved every bloody minute of it.

I'd seen it ages ago, of course, but I'd forgotten what a good holiday flick it is. We laughed, cursed Hugh Grant's character for being a scoundrel, laughed some more, and then Emily teared up at the end, while Bridget was running through London in her knickers, trying to find Mark Darcy before it was too late.

Fine! Maybe I teared up a little, too.

But then, it's a special thing...to be loved for exactly who you are.

Especially when you're a bit of an acquired taste.

I'm good at hiding my stranger tendencies from the world at large, but my crooked sense of humor, impatience for small talk, and random attacks of bluntness and foolishness give me away as an odd duck in the end. Most of the women I've dated would have happily marched me down the aisle—I'm a wealthy member of the peerage, whose ancestors had the sense not to marry a cousin too terribly often—but every last one of them expressed a wish for me to be "more serious" at one point or another.

They preferred the cool, aloof Oliver they'd known before they'd seen behind the mask.

But Emily seems to like impulsive, occasionally goofy "Olly" just fine.

By the end of the evening last night, she was snuggled up against me, her fluffy-sock-covered toes tucked under my thigh to stay warm, while we chatted our way through Elf, laughing at all the same places. Then, she fell asleep on my shoulder, muttering insane things in her sleep that made me laugh some more, and I sat there for far too long, wondering if love at first sight might be a thing, after all.

Though it isn't at first sight, obviously.

I've already seen her several times, including naked and writhing on my cock.

Which I'm *not* going to think about. I'm determined to show Emily I can abide by our "faking it" rules. I have to. I was the one who broke the initial trust. I lied about who I was and, in the process, exposed her to a level of internet bullying no human should have to endure.

Not to mention putting her livelihood at risk.

No, if we're ever going to find our way back to the bedroom, Emily has to be the one to decide it's time to change the rules.

But I *can* do my best to prove to her that I'd be a fantastic boyfriend, starting with taking her skating at the most festive rink in London.

No matter how much I'm dreading the bone-splintering impact when my ass hits the ice again and again...

"Oliver, there you are!"

I turn to see Emily bouncing through the crowd milling about the rink, her cheeks pink and a big grin on her face.

She's wearing that red coat that makes her look like a holiday elf, a thick white scarf, and matching mittens, proving she's ready to take this skate session seriously.

"How did the meeting go?" I laugh as she launches herself into my arms. "That good, eh?" I grin, taking advantage of the excuse to give her a proper squeeze before setting her back on her feet.

"So good!" she says, her breath rushing out with an excited flap of her hands.

"Come on, you have to give me more than that," I

insist. "I've been waiting on pins and needles." I shoot my watch a mock glare. "You are a full twenty-five minutes late."

She laughs. "Sorry, things were going so well, I lost track of time. She *loved* the concept artwork. Absolutely loved it, just like I hoped she would, and started coming up with ideas for the design right away. We're going to combine flowers and recycled fabric to make the ceiling in the dining area look like it's made of giant blossoms." Emily flaps a hand again. "It's kind of hard to describe without the sketches, but it's gorgeous and brilliant, and assuming Fletchers chooses my pitch, Belinda's on board. She promised she'd set aside an entire day for installation as soon as the venue's on lock. Gah! I'm so happy and relieved!" She presses mittened hands to her flushed cheeks, words slowing as she adds, "And I mean, maybe I'm crazy, but I think we might actually end up being friends."

"That's fantastic, Em," I say, grinning. "So chuffed for you."

"I'm chuffed, too." She giggles as she throws her arms around my neck again. "Sorry, I get huggy when I'm this excited."

"You'll hear no complaints from me," I say, adding in a whisper as I spot a giant lens in my peripheral vision. "But it looks like we have company. Paparazzi at eleven o'clock. Chap in the red hat trying to blend in with the tourists, and failing miserably."

Emily groans, "Jesus. They really are relentless, aren't they?"

"Completely," I agree, brushing my lips across her forehead as I murmur, "But we could use this to our advantage... Shall we give him something boring to photograph?"

Emily lifts her chin, eyes glittering. "I think we should. Something very boring, with no choking or humping in it."

"But still romantic," I insist, pulling her closer. "We have to show them we're an established couple, after all. Shall we Eskimo kiss?"

She grins. "No, that would be weird. And we're trying not to be weird, remember?"

"Oh, right," I say, feigning confusion as I ask, "So what's a non-weird couple thing we could do?"

"Well, I guess we could just kiss." Her smile fades as she presses up on tiptoe. "A nice, normal kiss...for the camera."

"For the camera," I agree, and then my lips are on hers and damn...

Kissing her is even better than I remember.

Kissing Emily in the dark under a softly falling snow was electric.

Kissing her across my penthouse, while I stripped her bare for the first time, was the sexiest thing to happen to my lips in a damned long time.

But kissing her on a sunny winter's day, under a clear blue sky, with nowhere to hide...

I'm not sure exactly why it hits so hard, but it does. Her lips are still warm and wicked and so skilled at unravelling me it's a little frightening. But this kiss is also gentle, curious.

The way she cups my face in her mittened hands, the way she whispers that I taste like peppermint and that she "loves a peppermint kiss." The way she sighs and melts closer when I curl my fingers into a loose fist at the nape of her neck, deep in the soft, luxurious underbelly of her magnificent hair...

It's sweet.

So sweet that when we finally pull apart, I can't help staring down at her for a long beat, wondering where she's been all my life.

And if she'll still be here next Christmas.

It's a completely inappropriate thought, but still...

"Should we try again?" I whisper. "Just to make sure he got the money shot?"

She exhales a shaky breath. "I mean, maybe. We wouldn't want to waste a perfectly good—" Her words end in a startled squawk as a pigeon zooms past, inches from our foreheads, making a beeline toward the popcorn a child just spilled on the ground.

"Good grief, that was close," she says, frantically patting the top of her head. "He didn't bless me, did he?"

Laughing, I ask, "Bless you? Shit on your head, you mean?"

"Yes," she says, huffing as she shoves at my chest with a grin. "My grandmother calls it getting 'blessed by the birds.' She swears being pooed on is actually very good luck."

I fake a disappointed sigh. "Oh, well, in that case, you'll be sad to learn that your hair is currently pigeon-poop-free. Which is sad for us both. Looks like the odds of you surviving an hour as my skate partner without sustaining multiple injuries just went down by quite a bit."

She takes my hand in hers with a laugh. "Oh, come on, you'll do fine. We'll take it nice and slow until you find your skate legs. Besides, how bad can you possibly be?"

Twenty minutes later, I've answered that question definitively.

Spectacularly bad.

Historically bad.

Potentially catastrophically bad if that kid in the yellow jumper knocks into my leg again. I barely avoided crushing him into a greasy spot on the ice the first time.

If he rolls the dice again...

"Must not crush children," I mutter beneath my breath. "Must not crush children or the elderly or break every bone in my body."

"Look up, Olly," Emily calls out from up ahead, where she's skating backward, just like that cheeky little toddler.

Making it look easy. Effortless. Graceful.

Meanwhile, I'm hunched over, death-gripping the barrier while a group of French teenage girls glide past, filming my wretched lurching with a mixture of giggles and insults.

"No, I do not have two left hands. That doesn't even make sense," I call after them in their mother tongue. "And I speak excellent French!"

They only laugh harder before skating away, one of them lobbing a final kill shot over her shoulder.

I growl and mutter, "Cruel. The French are a cruel people."

Grinning, Emily asks, "What did she say? I thought I heard something about a cow?"

"She said I sound like a Spanish cow," I explain, sucking in a sharp breath as my right foot nearly shoots out from under me again. I cling tighter to the barrier as I add, "Meaning my French accent is shite, I suppose. Or that I'm trying too hard. Maybe both. You can never tell with the French."

"Well, the trying too hard part is accurate, anyway," Emily murmurs gently. "All this tension is only making things harder, Olly. Can you try to relax your shoulders? Just a tiny bit? And bend your knees?"

"No, I can't, Emily. I've clearly lost all management of my limbs," I shoot back, only half joking. "I think that should be obvious by now."

My legs truly seem to have forgotten that they're attached to the same body, each one determined to strike out in different directions when I least expect it.

Emily emits a sympathetic hum that somehow makes me feel even more pathetic. "Okay. But you can at least stop looking at your feet, right?"

"But, if I don't look at my feet, how will I know what fresh betrayal they're planning?" I shuffle forward another few inches, arms windmilling wildly as my legs go rogue at the same time, once again.

"Here, let me help," she says, reaching for my hand.

Despite myself, I cling to her like a lifeline, allowing her to pull me a few inches away from the edge. "No, I can't. What if I fall and—"

"Oi, mister!" A small voice pipes up beside us. "My baby sister skates better than you!"

I look down to see Yellow Jumper circling me like a tiny shark, clearly intent on making mischief with my legs, once again.

"Good for her," I manage through gritted teeth. "Does she give lessons?"

"She's two," the boy says, with a hard roll of his brown eyes. He circles again, making my jaw clench so tight, I'm about to crack a molar when he asks, "Are you drunk? Is that why you can't stand up?"

"I'm not drunk, and I'm standing just fine," I insist, immediately making a liar of myself by going down.

Hard.

The good news is that I manage to release Emily's hand before I crash to the ice. The bad news is that my elbows crack into the rink with enough force to ensure I'll have no trouble remembering to keep them off the table at Christmas dinner.

Hell, they might still be black and blue on New Year's Day.

"Bollocks," I curse, wincing as fresh waves of pain continue to course from my arms into my shoulders.

The boy cackles with glee. "Drunk and a mouth on ya. Wait 'til I tell my mum. She said proper gentlemen don't curse, but you sure do."

"Listen here, little mister, I—" I start, but Emily cuts me off with a smooth, "Let me handle this, Olly."

She crouches down to the boy's level, still ridiculously graceful on her skates, making me feel even more like a Spanish cow with two left hands who will never find his way back to an upright position.

"What's your name, buddy?" she asks sweetly.

"Nigel," the boy says suspiciously.

"Well, Nigel, let me explain something." She maintains her sweetness, but there's a thread of steel beneath her words as she adds, "Some people are good at ice skating. Some people are good at being kind. Guess which one you need to work on?"

Nigel's face goes red. "He looks stupid. Really stupid."

"And you sound mean," Emily counters. "Which do

you think is worse? Looking silly while trying something new, or teasing someone who's struggling?"

The boy opens his mouth, closes it, opens it again, then ends with a wrinkle of his pug nose and a sigh. "Okay, fine." Glancing back at me, he adds, "Sorry, mister. You look like a right wanker, but I should have kept that to myself. Happy Christmas."

"Happy Christmas, Nigel," I say, a bit of my hope for the next generation restored as he skates away.

Emily helps me to my feet and back to my emotional support barrier, while I fight a fresh wave of completely inappropriate affection.

But there's nothing fake about the warmth in my voice, as I say, "Thank you, Ms. Darling. No one's ever taken on a cheeky child for me before. I'm touched."

"My pleasure." She grins. "I'm glad he seemed to see the error of his ways. Now, let's get you to safety before you break a bone. Or your face. Or someone else's face."

"Told you," I accuse. "I'm the worst."

She laughs. "Not sure about that, but you're up there. If my sister were here, she'd be having an aneurysm." She pauses, glancing up at the sky as if in deep thought. "Makes me wish I'd done some filming. Maybe I can ask the French girls to air-drop me a few of their videos. I mean, I can *tell* Izzy all about your ice-skating stylings, but it's really something that must be seen to be believed."

"Wicked woman," I accuse as she puts her arm around my waist, bolstering me for the final stretch to the exit.

"Very wicked," she agrees, still grinning. "But I'll make it up to you with a hot chocolate, Twitchy."

"As you should." I sniff, playing up the petulance in

my voice as I add, "And I'll be wanting extra whipped cream. For my dignity. It requires extra whipped cream to recover."

We make it to the outdoor café beside the rink through a combination of Emily's patient skill and sheer luck. By the time I collapse into a chair and Emily goes to fetch drinks, I'm just grateful to be alive.

And to have holiday skating behind me for another season.

"Here, drink up," she says a few moments later, pressing a mug into my hand before settling into the wrought iron chair beside me. "You look like you've been through something."

"I have," I announce, wrapping my frozen fingers around the drink, which is indeed topped with extra whipped cream. She really is an angel... "You were there. You saw. It was even worse than usual. This might be it, Em." I stare dramatically into the distance as I add in a softly wounded voice, "This might be the year I take genuine trauma away from that ice."

"Understandable, considering the near-death experience of it all," Emily says solemnly, playing along as I suspected she would. "But the way you crawled to the barrier on your hands and knees after that first big fall? Inspirational, really. I wanted to clap. Slow clap. For a long, long time."

"Now, you're taking the piss," I say, glaring at her over the rim of my chocolate.

"No, I'm serious," she says. "I *would* have clapped. But I was too busy reassuring a little girl that you weren't actually dying. You just sounded like you were, with all the moaning and groaning."

"I hate you," I mutter.

She giggles. "No, you don't. And she was so sweet! She was really worried about you. And her mother—" Something buzzes in her pocket, and she breaks off with a smile. "Oh, I bet that's Isabelle now. We always joke that she has a skating sixth sense. She always texts when I'm ..." Her words trail off as she scrolls through her phone, the pink slowly leaving her cheeks.

"What is it?" I lean closer. "Bad news from home?"

"No, from here." She shifts the screen toward me, her lips pressing into a tight line. "I set up a Google alert for you, too, so..."

Once again, the headlines are plentiful, and as cheeky as Nigel before Emily gave him a good talking to:

*Featherswallow Heir Falls
from Grace (and onto Ass)*

DISASTER STRIKES NOBILITY AGAIN:
Oliver Just Can't Keep it Up...

*Watch: Britain's Clumsiest Aristocrat Endangers Children
at Holiday Event!*

But it's the last one that makes me go completely still...

*Britain's most Chaotic Couple Strikes Again: Could These
Two Hot Messes be Perfect for Each Other?*

The article includes a photo compilation: me crawling across the ice, Emily laughing so hard she's doubled over, us clinging to each other by the barrier, and finally, that kiss from before.

The one that was supposed to be for the cameras, but felt like coming in from the cold on a long winter's night...

She looks up, meeting my gaze, a question in her eyes that makes me hope she might be wondering what I'm wondering.

Could we be perfect for each other?

She pulls in a breath, but before she can speak, her phone rings.

Emily blinks, then glances down. "Sorry, I... It's Isabelle." A soft laugh as she shakes her head. "I told you, she always knows." She lifts the phone between us as she half stands. "Do you mind? We've been trying to connect on a call for days and—"

"Of course," I say, waving her off with a grin. "Go. Chat. I'll be happy here with my cocoa and no ice under my feet. Or my ass."

She grins, her eyes crinkling just for me, even as she answers the phone with a warm, "Hello there, baby sister. How are you? I miss you so much."

Her words fade as she wanders away, seeking a bit of privacy for her conversation, but I can't seem to pull my eyes from the ginger in the fluffy white scarf. She's just... beautiful.

More than beautiful.

She's beautifully familiar. After only a few days, I feel like I've known her for ages. Or like I've been waiting for her for ages.

With Emily, both might very well be true.

"Mum said I had to apologize again," a petulant voice announces near my elbow, making me flinch in surprise.

I turn to see a runny-nosed Nigel pouting beside me, his own hot chocolate moustacheoing his upper lip. "What's that?"

"Mum said I had to apologize again," he repeats, a little more irritably. But then, I can't really blame him. I don't enjoy repeating myself, either. "Because you're some big fancy royal fuss."

I soften. "Nah, I'm not a big royal fuss. No need to apologize to me any more thoroughly than you would to anyone else. You did an excellent job apologizing the first time. Tell your mum she should be proud, and there are no hard feelings."

Nigel brightens a bit. "Okay, good." He glances around, searching for something before he adds, "Where's your redhead boss?"

I grin. "My boss? Did she seem like my boss, do you think?"

He shrugs. "She's way better at skating than you. And she's pretty bossy." He glances sharply my way again, seeming to rethink the wisdom of that last comment. "But I mean, not in a bad way."

"Just a bossy way," I supply.

"Yeah," he agrees, clearly irritated again when I laugh.

"Sorry," I say. "I shouldn't laugh. She's my girlfriend, actually, but I'm quite happy to have her boss me around. As you said, she's way better at skating, as well as many other things."

He sniffs, drawing the dangling wet beneath his nose up a millimeter before he exhales, setting the snot free again. "I don't like girls."

"Why not? Girls are fantastic. Your mum sounds very nice. And you yourself said your sister's a demon on skates."

He shrugs. "Yeah, but they're different. They're family. I don't have to kiss them like in the movies."

"You don't have to kiss anyone like in the movies if you don't want to," I say. "Kissing is neither obligatory nor necessary for a happy life."

He snorts, a crooked smile curving his chocolate-stained lips. "Oi, you *are* fancy. And silly, I think."

I nod in agreement. "Quite. Happy Christmas again, Nigel. Keep asking the hard questions."

He laughs as he toddles away on his skates across the gravel, clearly thinking I'm at least a little mad.

And, of course, I am.

I'm pretending to be in love with a woman I'm actually falling in love with, all while also pretending not to be falling to the woman herself.

Something has to give.

And maybe it will soon.

Grandmother's holiday party is right around the corner, an event with a unique mixture of heartwarming, welcoming, mapcap, and romantic vibes that doesn't come along very often.

A man with his heart on his sleeve could do worse when it comes to setting the scene for a grand confession than a Victorian mansion with loads of tiny, intimate rooms and mistletoe hung in every one...

Chapter Twelve
EMILY

Two days later...

What am I doing?

Seriously.

What?!

"I have no idea," I mutter as I wait for Maya to get back on the line after the "two seconds" she said she needed to find a private place to talk at the office.

It's still afternoon in New York and Maya's working through the weekend, along with two of our most loyal support staff, preparing a killer pitch for a new corporate client nearly as big as Titan Media. They're doing their best to save our business.

Meanwhile, I'm...

Well, I'm *also* doing my best to save our business.

But I should be working harder! So hard, I wouldn't have time left over to watch holiday movies with the funniest, sweetest, sexiest man alive. Or to notice how amazing he looks in linen pajama pants—and nothing else—first thing in the morning. Or to spend magical afternoons with him at museums, or ice-skating, or catching West End matinees, or riding historic carousels, or falling madly in love with the way he makes even a trip to the grocery store feel like a fabulous adventure.

Heck, just falling madly in love with...him.

No!

I'm *not* falling in love.

I know this because I've *been* in love, and this isn't the way love goes. Love starts slow, like easing into a pool of perfectly warm water. Love sneaks up on you, step by gentle step, until all of a sudden, you turn around one day and realize that the guy getting toast crumbs all over your table is someone you'd like to keep around for a long, long time.

Or...at least that's the way love worked with Gabe and Stephen.

But Gabe and Stephen *didn't* stick around for a long, long time.

Gabe met someone he liked banging more than me—while we were still dating—and Stephan and I just... fizzled out. First, our Saturday mornings lost their shine, then our date nights and evening walks. Soon, we were both finding excuses to spend time apart. I stayed late at the office and joined a book club. Stephen signed up for a pickleball league, got a second job walking dogs uptown, and eventually decided a WhatsApp message while I was out of the country was the best way to end things.

Which was hurtful, but still a relatively peaceful way to end a love affair.

As peaceful as the way we fell for each other...

So, maybe you're ready for something less peaceful, woman! Maybe it's time love threw you into the back of an unmarked van, drove you out into the middle of bumfuck Swoonville, and dumped your body in a boiling hot spring of emotions, with no time to ease into your feels—or a commitment—at a leisurely pace.

"Stop. Please, stop," I beg the Inner Voice.

I can't let myself be kidnapped by a love van right now, not with so much on the line. Even if I land the Fletchers' gig, Darling Events isn't out of the woods. If Maya can't land this big fish, we'll need to book at least five major events this year to make up for the drop in revenue from losing Titan.

And that's just *this* year.

Come next year, we'll have to do it all again, to keep going big or go home.

And I know myself. I can't grow a business from low six figures to mid six figures while juggling a long-distance relationship. Olly and I are just five days into this...whatever it is, and I was already missing him like crazy this afternoon. I couldn't wait for him to get back from running errands for reasons that had nothing to do with our West End matinee plans and everything to do with the way Oliver's blue-gray eyes light up when he sees me coming.

And that was after just four hours apart!

After two weeks, two *months*, I'd be a wreck. A pining, sad, moping, low-functioning wreck, incapable of holding up my side of the business. Even if Darling Events were solely mine, I wouldn't want that to happen. But it's not, it's Maya's, too. She's depending on me. She's been my friend since we were in junior high, and helping to grow Darling Events into a power player in the party planning scene for almost four years.

I can't let her down.

Not even for a man who might actually be my perfect match if he didn't live half a world away...

"Okay, I'm back!" Maya breathes into the phone, making me flinch and start pacing again. "What's up, buttercup?"

I've been dressed for Oliver's Grandmother's party for a while now, but left my heels by the door—the better to comfortably wear a hole in the carpet while having an emotional meltdown.

"I'm freaking out, that's what's up," I whisper-hiss into the receiver, glancing at the clock on the nightstand.

Eighteen minutes until we need to leave.

Eighteen minutes to get my head on straight before I have to pretend to be Oliver's girlfriend in front of his entire family, his grandmother's friends, high-profile society mavens, a Duchess, and an *Earl* who might be stopping by for Christmas pudding.

No pressure or anything.

"I'm starting to think this was a bad idea," I whisper. "Maybe even a really bad idea."

"What? Why? And why are you whispering?" Maya's voice crackles through my single earbud. I left the other one out, the better to hear the stupidly hot man singing in a husky baritone in the shower down the hall. "And why are you freaking out? You calmed the waters at Fletchers, have two incredible caterers on board for them to choose from, and are well on your way to being besties with Belinda Moore. As far as I can tell, everything is coming up roses, baby. White roses with little sprigs of fir tree tucked around them for the holidays."

"Yes, but I've also made four appearances in the British tabloids in five days," I remind her. "The paparazzi doesn't seem to be losing interest. They sneak shots of us every time we leave Oliver's apartment."

"But you look adorable in most of them, especially the carousel shots from yesterday," she counters. "And so happy! I haven't seen you smile like that since we ditched school to go to Coney Island senior year. It looks like you're having the time of your life being a pretend girlfriend."

"I am, and that's the problem!" I agree with a flop of my arm.

"Why?"

"I'm not supposed to be having fun! The fun is supposed to be fake. Just like the kisses and the laughter and the...other things. And Oliver is supposed to be a stuck-up snob who lied to me at a pub, not silly and sweet and hot and...perfect."

I pause at the window, staring at my reflection in the darkened glass.

The green dress Oliver bought me for the luncheon looks even more elegant and festive paired with dangly pearl earrings we picked up at a Christmas market stall. My hair is cooperating for once, falling in smooth curls around my shoulders, and I nailed the smudged gray eyeliner look all the cool South Korean girls are doing. I look like someone who belongs at a fancy Christmas party with a member of the aristocracy.

Which is another part of the problem.

My outside doesn't match my insides.

Not at all.

"Seriously, Maya," I add, my throat tightening as I

turn away from the window. "I think Oliver might be perfect. Like...for me. And that he might think so, too."

Maya makes an appropriately concerned sound, before ruining it with, "Oh, no, Em. A kind, funny, sexy as hell man with a panty-melting accent and ridiculous amounts of money wants to date you for real. How awful. Let me go fetch the world's tiniest violin."

"Maya, I'm serious," I say, flopping back onto the bed with a huff, staring up at the elegant crown molding on the triple-trayed ceiling. Even his ceiling is ridiculously fancy.

As fancy as I am not.

Not really. Not in real life.

"So am I," Maya says. "Hold on, I'm putting resin on my bow now."

"Seriously, this can't happen," I push on, ignoring the screechy "tiny violin" sounds she's making on the other end of the line. "Our business is hanging on by a thread, I'm already on the edge of burnout, and this is just the beginning of the marathon. We have miles to go before we rest, and I can't bring that level of hustle to my professional life, while navigating a high-profile, long-distance relationship in my private one."

"Okay. So?" she asks, thankfully ceasing her painfully squeaky version of "What Child is This."

I blink. "What do you mean, so? So...I can't date him. That's it. Even if he actually wants to, and I'm not being crazy. I just can't. We'd be doomed from the start. The business has to come first."

"Why?"

My heart record scratches to a stop in my chest, only to start pounding harder again a second later. "What?" I croak out, panic fisting around my throat. "What does that mean? You don't want to give up, do you?"

"No, of course not," she says, sending my breath rushing out in a huff of relief. "But that doesn't mean we have to let work take over our lives, either. I've been talking to my mom a lot the past few days, Em."

"Oh yeah? And what did the doc have to say?" I murmur. Maya's mom is a psychiatrist, the only nice psychiatrist I've ever met, actually.

Most of the other ones I've encountered give strong sociopath vibes, but maybe that's just a New York City thing. You have to be pretty crazy to practice psychiatry in one of the biggest, more feral cities in the world.

"She said that the years go by way faster than you think when you're young," Maya says. "And that, looking back on my life when I'm her age, I'm never going to wish I'd worked more. I'm going to wish I'd played more, dreamed more. Loved more."

My ribs squeeze around my fluttering heart. "Yeah. That sounds right, doesn't it?"

"It does," Maya murmurs. "And true. So...I say we keep pushing hard for the next few weeks, book what we can book, and if we aren't in a better place by the end of the year, we talk to the management company about breaking the lease."

I bite my bottom lip. "They could go after us for 22 months of unpaid rent, Maya. All at once. We'd be ruined."

"They could," she agrees, "but I seriously doubt they will, not if we agree to pay a penalty fee and forfeit the deposit. And yeah, that would hurt, but it wouldn't break us. Then, we go back to meeting high-profile clients over lunch for a while, until our bottom line recovers.

People love lunch, and buying lunch is a lot cheaper than a lease on an office space in DUMBO."

I nod, knowing she's right and...hating it at the same time. "It feels like failure, though, doesn't it? A little?"

"It does, but it would be a bigger failure to sacrifice what's left of our twenties to the Gods of Capitalism." She pauses before adding in a more pointed voice, "Or miss out on the guy of our dreams because we're too busy working ourselves to the bone just to keep our heads above water."

I exhale another shaky breath. "Yeah." I swallow hard before confessing in a smaller voice, "But I'm still scared."

"Of course, you are. If this goes hideously awry, it's going awry with the entire world watching. The paparazzi will probably snap pictures of you crying at the airport on your way home after the breakup. And of you stress-eating an entire pizza in The Village. And of you having a bad hair day in Central Park, while Oliver's already moved on with the Princess of Peru or whatever."

I sit up, frowning at the darkened window again. "Thanks for the visuals, friend. Now, I'm considering making a break for the elevator right now. Or just hurling myself out the window and being done with it."

She has the nerve to laugh, the wretched woman. "Sorry. But I'm here to keep it real. That's why you called me."

"It is," I mumble as I stress chew my bottom lip. "You're right."

"But it could also end in more pictures like at the carousel and the ice-skating rink," she adds in a softer voice. "In smiles and kisses and fun and two people being very happy together."

I release my lip and swallow. Hard. "Yeah. It could, I think. It really could."

"So, get out there and tell your fake boyfriend you don't want to fake it anymore," she says. "I've got to go. The grind calls. Talk soon. You've got this, Em. I know you do."

"Thanks," I whisper as we end the call.

After, I sit staring at my reflection again as my thoughts race. Then, I launch into list-making mode.

Because of course, I do.

Reasons Why Telling Olly I Want to be his Real Girlfriend is Still a Bad Idea

1. We still live on different continents (3,458 miles apart, give or take a mile, and who knows how far in kilometers).

2. He's from a noble family, has an obscene amount of money, a successful career, looks effortlessly chic in designer duds, and once dated a supermodel.

3. I'm from New Jersey, from a family that couldn't afford a beach club membership, have exactly four thousand, three hundred, and six dollars in my checking account, my business is in major struggle mode, and I look effortlessly uninspiring in off-the-rack suits, even my mother has hinted are too modest. I think in miles and pounds and inches and will likely

never successfully measure anything outside the United States. And cooking in Celsius? Forget about it. I've already nearly set his flat on fire trying to broil cheese on my toast at the wrong degree.

4. I hate having my picture taken, even when I know it's being taken, let alone a picture sneak attack. This paparazzi thing is already getting seriously old. Is that the kind of thing I could get used to dealing with for months? Years? Maybe even longer?

5. I still don't understand how serious this "fifth in line to the throne" thing is. I mean, I get that the chances of him becoming king are slim to none, but they aren't zero. And that means— should this *really* be my shot at happily ever after —there would also be a non-zero chance of *me* becoming...

"The Queen of Fucking England," I mutter aloud with a very undignified, unqueenly snort.

Yeah. That's *never* going to happen. Never.

I'm pretty sure someone would assassinate me first. Half the people in the U.K. don't like the monarchy much already, let alone if there was suddenly a lower-middle-class American from a crusty part of New Jersey on the throne.

Of course, it's much more likely that we'll never make it that far, that Olly will realize he's made a horrible mistake getting involved with a hot mess American and move on.

Even if the tabloids do seem to think that his mess and mine are a match made in heaven…

A soft knock interrupts my stress spiral.

"Ready to go, darling Darling? Time, tide, and my grandmother tolerate tardiness from no man. Or woman." Oliver's voice rumbles through the door, instantly making my thighs tingle.

I'm not sure if this is just a crush or something more serious, but it's certainly lust.

I'm already dying to see him in whatever sexy suit he's wearing tonight.

"Yes, just a second," I say as I stand. "Come in, I just need to put on my heels, and I'll be—" I cut off with another unladylike snort that becomes a full-throated chortle as Oliver steps into the room, doing a slow spin, the better for me to take in the full glory of his outfit. "Oh my God, Featherswallow. What in the Father Christmas is *that*?"

"This is the bet I lost with my grandmother at last year's party," he says. "We'd both been drinking. But I was certain she was the more inebriated party, and I would handily beat her at snooker. But alas…" He glances down at the most hideously festive Christmas sweater I've ever seen in my life.

And I grew up in New Jersey, so I've *seen* some shit when it comes to tacky.

But this…

It's aggressively red, like blood from a fresh, neon wound, with a massive gingerbread man across the chest. A gingerbread man who's clearly going through something, judging by the googly eyes pointing in two wildly different directions.

"Did it have a stroke?" I ask, barely suppressing another laugh as he flicks the bells forming a belt across the man's middle.

"Almost certainly," he says. "And I'm pretty sure its icing is infected with something. But it lights up *and* glows in the dark, so…there's that."

He presses a button beneath his armpit, and the gingerbread's icing begins to throb bright green, sending me into another fit of giggles. "Oh my God," I gasp. "This is worse than the reindeer sweater in Bridget Jones. You're totally Mark Darcy."

"And you're Bridget in a naughty little skirt," he says, his lips pushing into a pout as he glances at my lower half. "Are you sure you won't let me buy you a naughty little skirt on the way? I'm sure something's still open." He motions toward me. "I mean, you're gorgeous, but far too classy for the insanity to which you shall soon be subjected. I'm afraid someone will spill beer on you, and I'll never forgive myself for letting you ruin that perfect dress."

I arch a dubious brow, ignoring the way my cheeks heat at the "gorgeous" part of that statement. "I seriously doubt someone's going to spill beer on me, Olly. It's a holiday party at a Dowager Viscountess's mansion, not a kegger at a frat house."

He grunts. "You're right, it's more likely to be Christmas punch than beer. But I'd still feel better if you were wearing a hard-to-stain little black dress." His voice becomes a wicked purr as he adds, "A *very* little black dress."

"There he is," I murmur, close to purring myself.

"There's the bad man I met at the pub. I wondered where he'd gotten off to."

"He's been being a good fake boyfriend," Oliver murmurs, lifting a hand into the air. "And I solemnly swear, he'll still be a good fake boyfriend tonight. No matter how sexy you look with your smudgy eye makeup and berry-stained lips. Shall we?"

But maybe I don't want you to be good, Olly, I think as I step into my heels and take his offered arm.

Aloud, I say, "We shall."

But all the way down the elevator to the ground floor, all I can think about is how naughty Olly and I were in an elevator the last time we had a few beers.

And how much I want to be naughty with him again…

Chapter Thirteen

OLIVER

The thing about lying to my grandmother is that she always knows.

Everything.

Always.

All the time.

She is a mystical, all-seeing elf of a woman, who is also twice as plugged into social media as people half her age. The chances she'll guess that I'm trying to pull the wool over her eyes are significant.

But then, the fact that I'm genuinely mad about Emily and pretending *not* to be when we're alone is significant, too.

Hopefully, the two lies will cancel each other out, leaving everyone satisfied.

Or confused.

I'm certainly confused.

It makes sense that my stomach is in knots as Emily and I emerge from our cab and take the turn into Grandmother's front garden, where twinkling lights dance through the trees above the recently shoveled path.

"Shit, I forgot to ask—is there anything special I should know about British holiday party etiquette?" Emily asks, fingers digging into my arm through my coat, making me think she's feeling the stress, too. "I mean, obviously, she's Lady Plimpton until I'm told otherwise. And I won't hug her or compliment her outfit or do anything else repulsively American."

I laugh. "No one said hugging and complimenting were repulsive. They just make us uncomfortable." I shrug. "Until we're sauced, of course, then anything goes. Who knows, you might end up playing strip snooker with Grandmother before the evening is through."

She shiver-giggles. "Don't joke. I'm too nervous."

I pause halfway up the walk, turning to give her shoulders an encouraging squeeze. "Relax, you'll do fine. Better than fine. You're delightful at a party."

"How would you know?" she asks. "We've never been to a party together."

"But we've been to the pub, which is close," I say. "You've already proven you can hold your liquor and cut a serious rug on the dancefloor. And you're delightful all of the time. I don't see why you'd be any different at a party."

"I'm not delightful all the time," she says in a softer voice, her brow furrowing. "Remember the morning I yelled at you and said terrible things?"

"You didn't yell," I murmur. She hasn't brought up the morning after since... Well, since the morning after. The fact that she wants to talk about it now seems like a good sign. It's certainly an opportunity I don't intend to let slip through my fingers. "You spoke in a firm, but reasonable tone. And they weren't terrible things; they were true things. I *did* lie to you, but I don't plan on ever being that stupid again."

"You're not stupid. You're..." She trails off with a sigh that sends an increasingly familiar wave of longing rushing through my chest. "You're wonderful, and I'm having so much fun I—"

Before she can finish, the front door flies open and my grandmother cheers, "Happy Christmas! Oliver, darling, you're finally here! I thought I heard someone lurking in the garden!"

I turn to assure her that I wasn't lurking—just pausing for a chat that might have put me out of my "fake relationship" misery, if we hadn't been so festively interrupted—only to be drowned out by feverish barking.

A beat later, the usual Cacophony of Corgis explodes around her legs, streaming into the garden with the force of a tsunami. The corgi wave hits hard and fast, sweeping Emily and me both into an "avoid stepping on a paw or tripping over a puppy potato" dance as old as time.

Or as old as the corgi breed, anyway...

My grandmother is a corgi devotee. Such a devotee, she invites the Corgi Appreciation Society—and their pack of spoiled fur babies—to her holiday party every year.

I should have warned Emily, prepared her for the onslaught, but thankfully, she doesn't seem traumatized.

Quite the opposite, in fact. "Oh, my goodness, the precious!" She gasps like she's just been presented with the one and only, solid gold Labubu. "So much precious!" Then she's down on her knees in the snow in her lovely dress, collecting paw prints and drool.

"Jezebel, Jasper, come back inside at once," Grandmother demands of her own, poorly-behaved pups.

Who ignore her, of course, continuing to jockey for pets from Emily or mouthfuls of salty snow.

"You look just like Mr. Biscuit, yes, you do," Emily coos to a pumpkin-colored creature attempting to eat her hair. To me, she adds, "I had a stuffed corgi when I was little, Mr. Biscuit the Brave. God, aren't corgis the cutest things in the entire world?" She cups another grinning pup's snout in her hands as the curl eater makes a play for the strands by her ear. "Look at this face! I could just eat it."

"I think that one feels the same way about you," I tease. "Watch your hair. He seems to think it's made of bacon."

"Sir Reginald, no!" A sharp voice orders from the door. "Drop that young woman's hair this instant! No eating between meals. We've discussed this!"

A woman in what might be the ugliest Christmas jumper in history rushes down the front steps. Cats in Santa hats peer out at us from her chest as she pants, "So sorry." She snags Reginald by the collar, tugging him away. "He thinks anything red is edible. Last week, he ate half my nephew's Arsenal scarf."

"The scarf probably tasted better than their chances this season," I offer, helping Emily to her feet. There's snow in her hair and a ladder running up her tights, but she's glowing.

"Truly sorry," Cat Sweater offers again.

"Oh, don't worry. I'm—" Emily breaks off at the sound of a pained yip from the edge of the herd.

We all glance over to see a tiny, silky-haired corgi being bullied through the snow. Every time she tries to get to her feet, two much larger dogs knock her over again and snigger about it, proving humans aren't the only species with room for improvement.

"Play nice, you two," Emily says, sidestepping the mob. She shoos Lunk One and Lunk Two to the side before scooping up the trembling runt.

The tiny dog burrows into her coat like she's found salvation in Emily's bosom, which makes sense.

So did I, small dog, I think. *So did I...*

"Princess Fluffy Nugget, there you are, darling." My grandmother's best friend, Gretchen, appears in the doorway, looking even more thin and frail than she did last year, the poor thing. She's nearly ninety, but her former opera singer's voice still carries as she adds, "My poor little Nuggy. Always the underdog, but such a sweet girl."

"Aw, Nuggy, you are sweet. I can tell," Emily murmurs, nuzzling her face into the dog's furry head while the pup shivers with joy.

Suddenly, an image hits me with the force of Grandmother's punch: Emily in my flat—*our* flat—on a Sunday morning. Coffee in hand, a little runt of our own in her lap, dog toys scattered across the floor as we finish breakfast and debate how to spend the rest of our morning. Perhaps a walk through the park for ice cream and people watching? Or a trip to Camden Market, to let our fur baby sniff other dogs' bottoms while Emily and I peruse the antiques?

The scene is so clear, the longing so visceral, that I have to turn away for a beat to compose myself.

When I do, I catch Grandmother staring at me with thinly-veiled suspicion.

I'm making a mess of things before we're even through the door. Time to pull myself together and sell this fake romance.

"Happy Christmas, Grandmother," I boom with forced cheer. "May I present Ms. Emily Darling. Emily, my grandmother, Dowager Baroness Susanna Eugenia Plimpton, terror of Belgravia and president of the Corgi Appreciation Society."

On the landing, Emily shifts Nuggy to one arm and extends her hand. "It's wonderful to meet you, Lady Plimpton. Thank you so much for having me."

Grandmother takes the offered hand, pressing it between both of hers. "Oh, call me Suze, and the honor is mine, darling. Always fantastic to meet someone with the good sense to worship the corgi breed as God intended." She lowers her voice as she adds, "Though now that you've picked *that one* up, she'll never let you put her down. Princess Nugget is notoriously clingy."

Emily laughs as she hugs the dog closer. "Fine by me. She's adorable."

"Agreed. Now, come in before we all freeze," Grandmother commands, turning to shoo everyone back inside.

We follow her, corgis streaming between our legs.

"Be warned, Margot's spiked the punch again," Grandmother continues, "even though I told her it was obscenely full of rum to begin with. So, watch your intake, darlings. We don't want anyone passing out under the Christmas tree. Oh, and Oliver, remind me to get a picture of you in that jumper later. You're ridiculous, and I don't ever want to forget it. Nearly as ridiculous as your poor mother and her book club."

The warmth hits like a wall, a combination of Grandmother's preference for tropical temperatures and too many bodies packed into every corner. I'm helping Emily out of her coat without disturbing Nuggy, when my mother calls out from the next room, "I heard that,

Susanna. Leave him be. He's been through enough with the tabloids this holiday."

"Never," Grandmother calls back, good-naturedly. "Oliver knew what he was getting into when he challenged me at snooker. Just like you and your club knew when you foolish creatures tried to beat me at trivia." She waves me toward the drawing room. "Say hello to your mother, Oliver. And remind me to get a picture of her, as well."

Dropping our coats onto the overflowing pile on the table beside the also overflowing wardrobe, Emily and I head for the drawing room.

Stepping through the doorway, we're treated to a tableau of my mother's book club gathered around the piano, attempting to maintain their dignity while green and purple alien antennae blink on and off above their perfectly set hair.

They're launching into a slurred version of God Rest Ye Merry Gentlemen when Mother spots me and separates from the group.

"Hello there, darlings," she says, kissing both my cheeks before turning to greet Emily, her antennae bobbing. When she's done, she squeezes both our arms as she begs, "Please, be careful tonight. No bets with Grandmother this year. I'd love some sane holiday photos of the family next Christmas."

"I'll do my best, Mother." I press a kiss to the top of her head. "But you know how she is. She always makes a bet sound so sensible at the time."

"And you all always lose!" Grandmother calls from the next room, proving her hearing is as keen as ever. "Show Emily the tree, Oliver. Let's see if she's as lucky as you are."

"What?" Emily asks.

I start toward the sitting room. "You'll see. Come on, then, and we'll fetch a cup of punch while we're at it."

Emily grins, still cuddling Nuggy as we move into the sitting room. There, two Christmas trees sparkle on opposite ends of the makeshift dancefloor, where couples are swaying under a disco ball to the drunken carols drifting in from the next room.

"This is incredible," she whispers, taking in the festive madness. "It's like Downton Abbey had a baby with Studio 54."

"That's...disturbingly accurate." I guide her to the far corner, where Grandmother's primary tree stretches toward the ceiling. Every branch groans beneath the weight of decorations accumulated over multiple generations.

Nudging Sir Reginald away from the base, where he's trying to eat the red tree skirt, I clear the way for Em to step closer.

"Wow, what a beauty." Her jaw drops as she gazes up.

With a sleepy-looking puppy tucked against her chest and the fire casting her in a golden glow, she looks like she stepped out of a Victorian Christmas card. I want to tell her that *she's* beautiful, but there would be no excuse for that. There's no one close enough to hear the "performance," and I have yet to suck down a single cup of punch.

So, instead, I clear my throat and motion toward the branches. "All right, are you prepared to find a pickle?"

Her brows shoot up. "Excuse me?" Beneath her breath, she adds, "I'm not that kind of girl, Mr. Featherswallow."

"That's not what I heard, Ms. Darling," I shoot back,

because I can't resist an excuse to flirt with her. "But I wasn't talking about *that* pickle. I was talking about the pickle ornaments on the tree. When you're ready to start looking, I'll time you. Ten seconds to find as many pickles as you can. Two or more, and you'll have good luck secured for the new year."

Proving she loves a challenge, her eyes light up. "All right. Give me a countdown."

I lift my arm, arching a theatrical brow as I murmur, "In three, two, one, and go!"

Emily jerks her focus back to the tree, zeroing in on a tiny pickle with a glittering halo almost immediately. She follows her initial success by pointing out two relatively normal pickles, then a pickle in a diaper, and a pickle Santa with a giant sack of toys, proving she has excellent pickle-detecting radar.

"Time!" I shout, pretending to be scandalized as I announce, "You beat my record by two. What dark magic is this?"

She shrugs. "No magic. Just an excellent eye for detail, sir."

"And excellent luck guaranteed for the year," I agree, stepping over to the punch station to pour us each a glass. "Or so Featherswallow family lore would have you believe."

"I like Featherswallow family lore, so far," she says, shifting Nuggy to one arm as she accepts the drink. She glances around the room again with a stunned shake of her head. "I can't believe places like this really exist. I mean, I know they do, I've toured lots of historic homes, but..." She sips her punch. "I don't know, I guess I never imagined how modern life would play out for people who still live in places like this."

"Would you like the tour?" I ask, nodding toward the far door. "Fair warning, it includes a lot of dead people in frames, an offensive number of knick-knacks, and at least one allegedly haunted chandelier. Grandmother's had the electric people out to look at it five times, but they swear there's nothing wrong, and it only misbehaves when Edward's around. I think it's because he looks like my great-great-grandfather, who was apparently a bit of an arse."

"Knick-knacks and ghosts? Sounds like a good time to me." She glances down at Nuggy, who's fallen asleep against her chest. "Should I lay her down somewhere?"

"Not unless your arms are tired," I say. "She seems quite happy."

"They're not. And I'm quite happy, too," Emily says, holding my gaze for a beat. "Thank you so much for trusting me with your family."

"Of course, Darling," I say, voice gruffer than before. "You're a delight. My family is lucky to have you here to calm the corgi hordes and keep me out of trouble."

She arches a brow. "Oh, I don't know about that. We seem to have a knack for trouble."

"True." I loop my arm around her shoulders. "But at least there aren't any paparazzi here to take pictures this time."

"No, just your grandmother," she teases.

We slip away from the hubbub of the front rooms, and I guide her through one of the homes that shaped me. The Featherswallow country estate, with its grand history and faded furnishings, is my personal favorite, but I have so many fond memories of "The Little House," as Grandmother calls it.

Of course, it's anything but "little," only little by

comparison to the Plimpton manor home in Cornwall, and fifteen minutes later, we're just getting to the back of the first floor.

"This is where I got drunk on Edward's eighteenth birthday," I say as we move through the warmly lit library. "I was only thirteen and terribly jealous of the big boys having their first pints." I motion toward the window seat. "Then I was terribly sick over there, and Grandmother was terribly mad. But she didn't tell my parents, for which I was grateful. She just made me clean it all up and go for a long, vigorous walk with her the next morning while I was hideously hungover." I shudder at the memory. "Scared me away from alcohol for years."

"Wise woman," Emily murmurs, pulling in a deep breath. "It smells so good in here. I love the smell of old books."

"Me, too, but I love the smell in the next room even more." I lead the way around the corner, down a short hall, and into the glassed room where I played dinosaur hunter as a child, prowling my prey through the flowers and ferns.

The solarium unfolds before us, dark beneath the winter night sky. But even in December, it's warm and muggy, humid with the breath of hundreds of plants. Orchids climb the walls. Palms brush the ceiling, and roses perfume the air with memories of summer.

"Oh, wow," Emily breathes. "This is…"

"Mad? Excessive? A violation of heating efficiency standards?"

"Fantastic," she finishes firmly. "It's like stepping through the wardrobe into another world."

She wanders deeper into the urban jungle, still carrying Nuggy like a spoiled baby. She stops next to a particularly large fern, studying its sprawling fronds in the moonlight. "I don't pretend to know a lot about plants, but this looks old."

"It is," I say, doing my best to ignore the fact that she's stopped beneath one of the many sprigs of mistletoe Grandmother has hung around the house every year.

Mistletoe isn't reason enough to break the rules…

Is it?

"That fern was planted by my Great-Great something Aunt Cordelia," I say. "It's over two hundred years old."

Emily turns to me, her eyes huge. "No way."

I lean against the potting bench on the wall. "Yes, way. Cordelia had quite the green thumb. She was also beautiful, brilliant, and an exemplary horsewoman. Half of London was in love with her, and it was assumed she'd make a spectacular marriage." I lower my voice dramatically, "Before it all came crashing down."

"Oh no," Em says in an equally dramatic tone. "What befell the poor woman!?"

"Her reputation was ruined by a lecherous earl with wicked intentions."

"Oh no, not a lecherous earl with wicked intentions!"

"We joke, but it really was quite awful. Apparently, in early summer, 1814, at the first ball of the season, Cordelia shared a kiss with the Earl of Swythemore. They were out in his rose garden, alone, safe from detection…or so they must have thought." I step closer as I whisper, "But by morning, the gossip was everywhere. Someone had seen them in each other's arms. The news spread through the Ton like wildfire. Within days, it had become a massive scandal, and Cordelia was on the verge of ruin. The only way to salvage her reputation was for the Earl to propose marriage."

Emily's eyes narrow. "Come on, Earl, don't drop the ball."

"Oh, he dropped the ball. Dropped it big time," I confirm. "He claimed she'd thrown herself at him, hoping to trap him into matrimony, and he was simply an innocent victim of her feminine scheming. Classic 'he said, she said,' but that was all it took to ruin a woman in 1814."

"It's about all it takes now," Emily says with a roll of her eyes. "But at least we can work to earn a living these days."

"Indeed," I agree, "Thankfully, Cordelia's father was a good egg. He didn't force her to marry one of the less appealing fellows she would have been able to land in her disgraced state. He allowed her to live here, with him, and arranged for her big brother to take care of her after he passed. She spent her entire life behind these walls, rarely leaving the house after her disgrace. But it wasn't all bad." I glance around us. "This was her haven. She became a skilled botanist. Created some beautiful hybrid roses and a strain of wheat that was resistant to mold."

Emily sighs as she sets her sleeping charge down on the potting bench. Nuggy snuffles before sprawling into a full sploot and continuing to catch up on her beauty sleep. "Well, that's good, but... Damn, being a woman has been pretty shitty for most of recorded history."

I nod. "It has. The patriarchy's a beastly business. Especially here, and especially in the 1800s. I like to think I would have been a decent sort, but noble men really could get away with murder back then, so..." I exhale a soft laugh. "I probably would have been a terrible rake who gambled the family money away at my club and ravaged innocent young ladies in gardens."

She cocks her head, her brow furrowing. "No, I don't think so."

"No?"

She shakes her head. "No. You're a good one, Oliver Featherswallow. A very good one, actually, even though you came off a tiny bit twatty at first."

"Your British slang is coming along nicely," I say. "But that should be 'a bit of a twat', not 'a bit twatty.' Please try to remember that in the future."

"Got it. I'll keep that in mind." She smiles, soft and unguarded, a smile that feels like it's just for me.

And suddenly I can't keep my guilty conscience to myself.

"I'm not always good," I admit in a huskier voice. "I've been thinking impure thoughts about you nearly every hour of every day. And I'm seriously tempted to use that mistletoe above your head as an excuse to ravage you in the solarium."

Her eyes fly up, landing on the pearl berries hung between two palm fronds.

When her gaze returns to mine, her pupils are wide, dark.

Determined.

"Well, if you need an excuse," she whispers.

She doesn't have to ask me twice.

One moment, we're frozen in the dark, a sleeping puppy snoring on the potting bench between us.

The next, she's in my arms.

Chapter Fourteen

EMILY

I pull him closer, and suddenly the green icing on his hideous sweater is lighting up the shadows, throbbing in time with each eager beat of my heart.

We shouldn't do this.

At least not without having a serious talk.

I have no idea what he wants, what *I* want. Or how this could possibly work with all the obstacles between us. But God, his lips taste even better than I remember. Like punch and holiday magic and Olly, this kind, clever man who is so much more than a "spare."

"Every time the tabloids call you 'the spare,' I want to punch someone," I confess as his fingers curl around the back of my neck.

"Why?" His thumb presses that spot below my ear, the one that sends shivers all the way down my spine.

"Because it's mean." I nip at his lower lip. "You're not a spare, you're a person. You're...Olly."

He hums low in his throat, kissing me harder before whispering against my lips, "I love it when you call me

Olly. It makes me happy and hard, all at the same time." He shifts his hips, proving he isn't lying.

I *do* make him hard.

And he makes me want like I've never wanted a man before.

But we're technically in public—in a room with glass walls, no less.

"What if someone sees? There could be paparazzi outside," I breathe against his mouth. But when he backs me against his Great-Great-Whatever Aunt's potting bench, I put up exactly zero resistance.

"They can't trespass on private property." His tongue spars deliciously with mine before he adds, "But that doesn't mean someone from the party couldn't walk in at any minute. This shows a staggering lack of judgment."

"It does. We should—" I break off with a shudder as he grips my ass in both big hands. "We should really..." He pulls me tight to his erection, making my breath catch on a moan. "I wouldn't want to..." His kisses my neck, my jaw, his breath coming faster as my head spins. "What about the rules?"

"Fuck the rules," he says, the roughness in his voice making me even hotter.

Which makes me kiss him harder.

Which makes him grind closer.

Which makes me forget why we were doing all this stupid talking in the first place.

Before I know it, my zipper is down. My bodice sags forward and my pulse spikes with a heady combination of panic and arousal—I don't want to get caught in flagrante delicto by his family or friends—but I also *really* don't want him to stop undressing me.

Still, I'm about to insist we find somewhere more private, I really am.

Then, he tugs my dress down around my waist, baring my breasts to the humid air as he murmurs, "So fucking beautiful, Em," and all capacity for rational thought flies out the window.

He sucks my nipple deep, and I cry out, fingers tangling in his hair as I arch closer to his wicked, wonderful mouth. He hums appreciatively against my skin as he squeezes my other breast, holding me prisoner as his thumb flicks back and forth across the sensitive peak until my knees give.

But he doesn't let me fall. He braces us both against the bench as he gathers handfuls of my dress in his fists, drawing my skirt higher on my thighs.

The hard wood digs into my back, but I barely feel it. I'm too focused on the scrape of his teeth, the pressure of his hips, the heat rolling off him as he frees my legs.

"Need you, Red, need you so fucking badly," he says, hooking a hand behind my knee and guiding my leg around his waist as he thrusts forward.

Suddenly, I'm tipped open, rocking against him as he grinds between my legs, shamelessly rubbing on him through our clothes like a teenager until the room starts to spin.

I bite his shoulder through his ridiculous sweater, smothering a cry as his fingers slip into my panties. "Fuck, Emily." He groans as he strokes through my swollen folds. "You're killing me. So sexy, the sexiest thing I—"

"Inside me," I beg, fumbling at the top of his pants. "Inside me, please."

"I don't have a condom, I—"

"I'm on the pill, and I trust you," I cut in, shoving his

pants down. "I don't want you to stop. Please, Olly, don't stop. I need you so much, it hurts."

"Never want to hurt you, love," he says as he pulls my panties to the side, clearing the way. "Never."

I reach for the top of his boxer-briefs, hands literally shaking, I'm so desperate to free his cock.

But before I can curl my fingers around the fabric—

I hear it.

A soft, questioning whimper from just a foot away…

Olly and I both freeze—me with my breasts out for show and tell; him with his pants around his knees—a scandalous tableau certain to traumatize innocent eyeballs.

If Nuggy's awake.

But surely, she isn't.

She was sleeping like the sleepiest puppy in Puppytown.

Slowly, we turn our heads in unison to find that Princess Fluffy Nugget is indeed awake, her tiny head tilted at an angle that seems to demand to know what the heck we think we're doing.

With her big brown eyes glinting in the moonlight, she looks like a cartoon character who just woke up in a porno, and I can safely say I've never gone from turned on to traumatized this fast.

"Oh my god, Oliver," I say in a rush, scrambling to pull my dress back into place. "Oh my God!"

"What's wrong?" he pants, still parked between my thighs

"She's awake," I insist, pushing at him with one hand as I hold my sagging bodice in place with the other.

He blinks. "She's fine. Just let me set her down on the floor, so she won't take a tumble, and—"

"We can't just set her down!" I bleat as I twist away, drawing my skirt back down to my knees. "We have to comfort her! Reassure her. Get her a treat or something."

At the word "treat," Nuggy's adorable fox ears perk up.

"What?" Olly winces as he adjusts himself beneath his boxers, still apparently utterly confused. "Why?"

"To make amends. Obviously," I huff, starting to doubt his moral compass. We were just caught humping in front of a precious *baby* for goodness' sake, where's his sense of decency? "For scaring her and corrupting her innocence."

"For what?" He laughs. I glare. He stops laughing. "You're serious." He blinks again before adding in a more cautious voice, "She's a dog, love, not a nun."

"She's a child."

"She's not," he counters firmly.

"She's very close to a child," I amend. "And I feel almost as terrible as I would if she were." I reach for my zipper, my breasts pushing forward as I nudge it up. Olly's gaze drops to my cleavage, and I stomp the tip of his shoe with my heel. "Stop staring at my boobs, give her a cuddle, and tell her it's going to be all right!"

Oliver rolls his eyes, but he's smiling as he insists, "She's fine, woman! Seriously. Look at her." He motions to the dog. "She's already forgotten everything but that treat you mentioned."

Nuggy yips and rises onto her stubby legs, silky tail wagging.

"Pick her up, Olly," I say as I continue to do battle with my zipper. "Don't let her jump off the bench. It's too far, she'll hurt herself. Corgi spines are delicate."

"Why don't I attend to your zipper, and *you* can

attend to the not-at-all traumatized *adult* corgi, who had her first litter last year, and is fully aware of how babies are made?" He shifts behind me, his breath warm on my shoulder as he adds, "You nutter. Who knew I'd brought a dog fiend into my home?"

"I'm not a fiend, I'm an appreciator," I say, smiling as Nuggy bounds eagerly into my arms once more. I cuddle her, kissing her silky head as I murmur, "Did you really have puppies, Princess? I bet they were the most beautiful puppies anyone has ever seen."

"They were wickedly cute," Oliver assures me. "But all claimed by Gretchen's grandchildren and great-grandchildren before members of The Appreciation Society could throw their hats into the ring. Grandmother was terribly upset. Personally, I think things worked out for the best. Jasper and Jezebel are awful bullies. They wouldn't have been good older siblings." He finishes with my zipper and smooths my skirt. "There. Decent again, once more. Much to my dismay."

I turn, grinning at his tragic expression. "Oh my, your face."

He sighs, playing it up as he adds, "Indeed. I suffer, Darling. I really do."

"It looks like it," I tease, glancing down at his still throbbing sweater. "You're especially tragic in the lime green glow of it all."

He sniffs, lifting his nose in the air. "Yes, well, the fact that my partner in crime seems completely unaffected by the abrupt end of our passionate interlude might be adding to my despair."

"Don't despair," I murmur, nudging my arm against his. "Your partner in crime isn't unaffected."

He arches a brow. "No?"

I shake my head. "No. She just thinks we should wait to pick up where we left off until we get home. Where there's a bed and no dogs."

"Home, bed, no dogs," he murmurs. "That sounds good." He glances down, lips curving as he asks, "What do you think, Princess?"

I follow his gaze to see Nuggy licking his gingerbread man's googly eyeballs, and laugh. "I think she's starving."

"Indeed," Olly agrees. "We'd better get this puppy a treat before she's forced to feast on the toxic fibers of my Christmas jumper. Come on, you two. I know where Grandmother hides the best puppy treats."

I follow him out of the solarium, thoughts of "home" tumbling around in my head. Oliver's flat already feels homier than my studio in Queens ever has. I tell myself it's the luxurious furniture, fine art on the walls, and fantastic view of the park. That it's the elevator and the Egyptian cotton sheets and the bath outfitted with a spa-worthy jacuzzi and heated towel racks, but I know better.

It's just...him.

This man, who I'm falling for faster than I believed possible.

But maybe love doesn't play by the rules or slot neatly onto a list. Maybe love does what it damned well pleases.

Especially at Christmas.

After fetching Nuggy a jerky treat from a container by the back door, we rejoin the party.

In the drawing room, the fun—and the rum punch—has been flowing freely without us. Oliver's mother and her book club have progressed from carols to an interpretive dance performance of "The Twelve Days of Christmas." A woman with long gray hair embodies the partridge in the middle of the floor. The rest flap around her, their alien antennae bobbing as they make various bird sounds, while the men gathered around the piano belt out the lyrics.

"Altogether now, five golden rings!" the piano player shout-sings, prompting the entire party to make a circle with their arms over their heads.

Oliver and I join in on the next round, playing the "geese a laying" with an enthusiasm that has Gretchen giggling so hard that, as soon as we're done, Oliver offers to fetch her a lemonade from the buffet in the dining room.

"Oh, I'll come with you, it's nearly time for the pudding competition, anyway," Gretchen says, nearly tripping over Nuggy as we start down the hall.

Oliver catches her arm, and I scoop Princess Nugget up from the ground, sobering at the thought of Gretchen taking a fall. She's at an age where a tumble over her puppy could lead to serious consequences.

But she seems unfazed, beaming up at Oliver as we start toward the dining room again. "Oh, you're such a lovely boy." To me, she adds, "He always has been. Even when he was small. You've picked a good one, darling. And from such a fine family."

"A fine family with the finest puddings in the kingdom!" Olly's grandmother joins us, thrusting a wooden toy sword down the hall. She's red-cheeked, sauced, and obviously having a fantastic time.

And so am I.

If I weren't already falling for Olly, his wonderfully wacky family would have done the job.

In the dining room, the ancient wooden table groans under the weight of at least a dozen puddings. Some are architectural marvels. Others look like they've survived a bombing.

"Oh no, were we supposed to bring one?" I whisper once Olly has Gretchen settled in a chair near the head of the table.

He shakes his head. "Oh no, we aren't nearly old enough yet. Only those sixty and over have the necessary gravitas to bring a pudding. Even my mother was only recently granted pudding privileges." He nods toward the table. "That's hers there, the purple one with the silver filigree decorations. She's done something with vanilla and lavender, we should pretend to like even if it's awful. She's terribly nervous about her performance since her peppermint pudding flopped last year."

"Peppermint pudding sounds good to me," I say, joining him in the line to fetch samples.

"Sadly, it tasted like toothpaste," he says, handing me a China plate so fine I'm instantly terrified I'll drop it and owe his grandmother a small fortune. "But I think she might be onto something with the vanilla lavender."

"No favoritism," his grandmother shouts from a few feet in front of us. She turns to glare at Oliver over her shoulder. "And no poisoning the well, Olly. Let the girl taste with an open mind."

Oliver offers her a sharp salute. "Yes, Madame. Understood."

Once we've filled our plates and fetched samples for Gretchen, we find seats along the wall and begin working our way through the offerings. Number three is, Oliver assures me, a very traditional offering, heavy with suet and dark fruit. Number five features chocolate chips gone bitter in a sweet cherry sauce—someone's failed attempt at innovation. Number nine swims in so much brandy that the fumes make me lightheaded.

And then, we reach number twelve.

From the first bite, it dances on the tongue, floral notes elevating the pudding from heavy winter fare to something ethereal. It's his mother's lavender, I realize, perfectly balanced with vanilla and crystallized sugar.

I go back for a second taste, then a third.

Around me, I see Olly and the others doing the same, the room growing quiet as we all reach the same conclusion.

Even Susanna, who's clearly a fan of more traditional flavors, takes multiple bites with an increasingly thoughtful expression.

Finally, she mutters, "Well, bollocks," beneath her breath in a way that sends laughter rippling through the tipsy room.

When Edward tallies the votes, number twelve wins by a landslide. "Well done, Mum," he says, starting a round of applause.

Vivian stands, elegant even in inebriation, swaying only slightly as she bows, clearly honored that her experiment has dethroned years of Christmas pudding tradition.

Slowly, the party splits into factions again, some retreating to the veranda for a smoke, others to the drawing room for a drink by the fire. Oliver and I join the dancers in the sitting room, where the lights are turned down low and Bing Crosby croons from hidden speakers behind the tree.

He pulls me close, one hand spanning my lower back.

I rest my cheek on his chest with a happy sigh, and we begin to sway.

The Christmas tree lights blur into stars as my lids close and an impossible fantasy plays out behind my eyes. I imagine Oliver and I doing this next year, and the next, and the next, carrying on the Featherswallow holiday traditions, while turning making out in the solarium into a tradition of our own. I imagine us growing closer, older, eventually adding a puppy baby and maybe even a *baby* baby to the celebration. I imagine Christmases full of love and ease and holidays we'll "have to muddle through somehow," and how both will be beautiful in their own way.

I imagine myself at thirty-eight, fifty-eight, then with long white hair like my Irish gran, the other redhead in the family. I see myself working on my entry for the pudding competition, while Olly putters around the kitchen making coffee, teasing me about my thin chance at victory, sneaking a quick squeeze of my ass as he reaches for the mugs.

"What are you thinking, darling Darling?" Oliver asks as Bing Crosby fades and Judy Garland's voice fills the room.

It's "Have Yourself a Merry Little Christmas."

As if summoned by my thoughts...

The answer to his question sits on my tongue, dangerous and ready: *That you feel like home. That I already hate the thought of a holiday without you. That I'm pretty sure I'm still going to want your hands on me, even when I'm old and gray, and that I wish this night could go on forever...*

"About this song, actually." It's partly true. "And how it makes me happy and sad and heartbroken and hopeful...all at the same time."

His chest vibrates beneath my cheek as he hums in

recognition. "Whoever wrote it knew, didn't they? That pain comes when it comes. Even at Christmas."

"And that love sometimes makes the pain worse before it makes it better."

"The deeper the love, the deeper the loss," he murmurs. "But how lucky we are to love like that."

"Yes," I agree, my throat tightening as I lift my head. "I'm sorry."

"Why?" he asks, a sad smile curving his lips.

"I didn't mean to remind you of hard things," I say. "I know this is a difficult Christmas for you and your family."

"Stop. I've been thinking about Dad a lot tonight. It almost feels like he's here. And happy to see us happy." His voice catches as he adds, "He would have adored you, Red."

Fighting a wave of emotion too intense for a British holiday party, I smile. "I wish I could have met him and told him he helped raise someone very special."

His lips hook up on one side. "Me?"

"Yes, you." I roll my eyes, hopefully throwing him off my increasingly sappy scent as I add, "It's not every day you meet someone who, after just a few days, feels like a forever friend."

"Almost six days now," he corrects seriously. "But I agree. This sort of thing is rare. It's never happened to me before, actually. If I'm honest, I wasn't sure I believed it *could* happen."

"Me either," I whisper, pulse beating faster in my throat.

If I didn't know better, I would think he was about to...

Could he be about to?

"But I confess, I don't really think of you as a *friend*, Darling," he says, that Olly playfulness creeping back into his tone, even as his gaze remains open and honest and locked on mine. "I think about your breasts far too often for that."

I smile, relieved. It's too soon—and we've had too much rum—for any big declarations.

But it's exactly the right time to talk about boobs.

And other body parts...

"I think about your cock an awful lot, too," I whisper, loving the way his jaw clenches in response. He makes dirty talk so much fun, I can't resist adding, "And the fact that I didn't get a chance to taste you the way you tasted me. Doesn't seem fair, really."

"It doesn't," he agrees, eyes glittering with excitement for the new game at hand. "What a lout I've been. Can you ever forgive me?"

"I don't know," I say with a shrug, playing along. "It's selfish, really."

"Wickedly selfish, Red, you'll hear no arguments from me about that. But please, tell me what I can do to make amends? I simply must make things right between us."

I exhale a heavy sigh. "Well, maybe if we're in a cab in the next ten minutes..."

"Make it five." He grabs my hand, making me laugh as he bolts for the door, dragging me along behind him.

Chapter Fifteen
OLIVER

The taxi drifts through quiet streets, its engine a low purr against the silence of London at one a.m. Frost glitters on the iron railings of Belgrave Square, and somewhere a church bell chimes the hour, clear and somber in the cold air.

Emily doesn't speak.

Neither do I.

All our jokes evaporated as we tumbled into the cab.

It was as if we both suddenly realized how quickly we'll be home, alone with feelings neither of us knows quite what to do with.

We need to talk.

Frankly. Seriously.

But preferably *after* we do wicked things to each other in my bed.

I can't wait to touch her. Everywhere. I've been at least a little—sometimes *a lot*—hard since we left the solarium. Since I had my hand up her skirt, feeling how wet she was for me.

For *me*. Mine. Fuck, I want her to be mine. She

brings savage, caveman levels of possessiveness rising inside of me every time we leave the apartment.

The old guy at the museum with a soft spot for redheads?

Punch him in the face.

The blokes admiring her skill at the ice rink?

Death by thrashing of my poorly controlled limbs.

The usher who turned to stare at her ass as she walked away at the matinee earlier today?

Could have literally ripped his throat out with my teeth.

She is turning me into a savage, randy beast.

And a sappy one as well.

I nearly teared up in her arms on the dancefloor, and I can't even blame the rum. I only had two glasses.

No, it wasn't the rum; it was the way she understood. The way her understanding made my heart ache. The way the aching in my heart assured me that this isn't simply lust or a crush that will fizzle out when the holidays are through.

This is me, falling in love with a speed that's likely mad and certainly not wise.

But try telling that to my heart, which is already quite certain Emily Darling is the wisest woman he's ever met.

And has the most fantastic curves.

And the sweetest nipples.

And...I'm hard again.

Just in time to get out in front of my building.

Thank God for the darkness in the cab as I press a twenty into the man's hand and open the door, drawing my coat across my hips to conceal the situation in my trousers.

Emily takes my hand as we head inside, whispering,

"Just so you know. I meant what I said before. But if you're out of you-know-whats and want to find a twenty-four-hour pharmacy, I can look for one that delivers."

My cock twitches, proving he *can* get even more desperately erect, as I connect the dots. "No," I murmur, nodding as we hurry past George, the doorman. "I have plenty upstairs."

"Oh, good." She steps into the lift, waiting until the doors close behind us to add, "But we don't have to use them. If you don't want to."

"No?" I ask, sweat breaking out on my upper lip at the thought of nothing between us. "Are you sure?"

"I'm sure." She holds my gaze in the reflection of the mirrored wall. "I've never had sex without one, but I suddenly really want to."

I fight to swallow. "Yeah?"

"Yes," she whispers. "And I don't want you to pull out."

I curse and close my eyes. If I don't, I'm afraid I'll have her dress up around her waist before I can stop myself.

"Unless you don't like that idea?" she asks, clearly having misunderstood the reason for my wince.

"No," I wheeze, my pulse thudding in my ears as I pray for the strength to keep it together until we reach the fifth floor. "No, that was the hottest thing I've ever heard, Darling. Just...hanging on by a thread over here. And trying not to take you against the wall like an animal."

"Oh." She's practically purring as she adds, "I'm not opposed to a wall, but we should get inside first."

"Inside, yes," I agree, breath rushing out as the elevator finally dings. "Thank God." I wrap an arm around her waist, hauling her against me as we spin out into the hall.

I crush my lips to hers, tongue stroking deep as she fists her hands in my shirt. I kiss her with all the pent-up frustration of the past few hours. Hell, the past *week*. I've been dying to be back inside her since the morning she called me a liar and stormed out of that loft.

And now...

Finally...

I get my key in the lock by instinct alone, tossing it to the floor as soon as we're inside. "Thank Christ for doors," I rasp against her lips. "I love doors. So much."

"Doors are the best." She sucks in a breath as I jerk her coat down her arms, then drag her back against me, unable to bear being away from her for more than a second. She braces trembling hands on my chest. "God, Olly. I want you so much, I feel like I'm going crazy."

"I've barely slept," I confess against her lips, stripping off my coat as we stumble deeper into the apartment. "All I could think about was your beautiful body, all soft and warm under the covers just a room away. I've been wanking one off every bloody night, but it didn't help."

"I did, too," she breathes, making me groan. "I touched myself. Thinking of you. I've never come that hard from my own—"

"Fuck, Emily. Just...fuck." I pin her wrists over her head on the living room wall, grinding against her because I can't help it. That's how little self-control I've got left. "You should have told me. I would have been there in seconds to make you come again on my mouth."

She hooks her leg around my waist. "I wish I had. Shit, Olly, please. Now. Inside me now. I seriously can't wait. I can't."

I can't either.

I lift her, and she wraps her legs around me with a needy whimper that makes me absolutely feral. I stagger blindly into the coffee table, bruising my shin, but barely feeling it. I'm too focused on getting my ass on the sofa, with Emma straddled on top of me.

"Fucking clothes," I curse, shoving her dress up to give her more room to maneuver, shuddering in relief as her thighs spread on either side of mine.

"Hate them." She tugs my jumper over my head, then my undershirt, humming in satisfaction as she tosses the last terrible piece of fabric away. "There. God, there you are." She exhales a shaky sigh as her hands find my bare skin. "I've never wanted to be naked with someone this much."

"Likewise, Darling." I peel her dress over her head, losing the ability to breathe as it floats to the carpet, leaving her in nothing but those tiny lace panties.

"You are so beautiful," I rasp, skimming reverent hands down her sides to the curves of her hips. "I seriously can hardly bear it, Em."

"You, too." She presses down against me, her heat searing me through my pants. "You're beautiful, too." She bites her lip. "And so hard..." She braces her hands on my shoulders, rolling her hips against my cock in a way that realigns the universe as she whispers, "So why aren't you inside me, Oliver?"

Christ, my name on her lips is enough to make me savage.

I lean in, capturing her nipple in my mouth. I lick and suck and bite until she's crying out, her nails scoring into my shoulders as we rock together. I squeeze her ass, she tugs at my hair, and then we're kissing again, even wilder than before. This kiss is frantic, unhinged in the best way, and soon, she's squirming on my thigh with breathy moans, and I'm seconds from coming in my pants if we don't—

"Bed," I choke out, fingers digging into her hips to slow her down. "Let me—"

"No. Here." She fumbles at the close of my pants, her breath coming as fast as mine. "Now. Please."

Between us, we manage to free what's necessary and then, "Christ, Emily," I cry out as she sinks onto my cock, bathing me in pleasure so intense I can barely stand it.

It's too good.

Too right.

"Fuck," I gasp against her throat, holding her tight. "Don't move. Not yet. Just a minute, love. I need a minute."

She shudders, but stills, wrapping her arms around me. "I'm going to need all night," she rasps against my temple. "I'm never going to get enough of you, Olly. Never."

"Never, Red," I agree, voice raw, ravaged by the things she does to me. "But that doesn't mean I'm not going to try." Willing my cock to strap in and hold on, I whisper, "Now, ride me, darling. Ride me like you mean it."

Then she starts to move, and I'm lost.

Lost and so glad to be lost because I'm out in the wilderness with her.

She rides me like she's never needed anything as much as my cock, shameless and needy, and I have never been happier. Never. Because I need her just as fucking much. I grip her hips, thrusting up to meet her, driving deep into her sweet pussy, knowing no other will ever compare.

I am ruined for all other pussies.

All other women.

As her breasts bounce and her hair writhes around us like a living thing, I do my best to hold on, but she's a force of nature, and I've been on edge for hours.

But hell, I really don't want to go without her...

Reaching between us, I press my thumb to her clit. Rubbing, circling, silently begging her to come with me, and finally—*Oh God. Fuck! God, this woman*—she cries out, convulsing around me.

"Emily. God, Emily." I bury my face in her neck as I cry her name, shuddering hard, filling her while she makes desperately happy sounds that are music to my ears.

Afterward, we stay tangled together for a long time. Her, catching her breath in my lap with my cock still buried inside her. Me, wondering if it's too soon to ask her to marry me.

Or at least move in. Forever.

"Should we...talk?" she finally whispers against my shoulder.

"We should," I say, stroking her bare back. "But maybe later? In the morning?"

I can't talk now. I'm too close to the edge. I might actually ask her to move in with me, and that's not a conversation to be approached on impulse at two in the morning. I need to plan, prepare, and make an Emily-grade list explaining why this is worth the risk and all the things I'll do to keep her emotionally, physically, and financially safe as she transitions.

"I think so. We should probably conserve our energy," she says, the husky note in her voice enough to have me getting thicker all over again. "I still have things I want to do to you with my mouth."

Cursing, I mutter, "Your mouth on me may have to wait, love. You need to be fucked in a bed first. Most urgently. And I know just the man for the job."

I stand with her wrapped around me, making her giggle as I dash toward my bedroom, playing up the urgency to keep her laughing. And then, I lay my Viking goddess on my sheets and set about worshipping her the way she deserves.

Soon, neither of us is laughing...

I take my time, lingering on every kiss, every touch, memorizing the curve of her throat as her head falls back, the way her eyes burn into mine as I finally sink inside her again, inch by torturous inch.

"Oliver?" she breathes, cupping my cheek.

I'm still inside her, buried deep, and certain her body is the best place on earth. "Yes, love?"

"Is this the best Christmas ever?"

"Maybe just the best so far," I say, holding her gaze as I pull back and glide into her again, a silent promise that it's only getting better from here on out.

If she'll let me make it better.

If she'll stay...

"Yes," she whispers, rocking into my next stroke with a whimper. "Yes, right there. Just like that."

I roll my hips, grinding into the spot that makes her lashes flutter, slow and deep, drawing it out for both of us as long as I can. But eventually, need gets the better of me, and I can't help moving faster, faster, until I'm snapping my hips into her and she's urging me on with "almost there" sounds that are nearly as sexy as the way her flesh ripples as I give her everything.

Everything, everything...

Until she lets out a proper American scream as her

pussy clutches around me. The waves squeeze harder, tighter, drenching my cock as she comes, and that's all she wrote for me. Features twisting with the terrible beauty of it all, I cry out and shove deep, balls pulsing in the seam of her ass, I fill her again.

And it's just as fucking hot as it was the first time.

Note to Self: Add ruined for condoms to the list...

After the final shivers have faded away, I roll to the side, and she rolls with me, draping herself across my chest with a happy sigh. I smooth a hand down her spine, kiss the crown of her head, absolutely certain now that this is it.

This is the Great Love my father swore found a man when he was ready. This is the reason none of my other relationships ever felt quite right.

There was always something missing because none of those women was *her*.

None was my Emily, my darling girl...

Long after her breath has grown slow and even, I lie awake, staring at the ceiling in the moonlight. I should sleep. We have big plans for tomorrow. But I can't.

I'm too busy turning the problem of thousands of kilometers and an ocean over and over in my mind, too busy pondering visas and permits and all the legalities of building a life in another country with your favorite person, all of which suddenly seems bizarre.

How dare the government—*any* government—think they have the right to stand in the way of two people in love? It's ridiculous. Offensive. And I mean to write a strongly worded op ed about it for the Times...

As soon as I know for certain that Emily feels the same way.

Chapter Sixteen

EMILY

I wake with a start, jolted into consciousness by my phone, which is currently humming on the nightstand like a vibrator turned to the "ultimate annihilation" setting.

Oh God, not again.

What is it this time?

I fumble for it blindly, still wrapped in Oliver's arms. We shifted position sometime in the night, and his chest is currently warm and comforting against my back. All I want to do is throw my cell at the wall and go back to sleep, but notifications can be serious business these days, and the light filtering through the curtains is way too bright.

How long have we been out?

Fingers finally wrapping around my phone, I squint at the screen—9:47 AM.

Shit. We've slept late. Really late, which isn't a surprise considering we were up until the wee hours of dawn having fantastic sex.

But still, it's awfully early for—

"Twenty-three notifications?" I hiss, my stomach balling into a knot.

What fresh hell have we stumbled into now? Did photos of us mauling each other in the solarium break on the gossip sites this morning? It was dark in there, yes, but—as I *warned* Oliver—the walls were made of glass.

Why-oh-why did I think it was okay to get half undressed in front of an innocent puppy in a room *made of glass!*

Blinking panicked eyes, I scroll to the text thread at the top, a series of a dozen or so messages from Maya.

> Maya: HAVE YOU SEEN THE NEWS??? 😂

> Maya: You are SO in the clear after this.

> Maya: SQUEE! 🎉 Call me NOW!

> Maya: Or like…at a decent hour if you get this after two a.m. my time.

> Maya: I promised I'd meet my mother at church tomorrow. I have to catch the train to Jersey at the ass crack of dawn, even though Deedee and I were out dancing until one.

> Maya: But OMG, we had so much fun, Em! We have to go dancing 💃 as soon as you get back.

> Maya: Or maybe I'll fly over and we can go dancing in London on New Year's Eve!!! Doesn't that sound amazing?!

> Maya: 😊 God, life feels so…alive right now!

> Maya: It's probably the champagne. And I'll probably regret it tomorrow. Or…today. Shit, I have to be up in five hours!

> Maya: Okay, scrap calling me, just text when you're awake. I'll have my cell on silent so it won't disturb my beauty sleep.

> Maya: Love you, bye!

> Maya: And congrats again!!! 🎄

"Congrats?" I mumble with a frown. "On what, you maniac?"

But I should know better than to expect clarity from drunk Maya. She rarely parties, but when she does, she hardy parties.

She really should have known better than to promise she'd go to church with her mom after a Saturday night on the town.

Sending her "no hangover" vibes across the ocean, I tap back to the main message screen, hoping my other texts will be more illuminating.

But the missive from my mother—"Oh, honey, can you believe this? What's happening to the royals these days? Are they on drugs? You aren't on drugs, are you, sweetheart? Have you met the prince? Is he well? Mentally? Text me when you wake up."—only give me a slightly clearer picture.

"Something about the prince," I murmur, keeping that in mind for googling purposes as I check to see what Isabelle's had to say.

> Isabelle: OMG I'M DYING!! 😱 💀 This is so much more embarrassing than anything you and Oliver have done. Like, ten times more embarrassing. Maybe a hundred. Is that man okay?

> Isabelle: 😳 Seriously, is he okay?

> Isabelle: Have you met him?

> Isabelle: I mean, you know I've always thought he was crazy hot. 🥵 And he's still hot, but that was…weird. He might be having some kind of breakdown. Should Oliver check on him, do you think? If they're friends?

> Isabelle: Are they friends? If so, I NEED YOU TO INTRODUCE ME, EMILY! ASAP. 😍 I mean, yes, I'm engaged, but I had SUCH a crush on him growing up.

> Isabelle: Is it mortifying that I had posters of a man who's distantly related to your boyfriend all over my bedroom as a teenager? 🙈 Probably, right? Don't tell Oliver, okay? Just in case. 😅 Anyway, I hope you're having a great weekend! Call me when you get these. And good luck at the Fletchers' pitch tomorrow!! I'll be rooting for you. 🤞

I'm putting the pieces together—this must be about Prince Ronan, first in line to the throne, and my sister's one and only childhood crush—when Oliver mumbles against my shoulder, "What's up, buttercup? You're tense."

"I woke up to a bunch of texts and thought we were in trouble again," I say, opening a search window and typing fast, "but it looks like..."

I trail off as the results load.

"Oh my," I mutter, my eyes going wide. "Oh my God..."

"What? What's happened?" Olly sits up, peeking over my shoulder at the screen. "Oh, fuck." He chuckles as I scroll down a page of truly wild photos. "What the hell was Ronan smoking last night?"

"I don't know," I murmur, clicking on another headline—PRINCE IN BEASTLY SCANDAL: Ronan's Midnight Ride Shocks the Nation. "But it must have been something serious. Wait, it looks like there's video."

I roll over onto my back, holding the phone up so we can both watch.

The video is just grainy security footage, but it clearly shows the future king astride one of the Trafalgar Square lions at 2:54 AM. He's singing what sounds like "I'm Henry the Eighth, I Am," wielding a kebab like a saber, and tossing chunks of meat at the security guard trying to bat him down with a traffic cone.

"Bloody hell," Oliver says, squinting. "Is he naked?"

"No, I think he's wearing underwear." I narrow my eyes. "Or a diaper? Is that a diaper? God, why was he wearing a diaper?"

"No fucking clue. Christ." Oliver runs a hand through his hair, making it stand up at even more ridiculous, adorable angles. "But I bet the Palace press office wishes *they* were wearing nappies right about now.

They'll be shitting their collective pants. What happened? Is there any explanation in the articles?"

"I don't know. Let me look." We scroll through article after article, of which there are *many*.

Every British news outlet has abandoned all other stories, and #LionKing is trending on social media worldwide. There are already memes, including one of Ronan's face photoshopped onto Mufasa's body, that makes me snort coffee through my nose once we've moved our research to the kitchen.

"Okay, finally a hint of a motive." I tap my croissant to my screen as I read, "Palace sources suggest Prince Ronan was celebrating the English rugby win, when a night out with friends got 'boyishly' out of hand."

Olly grunts. "Celebrating by riding a stone lion in a diaper?"

"Not the way I'd celebrate," I agree. "But maybe?"

He grunts again, wagging his pastry back and forth in the air. "Nope. I'm not buying it. And what's that 'boyish' bullshit? He's nearly thirty. He hasn't been a 'boy' in nearly a decade. I call foul. This reeks of a press office cover-up up and damn it, I intend to get to the bottom of it."

My brows fly up my forehead. "Really? You do?"

Oliver grins as he slouches back in his chair, propping his slippered feet up in the seat beside mine. "Nah, not really. I mean, I hope the man's all right, but he's a second cousin, and we've never been close. I'm just glad to be out of the spotlight."

"Same," I say, even as a tinge of disappointment creeps into my chest.

I'm glad to be in the clear, I really am, but...

Well, without an excuse to *pretend* to be an item, Olly and I will be left with no other option than to have The Talk, and talking feels way scarier in the cold light of day. Last night was intense, and I didn't get nearly enough sleep, and I can't afford to have a falling out with Olly right now.

And maybe we won't fall out. Maybe we'll manage The Talk beautifully, but with the Fletchers' meeting bearing down on me in less than twenty-four hours, is it really worth the risk?

"So..." Oliver says, his smile fading as the vibes in the kitchen grow increasingly complicated. "I suppose we should—"

"Still go sledding," I cut in, heart racing as I force a cheery smile. "Don't you think? I mean, it's already booked, and the paparazzi have been stalking us like crazy. Someone at the sled rental could have tipped them off, and cameras could be trained on the hill right now, waiting for us to arrive."

Oliver sits up, brightening. "You're right. I mean, just because we're off the radar for now, it doesn't mean we're in the clear. If we book sleds and don't show up to use them, the paparazzi might start to wonder if there's trouble in hot mess paradise."

I grin. "Right. And there's fresh snow. It would be a shame to waste it."

"And I could use some exercise after all that pudding."

"God, yes," I agree, laying a hand on my stomach. "I think I gained ten pounds overnight."

"Bollocks, you look fantastic, but sledding would still be good for our health. Cardiovascular fitness and all that."

"So we'll go," I say with a breezy shrug. "Just in case. Just for fun."

"Absolutely for fun." His gaze locks on mine with an intensity that makes me tingly…and a tiny bit nervous. "Speaking of fun, I had a lot of fun with you last night, Darling."

Shoulders tensing, I nod. "I had a lot of fun with you, too."

"I'd be up for more fun in the shower before we get dressed," he says, sending relief rushing through my chest.

Talking feels like too much right now, but sex?

Sex, I can absolutely handle.

He nods over his shoulder as he rises from his chair, playing up the casual in his tone as he adds, "Simply in the interest of conserving water, of course."

"Of course," I agree.

Ten minutes later, we're "conserving water" so loudly I'm pretty sure the neighbors can hear, but I can't seem to keep it down.

He's just too good.

Way too good to say goodbye to in just a few weeks…

But there are so many obstacles in our way, obstacles that seem far more intimidating without Christmas punch in my system.

Pushing the thoughts from my head—I can't think about stressful things until after the pitch is over—I phone the airport, yet again, only to discover that my luggage is still missing in action.

Because of course it is.

That's just the Emily Darling Luggage Curse in action.

Oliver immediately offers to take me shopping. Again. This time for snow frolicking clothes. I try to refuse—he's already been far too generous, and I can just wear a pair of his ski pants, rolled up at the ankles—but he won't take no for an answer.

So, fifteen minutes later, we're in a swanky outdoor shop not far from Fletchers, buying a brown snowsuit with white trim that makes me unreasonably happy.

Just like the man who takes my hand on the sidewalk as we head for Hyde Park...

Three hours later, I'm even happier.

And grateful for the snowsuit that's kept me warm and dry as I've taken tumble.

After tumble.

After tumble.

Turns out I'm not as good at sledding as I remember, but that hasn't made the day any less fun.

"Your steering remains alarmingly subpar, Darling," Oliver says, standing over me as I lie in a snowbank at the base of Primrose Hill, laughing so hard my ribs are starting to hurt.

"Sorry," I wheeze. "I swear, that hedge came out of nowhere."

"Nonsense, you were aiming right for it," he insists, fighting a laugh as he thrusts an arm toward the top of the slope. "I watched it all happen from up there. With horror, I might add."

"I got distracted." I swipe giggle tears from my cheeks. "There were puppies in Christmas sweaters on the path."

"You and puppies," he mutters as he reaches down to

help me up. "You need a keeper woman. Come on, let's turn these in. Before you break a bone."

"No wait, can't we go again?" I ask hopefully. "I promise to make it all the way to the bottom this time."

"No, not a chance, you're a menace to society." But he's already turning around, pulling both our sleds back up the hill. "No more steering for you. We'll swap these for a double, and I'll take the helm."

"So bossy," I murmur, rather enjoying it.

Nearly as much as I enjoy his backside in his ski pants...

"Someone has to keep you from terrorizing innocent shrubbery," he says, before tossing over his shoulder in a sultrier voice, "And if I catch you ogling my backside again, you're getting a spanking when we get home."

Grin stretching wider, I ask, "You promise?"

"Naughty," he says, faking outrage. Badly. "You're very naughty, Ms. Darling. And I, for one, am appalled."

"Deepest apologies, Mr. Featherswallow," I say, faking penitence just as badly. "I'll do my best to mend my wicked ways."

I don't, of course, and manage to "get caught" staring at his bottom three more times before we give up the ghost on sledding an hour later. By then, my fingers are numb in my mittens, and Oliver's nose is adorably red.

So, we decide to wander down to Borough Market for a hot chocolate to warm up. Oliver insists on buying the most ridiculously overpriced artisanal cocoa available, and soon my nose is covered in hand-churned whipped cream and flecks of gold leaf.

But damn...a buttered bourbon hot chocolate with extra vanilla crème is something everyone should experience at least once in their lives.

We meander through the market, where holiday music piped through the speakers wars with noise from the crowd and a busker playing saxophone down the street. The air is full of delicious smells, and soon we're buying smoked honey sausages and bags of freshly fried truffle chips to go with our hot chocolate.

As food pairings go, it doesn't make much sense, but is weirdly fantastic.

Kind of like us...

"Where to next?" he asks as we emerge from the market.

"Dealer's choice." I glance up and down the cobblestone street. "You obviously know the city better than I do." I turn back to him. "But I'm not quite ready to go home yet, if that's okay with you."

"You need more holiday adventure," he declares, understanding immediately, the way he so often does. "Right then, let the adventure continue."

He takes my hand, leading the way until we reach streets I start to recognize. We end up in Covent Garden, where the Christmas decorations are copious, over-the-top, and perfect. Mistletoe hangs from every archway, silver bells chime in the wind, and a woman in a gorgeous velvet gown plays violin near the main tree.

It's God Rest Ye Merry Gentlemen, one of my favorites, but I swear it sounds even more magical than usual.

"Dance with me, Darling?" Oliver murmurs, pulling me into the small crowd already swaying beside the tree.

"Love to," I say.

As "God Rest Ye" transitions into an instrumental I can't quite place, we continue to sway, lost in each other's arms. Meanwhile, the tourists wander by without a second look. We're just another couple falling in love in London at Christmastime. And even with all the obstacles and complications waiting in the future, right now, I couldn't be happier.

Well, maybe a tiny bit happier…

"Take me home?" I whisper.

"I thought you'd never ask."

We head off again, through streets growing chillier as the winter sun turns in early for the night.

By the time we get back to his flat, my aching joints are feeling every fall on the sledding hill, and my jaw hurts from smiling. I grab two ibuprofen and a heating pad for my knee, while Olly orders Thai food. When it arrives, we head for the couch, spreading containers across his coffee table like a feast.

We've decided to watch The Muppet Christmas Carol—continuing our holiday movie marathon with a childhood favorite—but as we're flicking through the channels, we stumble across Love Actually and get sucked in.

"I don't know why I've watched this so many times," I say forty minutes later, full of green curry and feelings. "It always makes me cry."

"But a happy cry?"

I cock my head, considering. "I mean, yes. Partly. But sad, too. Not everyone gets their happily ever after. At least not the happily ever after I wanted for them."

He grunts. "Yeah, Laura Linney deserved a good shagging."

I snort. "Totally. She deserved a fantastic shagging and to turn her stupid phone off every once and a while. But I guess boundaries weren't a thing back then?"

"And they clearly had no idea what the word 'fat'

meant." He gestures toward the screen, where the Prime Minister and Natalie are getting caught kissing at the holiday pageant. "That woman is the furthest thing from fat. If anything, she's a touch too thin for my liking." He sniffs, pretending not to notice me staring at his profile as he adds, "But then, I *do* like a curvy girl. As you know."

"I do," I murmur. "I know that very well." He turns to me, but instead of the kiss I can tell he's expecting, I whisper, "What if the presentation goes badly tomorrow? What if I drop the ball and fuck it all up?" I exhale a shaky breath. "Sorry, I've entered the 'stressing about Monday' portion of Sunday funday."

"No need to apologize." He smiles as he gathers my feet into his lap, rubbing my arches in a way that feels absolutely delicious. "I seriously doubt that will happen, Em. You're quite possibly the most prepared person I've ever met."

I nibble my bottom lip. "I know, but what if it does? Or what if they just like someone else's pitch more than mine? I was hoping to use this as a springboard to get more business in the U.K., and maybe even open an office here someday." I shrug. "That's probably a pipe dream, considering the state of our finances right now, but..."

"I don't think so." He gives my foot a reassuring squeeze. "From what you've said, all it would take to turn things around is one big client to replace the one you lost. Right?" I nod and he continues, "Well, then. I see nothing but blue skies ahead. First Fletchers, then a big, juicy, corporate client who can't get enough of your fantastic work, and then..." He blinks, pondering for a moment before turning to me with a straight face and declaring, "Well, and then, the world."

I roll my eyes, but I'm laughing as I give his shoulder a

shove. "Thanks, but I think I'll leave that to someone else. I don't want to rule the world."

"What do you want, Darling?" he murmurs.

You, I think. *Just you.*

Aloud, I say, "Another shower, I think. I'm dirty again, Featherswallow."

"Yes, you are," he agrees, tugging me up from the couch. "And so am I.'

We strip on the way to his room, leaving a breadcrumb trail of clothing across the flat. He proves how dirty—and wonderful—he is, and I prove I wasn't kidding about that driving need to wreck him with my mouth.

And as we head to bed at a reasonable hour, teeth flossed and brushed, and my hair in my curl bonnet to protect it from frizz, he proves that even a normal bedtime is fun with him around.

Falling asleep beside him, I think this might be what it feels like when everything finally comes together.

When Fate mixes with Christmas magic and suddenly, all the obstacles melt like snow on a sunny morning.

I should have remembered that Fate has a twisted sense of humor.

And that magic often comes at a price...

Chapter Seventeen

EMILY

Monday morning dawns bright, but freezing cold, with the temperature barely scraping 1 degree Celsius, which is pretty darned cold in Fahrenheit.

I think...

It *feels* cold, anyway.

"Note to self: New Year's Resolution, learn Celsius," I mutter as Oliver and I head up the stairs to the Fletchers' administrative offices on the fifth floor of a gorgeous Georgian building. He's meeting his brother for coffee at a café nearby and insisted on walking me "for luck," and to protect my cream pants from the London muck.

He walked on the "mucky" side all the way from his flat, hustling me out of the way of lorry splashes, proving he's the best fake boyfriend ever.

Except that maybe he's my *real* boyfriend now?

Maybe?

We haven't nailed that part down just yet, but we will. Soon. Once this presentation is over, I'll have the bandwidth to tackle other big discussions, and I've already started work on a "Why We Should Give Long Distance a Shot" PowerPoint, with multiple lists to accompany the presentation.

Partly because list-making is in my soul.

Partly because I know it will make Olly laugh, and I love to make him laugh.

I just…love him. Period. I don't care that we've been an item for barely a week and half of that was spent faking it. I'm not here to second-guess a holiday gift from the romance gods. I'm here to rock this presentation, go last-minute holiday shopping with my hot British boyfriend, and dance the night away at his office holiday party tonight.

And tomorrow, we're doing Christmas Eve dinner at his brother's house, then Christmas day luncheon and White Elephant presents at his mother's, and then—assuming my luggage is still lost in the Twilight Zone—we're going to hit the Boxing Day sales to buy a party dress for New Year's Eve.

Oliver is already insisting that it must be sparkly, with a very naughty, very cheeky skirt…

I sneak a peek his way at the top of the stairs, still unable to believe this gorgeous, funny, fantastic man is mine.

Or about to be mine.

Mostly mine?

"Don't be nervous, you've got this," Oliver says, clearly misunderstanding the reason for my anxious expression.

"I'm not, just hyperventilating slightly," I lie as we start down the hall. "That was a lot of stairs."

"Damn straight," he grumbles. "If I'd known there were that many, I would have skipped the stair climber this morning. The holidays are for phoning it in at the gym. I only like to do as much exercise as is strictly necessary to keep the pudding and wine from going to my waist."

I grin. "Well, you're doing an excellent job so far. Your abs looked delicious in the shower this morning."

He makes a growling sound low in his throat as he sways closer. "Stop. Don't talk about it, or I'll have to ravage you in a broom closet before the meeting. Those leggings you wore on the treadmill should be illegal. And the way your bottom jiggles when you run..." He shudders. "Christ. I nearly dropped a barbell on my throat."

I arch a brow. "In the immortal words of Beyonce, I don't think you were ready for that jelly."

His arm sneaks around my waist. "No, I most certainly was not. But I will be next time, I promise. I'll arrange to get on the machine behind you and think wicked thoughts the entire time."

I fight a giggle, gently pushing him away as the boardroom entrance—and the prim-looking receptionist seated outside—come into view.

"You've got this," Oliver repeats, giving my elbow a squeeze, his hand warm and reassuring through the cashmere. "Remember, they're already fans, or they wouldn't have asked you to fly all the way across the ocean to pitch. They *want* what you're selling."

"Right." My voice sounds steadier than I feel. "They want my Dickensian-meets-modern-sustainability with a top note of lush fairytale party planning genius."

"Exactly! Damn, listen to how inspired that sounds. How could they resist?" He turns to face me a few feet from the desk, and honestly, it should be illegal for anyone to look this good at nine in the morning. His charcoal suit makes his eyes swirl like blue-gray storm clouds, and his hair is defying the laws of physics with a mix of floppiness and structure that proves fifty-pound hair product really is worth the splurge if you can afford it.

He gazes deep into my eyes, into my soul, before whispering, "Are you ready for your pre-meeting cheerleading session?"

I nod, shaking my arms loosely at my sides. "Yes, please."

"You are Emily Bloody Darling, ferociously prepared, adorably feisty American, with fantastic ideas and crackerjack execution, and you are about to slay that meeting to absolute death."

"To absolute death," I echo. "With my thirty-seven PowerPoint slides and sexily embedded video montages."

"Hell yes, you beastly little organization freak," he agrees, making me cover my mouth to suppress a laugh. "There will be no survivors. How could there be?"

"Get out of here," I whisper, waving him off. "Before you give me the hiccups. I always get the hiccups when I laugh when I'm nervous."

"All right, good luck." He kisses me, soft and quick on the cheek, but it still makes my knees wobblier than the stairs. "Go, dazzle them with your brilliance. Then text me when you're on your way to the café, and I'll have a second coffee waiting when you arrive."

"You really are the best," I say, meaning it.

He winks as he turns to go. "Remember that when I'm three sheets to the wind and humping your leg on the dance floor tonight."

I wink back. "Oh, I will. I'm looking forward to it."

Then he's gone, striding back down the hall toward

the stairs with that relaxed confidence that makes every woman we pass on the street stop to stare.

Which is fine.

They can stare all they want, but that gorgeous man is coming home with me.

With a private, slightly smug smile that feels good, if I do say so myself, I square my shoulders, check in with the receptionist to ensure I'm clear to go in a few minutes early, and push through the heavy doors.

Inside, the boardroom is mahogany and history, a monument to Timeless Business Decisions. The conference table could double as a small skating rink, and the view of London through the floor-to-ceiling windows makes me dizzy.

Or maybe it's the ring of very posh and important people who pause sipping their tea to look up at me as I step inside that has my head spinning a little.

Ignoring the spike of anxiety dumping into my blood, I force my warmest smile. "Good morning, everyone, Happy Christmas."

"Good morning! And Happy Christmas to you, Ms. Darling!" It's Christoph, my main point of contact, looking even more luxuriously gay in person than he does on his social media. He rises from the closest chair, his brown eyes warm behind designer glasses that match his three-piece suit. "So lovely to finally meet in person."

"Hello, Cristoph. Likewise," I say, clasping his extended palm.

His handshake is firm, but in a comforting way, and I already feel more at ease as he turns to introduce me to the rest of the table, including his boss, James, the CEO of event coordination, two executive assistants here to take notes for *their* bosses, and a woman from the budget department.

"We were all so impressed by your Brighton wedding," Christoph continues as we finish pressing hands across the table, and I start to set up. "The way you handled that seagull showed real grace under pressure. Especially knowing a Brighton seagull the way I do." He glances to the rest of the table as he adds in a confidential voice, "Big as dogs and twice as aggressive. I had one steal the celery right out of my Bloody Mary while I was there last summer."

The table titters with laughter, and I make a mental note to send Christoph a thank-you gift for being such a wonderful warm-up act. He's getting everyone loose, relaxed, and ready to receive my message of party wonder.

Now, all I have to do is deliver.

"Can we get you anything before we begin?" he asks, motioning toward a sideboard against the wall filled with hot drinks and pastries. "Tea? Coffee? Cranberry tart?"

"No, thank you. You can just dim the lights if you don't mind." I tap my laptop to connect to the conference room's display with another smile. "I've already eaten my way through multiple servings of Christmas pudding since I've been in London. I have to slow down before I go into sugar shock."

The table titters again, for which I'm grateful.

My joke wasn't as good as Christoph's, but they seemed to appreciate *my* appreciation of British holiday desserts.

It's as good a segue as any...

"Speaking of sweets, I have some fantastic options for the gala menu near the end of the presentation," I say as Christoph hits the lights and returns to his seat, beaming up at me with what looks like genuine excitement. "London caterers are truly masters of their craft. And so creative."

The first fifteen minutes of the presentation prove that my anxiety dreams last night were meaningless manifestations of stress, not prophecies foretelling certain doom.

My laptop doesn't spontaneously combust—a Christmas miracle given my history with technology—and the emergency binders stay tucked away in my big briefcase as I move from slide to slide.

By the time I reveal the design concepts Belinda and I developed during our meeting—a magical entrance, enchanted conversation nooks, and a ceiling of oversized flowers for the dining area that gives posh Alice in Wonderland vibes—they're all leaning forward, tea and tarts forgotten.

"Guests will feel like they're entering a secret garden from a fairy tale," I say, clicking to the rendering that made Belinda gasp when she first saw it. "Attendees enter through a tunnel of wisteria. And at the tables, the ceiling blooms with giant peonies and rose vines, all in blush and cream with touches of gold."

James, the CEO, fetches his glasses for a sharper look. The silver-haired woman beside him stops taking notes to grin at the illustrations as they materialize and fade on the screen.

"And for added magic," I continue, blood rushing with that presenter's high that sets in when you know your audience is with you, "Hidden LED strips make the flowers seem to breathe. Subtle. Romantic. Like being inside a music box made of petals."

I click to slide fifteen. "All with an eye toward

sustainability, of course. In addition to actual florals, we'll use recycled fabrics and found elements from London parks for the installation. And when the party's over, the flowers will be donated to local care homes, courtesy of Fletchers, bringing holiday cheer long after the gala ends." I smile as I add, "And goodwill toward their favorite place to shop during the holidays, of course."

A knowing smile curves James's lips, and Christoph shoots me a subtle thumbs up beneath the table.

I've just finished with slide twenty-three—the custom menu designs—when James calls for a short break.

"Brilliant work so far." He stands, glancing down at his phone. "Let's take five before we move on." He lifts his cell with a sheepish smile as he moves toward the door at the back of the room, "It's my daughter. She's about to go on as Clara in the Nutcracker at her school and needs a pep talk from Daddy."

Heart melting, I make happy shooing motions. "Of course, no need to apologize. That's fantastic. Please tell her to break a leg for me."

"Yes, from all of us!" Cristoph agrees, rising with a wink. He squeezes my arm before adding in a softer voice, "So good, Emily. I have chills. Seriously."

"Thank you," I say, beaming.

"Can I get you a coffee now?" he asks. "Or tea? We have a fantastic smoky Earl Grey."

I wave him off. "No, thank you. I'll get one when I get back. I'll just pop down to the loo while we're waiting."

He nods and lifts a hand. "Of course, no rush. You're so organized, we're running way ahead of schedule."

My knees only shake slightly as I push back through

the main doors into the hallway, heading for the bathrooms I spotted on the way in.

Things are going so well! They're engaged, excited, and seem to love my ideas. I just need to make sure I don't lose my momentum during the last inning, and this might really happen. I might land the Fletchers' gala and pave the way for more UK business sooner than I ever imagined!

I use the facilities, wash my hands, and reapply a light coat of lipstick before starting back, only to find a man in a gray jumpsuit busily mopping the marble floor in front of the boardroom doors.

From behind her desk, the receptionist shoots me an apologetic glance.

"Sorry, it'll be slick." She motions to her left. "If you go this way and turn at the first hallway, you can go in the back."

I smile, taking the turn, she indicated. "Of course, no problem. Thanks so much."

I'm halfway down a much smaller, more intimate hall, running through my mental list of what's still left to cover, when I catch a conversation drifting from an alcove up ahead.

A voice that sounds like Christoph's says, "especially for an American," and my steps slow like I've hit wet cement.

My stomach drops, but before I can decide whether to cough to alert them to my presence or go back to the entrance to the hallway and make more noise on my way in, I hear the silver-haired woman—Anne, I think her name was—trilling, "Oh, I know! She's just delightful. I couldn't be more impressed. And everything's so finely woven together with the theme, down to the last detail."

LILI VALENTE

I bite my bottom lip, face flushing with happiness even as a panicked voice in my head warns to get out of here before I'm caught eavesdropping.

"So creative," the other secretary, Tabitha, agrees. "Though, I must say I'm a bit surprised."

"Oh, stop," Christoph says. "You saw what she did with that wedding. I'm not surprised at all. I knew she'd knock it out of the park."

My head is at serious risk of growing at least one size this day when Tabitha adds, "No, I just meant that most people don't try so hard when they know the job is already in the bag."

My smile freezes, then swiftly begins to fade.

In the bag?

What is she talking about?

As if answering my question, Anne flutters, "Oh yes, quite. That boy we were made to hire for the Summer Sale promotion certainly didn't put himself out, did he? But if your father's well-connected..."

"It doesn't matter," Tabitha finishes. "And remember when Lord Gentry forced Thomas to showcase his daughter's winter collection on the design floor?"

Christoph groans softly. "Don't remind me. Those graffiti gowns with the holes in the pits? Hideous. An embarrassment for everyone involved. But Ms. Darling is different. She was invited to pitch ages before Featherswallow called to bully James into giving her the job."

My eyes go so wide they start to sting.

What?!

I must make a sound—a wheeze, possibly, or my jaw cracking as it drops in shock—because suddenly the voices hush and Christoph swings out of an open door just ahead.

His face shifts quickly from surprise to guilt to a "nothing to see here" grin as he spies me.

"There you are, Emily," he says, his warm smile back in place. "We were just talking about what a wonderful job you're doing. We couldn't be more thrilled with the presentation."

According to what I overheard, it's the truth.

But it isn't the whole truth, and we all know it.

My smile is wobbly at best, and my "Thank you so much" sounds like I'm apologizing for existing. "The receptionist told me to come this way. A man was mopping and..."

I trail off, silently willing the floor to open and swallow me whole.

Or for time to unwind, take me back five minutes, and ensure I get back to the main doors before the mopping starts. Or that I never went to the loo in the first place.

I didn't have to go that badly! And if I hadn't left, I never would have heard...

I wouldn't have to know...

Tabitha and Anne emerge next, both of them looking even guiltier than Christoph. Anne, clearly the mother hen of the group, apparently feels compelled to apologize.

"We shouldn't have been gossiping, sweetheart," she says, patting my shoulder as they herd me back toward the boardroom. "I'm not sure what you heard, but we didn't mean a thing by it."

"Only good things," Christoph assures.

"Exactly," Tabitha agrees. "Lovely things."

"And no one gets anywhere in this city without connections," Anne adds. "There's no shame in using them to open doors. If I had a connection to a Viscount's family, you can bet I'd have much better seats at the opera."

"And I'd have a standing invitation to that polo party they throw every summer," Christoph says. "I can't get enough of short men on horses."

Tabitha titters. "Oh, me, either. But that's probably because I'm not much bigger than a Hobbit myself."

I force myself to laugh along with them, pretending to move on as I resume my place at the table, but inside I'm spiraling as every success of the last week rearranges itself in my mind:

Belinda suddenly being willing to see me again after I turned her baby Jesus into petal confetti?

Oliver's doing.

The meeting slots with those "impossible to get" caterers that miraculously opened like the Red Sea?

Oliver again.

The way Christoph brushed aside the scandal as soon as I explained that Oliver and I were dating?

Well, that was all Oliver's idea, too.

And yes, my PowerPoint is perfect, and they all seem genuinely impressed with my work, but would that have mattered if I didn't have the fifth in the throne pulling strings for me in the background? Would I still be on the verge of landing this job if it were just me, Emily Darling, the American party planner, being judged on my own merit?

Or does this win really belong to my fake boyfriend?

The fake boyfriend who lied to me—again—and made mortifying phone calls behind my back.

Why did he do this?

I thought he believed in me?

But maybe all that's a lie, too...

James returns with an update on his daughter—ready to take the stage like a champ—Christoph dims the lights once more, and I pick up where I left off.

But the magical flow state is gone. I feel outside myself, like I'm watching the woman in the red sweater present from the ceiling along with the ghost of my professional dignity.

I fumble the remote, nearly dropping it, and click too fast through the budget breakdown. And then, there goes slide twenty-eight without its carefully planned transition or my joke about accountants. My voice sounds thinner than it did before, like someone let half the air out of a balloon.

But they don't seem to notice the change in my energy.

Why would they? This isn't a real evaluation. It's theater, and everyone knows their lines but me.

Finally, it's time for slide thirty-seven—my big finish, the final rendering of the transformed space. James actually applauds. *Applauds.*

I just wish I could believe his enthusiasm was real.

"Brilliant," he says, exchanging a pleased glance with Christoph and the others. "Absolutely brilliant. I think I speak for the committee at large when I say we're thrilled to offer you the contract."

The others murmur agreement like a Greek chorus, and Christoph assures his boss that he'll have the contract drawn up immediately. We briefly discuss timeline concerns, and the date I'll need to submit my budget for approval—things that should have me doing an inner victory dance.

But it all feels hollow.

Embarrassing, even.

More handshakes. More congratulations, and Christoph walks me to the door with a final assurance that he'll be in touch before I fly out, so we can finalize the contract in person before I leave.

I wave, keeping my smile firmly fixed until I'm down the hallway.

And all five flights of stairs.

I make it to the lobby, through revolving doors that feel like they're trying to trip me, and around the corner to where a row of black cabs wait like patient beetles.

Then, I run.

My sensible heels click against pavement, probably destroying the leather— definitely destroying my ankles —but I don't care. I need to move, to put distance between me and that boardroom, between me and the truth that's burning a shameful hole in my stomach.

Two blocks. Three, and then a small park appears. I try the gate, breathing a sigh of relief when it opens beneath my hand. I close it, wrapping my coat tighter around me as I find a brown bench hidden behind the hedge.

I sink down on it with a sigh, fighting tears as I pull my cell from my briefcase.

I'm supposed to text Oliver, but I have no idea what to say—

I got the job...but only because you rigged it without telling me

How could you embarrass me like this, Olly? How could you go behind my back that way? When you know how much I hate lies?

Do you really think I'm THAT inadequate?

How can I ever trust you again?

I turn the phone off instead.

And sit.

And shiver.

And do my best not to sniffle.

After a while, a mother pushing a stroller passes by on her way to the gate, shooting me a very British look of concern—worry mixed with a strong desire not to get involved.

But I can't blame her.

I probably look like I'm on the verge of a breakdown. I feel like I am, but I don't know what's making me more upset. Losing the satisfaction of a job well done…

Or losing my trust in Olly.

"Congratulations, darling Darling, you did it," I whisper to the empty park, mimicking his posh, lying voice.

The words taste sour in my mouth.

I close my eyes, and for the first time since I landed in London, I admit the truth…

I don't belong here.

And I never will.

Chapter Eighteen
OLIVER

Edward and I wedge ourselves into the corner table at Café Bohème, the kind of place that thinks mismatched chairs with peeling paint are a design choice rather than evidence of financial distress.

The café is practically drowning in Christmas—fir boughs strangle the light fixtures, the top of the bar is lined with leering nutcrackers, and a mechanical elf in the corner giggles every time a server hustles by on their way to the kitchen.

It's over the top in a way that would normally make even a holiday fan like myself twitch a bit, but this year...

Well, this year, I don't mind it.

But I *do* mind that the table rocks every time Edward or I so much as breathe, threatening to send our flat whites sloshing over their rims. I also mind the sauced Father Christmas murdering "Love is All Around" on the bagpipes outside, each wheeze of the bellows perfectly timed to make conversation impossible.

"For the love of—" I wince as he honks out a note

that could curdle milk. "Is busking whilst pissed a holiday tradition now?"

"Should I go ask to see his license?" Edward asks, steadying his cup as the table lurches again. "Somehow, I doubt he has one. That might scare him up the block."

I sigh, shaking my head. "No. It looks like he's taking a smoke break. We've been granted a reprieve."

"Thank God." Edward rubs his temples. "I'm already battling a headache. I'm getting too old for holiday parties every night."

I grin. "Matilda's office celebration was a banger, was it?"

He snorts. "Hardly. That's why I ended up having that third Scotch. Not all climate scientists are as riveting as my lovely wife."

"I bet," I say, chuckling. "Feel free to skip my soiree tonight if you need a night to recover."

Edward arches a brow. "Really?"

"Really," I say. "I mean, I can promise you better music and food, but architects aren't really known for our riveting small talk, either. And I know you have a lot more on your plate this holiday season, now that you're a husband and head of the family."

My brother's shoulders sag. "Thank you for understanding. I think a night in would do us both some good. Poor Matty's been exhausted by the shopping this year." He arches a wry brow. "Apparently, our family is a bit 'odd' and difficult to buy for."

I feign confusion. "Really? Us? Odd? I thought every family had a cutthroat pudding contest and a collection of horny holiday antiques displayed in the entryway of their ancestral home."

He winces. "God, don't remind me. I thought Matilda's mother's eyeballs were going to pop out of her head the first time she saw the elves with the giant you know whats..." He motions vaguely to his crotch, then up toward the ceiling in an arcing motion.

"Oh, I know," I say, grinning. I can't wait for Emily to see them. I expect she'll laugh her head off.

I hope her meeting is going well. Once she lands the job, the rest of her time in London will be fun, frolic, and festive, smooth sailing.

And when it's time for her to go...

Well, we haven't discussed our options just yet, but if things are still as fantastic between us as they are now, maybe I'll go with her for a month or two. I can work from the New York office, and it's not like London is any fun between Christmas and when the tulips start popping in March anyway.

And by then, maybe Emily and I will have hammered out a long-term game plan to get her living in the U.K. for good.

It's certifiably insane to be plotting plane flights and visa options a week in, but I really, *really* don't like the thought of saying goodbye to this woman.

My woman.

At least, I'm hoping she'll soon officially be mine. I have quite a romantic "be my girlfriend" plan plotted for tonight, involving the office rooftop, an antique ring on a chain, and a cheeky poem to keep things from feeling too over-the-top. I think she'll love it, and I'm nearly certain she'll say yes.

Please, let her say yes...

"Speaking of elves with giant dongs," Edward says, pulling me from my moony "man in love" thoughts, "what fresh hell are you planning to unleash at the White

Elephant this year? Mother made me promise to make sure you didn't take things too far. She's worried the fire department might not make it to the house in time. They've cut staff in the village, you know."

I sigh. "I've told her a hundred times—that wreath bursting into flames was a freak accident. I still have no idea how it happened. It was nowhere near the candles on the table. I can't be blamed."

"She's pretty sure you can," Edward says. "The fire was your fault for bringing a cursed object into our home in the first place. Seriously, a Victorian hair wreath, Olly? Could you be more morbid? And at Christmas, too."

"In my defense, I wasn't aware the hair was harvested *after* the Victorian was deceased," I say, sipping my coffee before muttering behind the rim, "Or that the particular hair in question might have belonged to a woman who murdered people with soap."

Edward makes a soft, but deeply horrified sound.

"Soap is a bizarre way to kill people," I double down. "And we probably did the world a service by bringing that wretched thing into a happy home where such cursed darkness couldn't possibly survive. So, it promptly burst into flames, never to wreak havoc upon the living again."

My brother's lips twitch, but he still looks decidedly unamused. "Right. Well, in any event, I've made Mother a promise, and I intend to keep it. We all know this year is...difficult. For all of us, but especially for her."

Sobering, I nod. "Yes, of course." I study what's left of the foam in my cup, debating for a moment before I add in a cautious voice, "Though, to be frank, it hasn't been as miserable as I thought it would be. At Grandmother's on Saturday, I..." I shrug. "I would have sworn I felt him there with us."

"Me, too," Edward says, meeting my gaze for a quick beat before looking away. "I thought maybe it was just the grief playing tricks, but..."

I shake my head. "I don't think it was. I mean, you know how much he loved a party. Especially a Christmas party."

Edward smiles, sadly, but fondly. "He was a beast this time of year. Remember how he kept stealing Mother's mulled wine last year, even though he wasn't supposed to drink with his medicines?"

"And laughing like an imp," I add, throat tight. "*He* always appreciated my extra effort for White Elephant." I sigh. "I think he'd be especially delighted by this year's offering."

My brother's gaze sharpens on mine. "Which is?"

Fighting a grin, I demure, "I don't want to ruin the surprise. I promise, it isn't cursed or flammable, and was obtained through...mostly legal means."

His brows shoot up. "Mostly legal? What does that mean? Either something is legal or it's not, Olly."

"I would argue that there are actually shades of gray when it comes to—"

"Oliver, I swear, if the constable shows up at our Christmas luncheon, I will be forced to... I, well... I will have no choice but to..." He huffs out a breath. "I don't know what I'll do, but something will have to be done."

Taking pity on my poor, uptight brother, already buckling under the strain of his new title and responsibilities, I decide it's worth breaking tradition to put his mind at ease. "Relax, Eddy. It's just a Westminster speedbump. For mother. I drew her name again this year."

"What?" He blinks, then frowns as he connects the

dots. "You mean one of those hideous concrete sleeping policemen?"

"The same," I say. "I bribed a man in the public works department to liberate one for me. I hid it in the old larder at the country house, wrapped in paper and topped with a big red bow, ready and waiting for the big reveal."

"Oh God, she'll hate it," he says, looking torn between amusement and revulsion. "She's been complaining about how tacky they are for at least a decade."

"Oh, much longer than that," I agree cheerfully. "I remember her grousing about them when we were small. I'm going to offer to put it in the garden for her, right next to that rhododendron she loves so much."

Edward snorts. "She'll send it straight to the attic with all the other things she's too embarrassed to have downstairs. You're going to end up lugging fifty pounds of solid concrete up three flights, mark my words."

"Likely. But it'll be worth it," I say, glancing at the clock on the wall above the giggling elf.

10:12. Huh. Strange that I haven't heard from Emily...

The presentation was scheduled for forty-five minutes, tops. They had someone else coming in to present at ten.

I flip my cell over on the table to see if I missed a notification, but I'm still all caught up.

"Nothing from Em?" Edward asks.

I shake my head. "No, but maybe the meeting ran long. I'm sure she'll text soon."

Edward smirks. "Well, well...looks like Matilda was right."

"Right about what?"

"It's serious this time," Edward says. "You and your American. I said it couldn't be, or you would have said something after you two met in New York, but..." He shrugs. "Looks like I was wrong."

Guilt twists through my gut. I hate lying to Edward. I also hate breaking promises, but surely, Emily will understand. And Edward can be trusted. He'll take our secret to the grave if I ask him to.

"About that..." I exhale. "There might be more to the story." I fill him in on what really happened—the night Emily and I met, the instant scandal, the fallout for her business, and our decision to tell a few white lies in the name of making the scandal seem less scandalous.

By the time I finish, his eyes are as round as our coffee saucers. "Well, hell. That's completely mad, but...it looks like your plan worked."

"Thanks to Ronan and his midnight ride upon a concrete lion," I add.

"I mean, that didn't hurt," Edward agrees with a laugh. "But you were well on your way to putting the scandal to bed on your own. You're a charming couple. And for two people who have known each other such a short time, remarkably natural together."

"It's so easy to be with her," I agree, hating how mundane that sounds. "I know that doesn't seem like a meaningful thing, but it is. For me, at least. I've never felt so comfortable with a woman. Or so...happy." I exhale, frustrated. "I don't know, I'm doing a shit job of explaining it, but it's special. *She's* special."

Edward's lips curve into a slightly patronizing smile. "Aw, my baby brother's in love."

"Oh, shut it," I say, rolling my eyes. "I know it's too soon for that. I'm not completely mad."

"Who says it's too soon?" he counters, surprising me. "I knew I was in love with Matty ten minutes into her speech at that climate conference. I took one look at that gorgeous, nerdy science girl, passionately defending the preservation of habitat for endangered grouse and...that was it. I had to know her. I followed her around the cocktail party afterward like a puppy, wagging my tail until she finally noticed me and let me fetch her another glass of champagne."

"That's a sweet story," I say.

"It's a true story," Edward assures me. "And I've never regretted going all in, right from the start. Connections like that are too precious, and too rare, to risk letting them slip away. But then, I've never been the best at navigating social situations in the typical way. You're definitely the cool one."

I exhale a self-conscious laugh. "I don't know about that. Better at playing at it, maybe, but deep down... Well, I don't think I ever realized what a relief it would be to completely drop the mask with someone."

"Someone who clearly adores you without it," Edward murmurs. "I'm happy for you, Olly. Truly."

I glance up, grateful for this rare, vulnerable conversation. Edward and I have always been close, but we're also British and from a noble family. Sharing our deepest, squishiest feelings isn't something society encourages for men like us. We do share an "I love you" now and then, but it's always a little awkward, and we move on quickly. Like at the luncheon.

He'd never told me how much our night cleaning the

birds meant to him before. His speech was the first I'd heard of it.

Suddenly, I want to tell him that we should talk more often. Really talk. And I can't help but feel like Emily is part of this, too. She really is breaking my heart open in strange and wonderful ways.

Before I can find the words to express my thoughts, however, my phone rings.

I reach for it, a little embarrassed at how disappointed I am that it's not Em.

"Grandmother," I tell Edward as I silence the ring. "I should step outside and take it. You know how she is. If I don't answer, she'll keep calling until I do."

Edward glances around at our mostly empty corner of the café. "I think you're fine to take it here. You won't be disturbing anyone." I hesitate, and he adds with a nod toward the door, "And if you step outside, you might have trouble hearing. Looks like Father Christmas is strapping back into his pipes."

Nodding, I agree, "All right, I'll be quick." Accepting the call, I say, "Good morning, Grandmother. How are you on this lovely Monday?"

"Oh, Oliver, darling, *I'm* lovely on this lovely Monday!" she gushes with a giddiness that's rare for her. At least when she's sober and discussing something other than her dogs and whatever adorable thing they've just done. "And I have wonderful news! Well, not wonderful for dear Gretchen. She's taken a tumble, the poor thing. Princess Fluffy Nugget was mucking about underfoot again, and one thing led to another, and now we're in the A&E."

"Oh, no," I say, frowning. "Is she all right?" A tumble can be a serious thing at Gretchen's age.

"She's fine," Grandmother hurries to assure me. "Just a hairline fracture on her wrist. Her hip is fine, thank God. That's always the major concern for people of a certain age. But this has solidified a decision she's been wrestling with for a while now." Her voice takes on that gushy note again as she adds, "She's decided it's time to rehome Nuggy to a younger family, and she's chosen yours, darling!"

I blink. "What? Grandmother, you know I adore furry things of all—"

"I know you do, darling," she cuts in, steamrolling on before I can explain that adopting a dog might be difficult at the moment. "You've always been fantastic with animals. But if I'm frank, it's Emily who Gretchen truly wants for Nuggy. They had such a powerful connection at the Christmas party. We all agreed it's Fate that brought her into Nugget's life at the perfect time. But since you and Emily are together, you'll get to share in the joy, too. Oh, I'm so happy for you both. Can you put Emily on the line? We should discuss how we move forward from here. There will be papers to sign, of course, and Gretchen would love it if Emily would—"

"Emily's not here, Grandmother," I cut in. "She's still at her pitch meeting for Fletchers. And I know she adored Nuggy, but I can't, in good conscience—"

"Oh, that's right. That's today. How could I have forgotten?" she asks with a laugh, clearly planning on ignoring my protests until she gets her way. As usual. "Well, she should be done soon, and news that she's going to be a dog mum will only add to the causes for celebration."

I roll my eyes at Edward, earning a wince of sympathy from my brother, who can no doubt hear every word. It's not like Suze is making any effort to keep her voice down. "She might not get the job, Grandmother. But if she does, and if an opportunity to discuss the possibility of—"

"Oh, pish, of course she'll get it," she cuts in. "She's already got it. It's in the bag, as they say. The meeting was a formality."

My stomach tightens as dread creeps in, like a cold breeze through poorly insulated boards. "What do you mean?"

"I placed a call, Oliver. As soon as I heard your American was here to pitch for the gala," she says, sounding pleased with herself. "Did you think I wouldn't? You know I've been dear friends with James and his family for years. And what are connections for if not to use them? Emily will be planning that gala and likely several more high-profile events before I'm through."

"Grandmother, you should have spoken to me first," I say, torn between patience for the quirks of the older generation and the part of me that's positive Emily will be furious. "This isn't the way things are done. Not anymore."

She makes a dismissive sound. "Oh, pish, Olly, of course it is. This is exactly how things are done. Don't be naïve. And an American in London needs all the help she can get."

"I have to go," I say, dread swelling larger as I begin to suspect this might have something to do with the fact that Emily hasn't texted. "We'll discuss this later."

"I just wanted to make it easier for you two to be together," Grandmother says. "I thought you'd be pleased."

"This isn't about me," I say. "This is about respecting

Emily's boundaries when it comes to work and our relationship and dog ownership and everything else." Before she can reply, I add firmly, "I'll call you later. Please tell Gretchen I hope she feels better soon, but that I can't confirm anything about the dog at this time."

And then, I do something I've never done before—I hang up on my Grandmother.

"Well, shit," Edward says, the rare curse confirming this is bad.

Perhaps even very bad.

I try to pull in a deeper breath, but my chest is tight, and it suddenly feels like the tinsel-covered walls are closing in.

"Do you think she realized it was rigged somehow?" Edward asks.

I shake my head. "I don't know. But I need to talk to her. In person," I say, scrolling over to my Find Your Folks app. "Is it creepy to track her down with technology?"

"Yes, but desperate times call for desperate measures," Edward says. "And as long as she shared her location with you willingly."

"She did. It was actually her idea, in case we..." I trail off as I find Emily's dot on the screen.

It's moving. Fast. And not toward the café or the flat. She's clearly in a vehicle, headed west.

Straight for the airport.

"She's headed to Heathrow," I say, already out of my chair and reaching for my coat. "I have to go."

"I'll drive you," Edward says, on his feet beside me. "My car's in the garage at the end of the block, by the hotel."

We explode out of the café just as Bagpipe Father Christmas launches into a torturous version of Jingle

Bells. The street is packed. Holiday shoppers swarm the sidewalks, and a massive group on a historic walking tour clogs the corner, making it take twice as long to get down the block.

By the time we reach the garage, panic is setting in fully.

Emily must have found out about Grandmother's interference somehow, in a way that made her feel so thoroughly betrayed that she headed straight for the airport without saying goodbye.

It must have been something truly awful.

And she probably thinks I had something to do with it.

Fuck!

Please don't let her get on a plane, I beg the universe as we finally reach Edward's car and begin the impossibly slow crawl out to the street. *Please, please, please.*

She has to at least give me the chance to explain.

Right?

"She's not going to want to hear a word out of my mouth, is she?" I ask Edward. "She's going to think I'm a liar who can't be trusted."

"No," Edward says. "She's a reasonable woman. Surely, she'll—"

"I lied to her the night we met," I cut in, needing to confess my sins. Needing Edward to know just how dire this could be. "I lied about who I was, and she was so angry, she tried to end it immediately. Even though we'd just had a fantastic night and even more fantastic...you know."

Edward sobers, then grunts, offering no further comfort as he cuts through side streets, moving fast toward the motorway.

But his silence is a response of its own.

It means, if I want a shot in hell of getting through to Emily, I'll have to pull out all the stops.

Which gives me an idea...

A wild, mortifying, but possibly irresistibly romantic idea.

I glance at my brother, who's wearing an only moderately festive holiday jumper. It's red-and-white striped, with a tiny holly leaf embroidered on the chest above his heart, but it will have to do.

I strip off my suit coat, tossing it into the back as I reach for the top button on my shirt. "I'm going to need your sweater, Eddy. As soon as we pull up, just strip it off and toss it over, all right?"

He casts a startled look my way before turning his attention back to the road. "Do I want to know what you have planned? Or will I want plausible deniability?"

"Definitely the latter," I say. "I'm going to do something mad, but...it's for love, so it's forgivable, right?"

"Love makes most things forgivable," he agrees. "And I think she'll forgive you, Olly. Once you explain. I really do."

I hope he's right, but just in case...

Well, I intend to put all my cards on the table and see if love really *is* all around.

Or if I'll be spending the rest of my Happy Christmas miserable and alone.

Chapter Nineteen

EMILY

I'm in hell.

The Brit Air queue at Heathrow, two days before Christmas, is a special circle of travel hell. And bizarrely, all of the people suffering in the line ahead of me *chose* to enter it of their own free will.

I would rather spend the holidays alone in a hole than travel this close to the big day.

But I can't spend them in London, so...here I am. In hell, inching forward at a snail's pace and praying the woman at the counter can be convinced to sell me a ticket this close to takeoff. It's too late to buy one online, but still three hours before the plane is set to board, and I don't have any luggage to check.

I don't have any luggage at all.

It's all either lost or abandoned.

I couldn't bring myself to go back to Oliver's flat to fetch the rest of my things. I couldn't risk seeing him again, being forced to confront him and the evidence of my own stupidity.

I'm not ready to face that yet.

The depth of my naïveté is too painful.

I can't believe I trusted that he truly thought I was "brilliant." Can't believe I assumed he knew me well enough to realize his interference would be offensive, let alone well enough to have real feelings. I can't believe I thought he was in love with me, and I really can't believe I *still* think *I'm* in love with *him*.

Or that the end of a fake, week-long relationship can possibly hurt this much...

The pain gnaws away in my chest, stealing all the holiday joy, leaving me feeling truly wretched and alone.

I have to get home. As quickly as possible.

Home, where I can lock the door and hide under the covers and cry the pain away in peace without any paparazzi around to document my shame.

Hold it together, Darling. Just ten more hours, give or take, and you can crumble in private, as God intended.

As the line inches forward again, I clutch my coat and briefcase for strength, thanking the benevolent forces of the universe that I always carry my passport on my person. The guidebooks tell you not to, but I find I'm asked for my passport far more often than one might assume—at hotels, museums, the pharmacy after I forgot my birth control prescription the last time I was here.

The world is an increasingly distrustful, passport-checking, outsider-hating place.

Maybe that's why Oliver did what he did, because he knew an outsider wouldn't get anywhere in London without help. Maybe it wasn't because he secretly thinks I'm a loser.

But even if that's the case, it doesn't matter. A lie is a lie, and I'm a list maker, a fact checker, a source verifier, not a liar. I can't build a life with someone who lies and manipulates, even if they do it with good intentions.

No.

This is it.

The end.

And I'll be flying home a far sadder woman, which is especially tragic considering I didn't even *realize* how sad I was before. It wasn't until Olly reminded me how incredible it feels to dive headfirst into the joy of the holidays, into the joy of falling in love, that I realized I've been cut off from that deep well of happiness for a long time.

I've been stressed out and on the edge of burnout for far too long. I was living a gray, faded life until Olly reminded me how gorgeous things are in color.

And now...

Now, it's back to a plate of gray with extra sad sauce.

"Next!" the agent calls. The line creeps forward a few feet, but the couple in front of me is too busy arguing to notice.

"We should have taken the earlier train," the man hisses, American accent sharp with frustration.

"I'm not the one who takes forever to pack," his wife shoots back. "You should have done it last night, like I told you."

He rolls his eyes as he mutters, "Because you're always right. Jill is perfect and *always* right."

"I am right," she says, hurt creeping into her voice. "At least about things like this. That's why you ask me to plan our trips and keep us on schedule. But if you don't think I do a good job of it anymore, then we can—"

"You did a great job," he cuts in with a sigh. "Sorry. I'm just stressed about missing the flight. And mad at myself for not listening to you last night."

"It's okay," she says. "I'm grumpy this morning, too. I'm not ready to go back."

"Me, either." He pulls her into a hug, oblivious to the dozens of eyeballs boring into his back, willing them to grab their suitcases and move along. "But we'll come back soon. And next time, we'll make it to that castle you wanted to see on the west coast. I promise."

My throat tightens.

I want someone to hug me and promise to take me to a castle on the west coast.

Someone like Olly, who never rolls his eyes at me or treats me with disdain, even for a second.

No, he just lies to you and treats you like a loser who can't succeed without her sexy British boyfriend pulling strings for her in the background.

"Well, isn't that better than being a jerk?" I mutter beneath my breath.

"Next, please," the agent calls again.

Jill, who is always right, and her moderately dickish husband finally move up.

So do I, but I'm no longer certain I want to be in this line. I am, for better or worse, completely straight, and most straight men are a pain—as Moderately Dickish has so helpfully reminded me.

Even the ones who don't act like cranky, petulant children in line at the airport aren't usually anything to get excited about. My best experiences with men have been steady, mostly fun friendships that petered out when my partner cheated or dropped the emotional ball. My worst have involved brushes with staggering emotional immaturity, insufferable entitlement, or deep-seated resentment of women.

A lot of straight men seem to loathe women, to feel

threatened by us despite the fact that women are the ones who've spent thousands of years being subjugated, attacked, or un-alived by men.

Finding a decent partner is difficult.

Finding one who gives you pep talks, makes you laugh, and isn't weird, selfish, or dysfunctional in bed is practically unheard of. Add in the rich, handsome, and highly successful parts, and Oliver is a unicorn.

Hell, he's something even more rare and magical than a unicorn.

He's a unicorn holding a four-leaf clover during a solar eclipse, under a sky of dazzling northern lights, during a once-in-a-lifetime planetary alignment.

And he might be my best and only shot at a once-in-a-lifetime love.

But the lies! The uptight, stressed-out voice in my head demands.

But is she stressed out because the lying is really a dealbreaker or because falling in love this fast is a threat to everything the rational, list-making side of my personality holds dear?

I'm about to do what must be done to get to the bottom of this—namely, get out of line, find a quiet place to sit, and make a very detailed list—when a sharp bark of laughter echoes through the air.

It's followed by another, higher-pitched giggle, and behind me, an excited murmur ripples through the crowd.

Probably another celebrity sighting. London airports are apparently full of them. There were two soccer players and a pop star here when I first arrived last week. I had plenty of time to witness the fuss everyone was making over them while filing the report on my luggage.

The murmuring gets louder.

More laughter.

Then two security guards rush past our line, radios crackling.

I turn, growing concerned, just as a Cockney accent rises above the crowd. "Aw, let him be, copper! Can't you see the bloke's in love?"

"Good Lord," a woman gasps. "Is he in his smalls?"

Pushing up on tiptoe, I look where everyone else is looking, my heart lurching when I see the source of all the uproar.

It's Oliver.

Jogging through the terminal in a Christmas sweater and...nothing else.

I mean, he's wearing his boxer briefs, but no shoes, no coat, no suit pants or jacket. He's basically half naked in the airport, holding what looks like a large piece of a cardboard box, while confused looking security guards trail behind him.

Every cell phone in a hundred-meter radius is instantly out and aimed his way, documenting what appears to be the complete mental breakdown of the fifth in line to the throne, hot on the heels of the Lion King breakdown of the first.

But I know he isn't having a breakdown.

I instantly understand what this is, and the sweet, crazy bravery of it brings tears to my eyes.

Someone at Heathrow central command must get it, too. Because a split second later, the opening notes of "Ain't No Mountain High Enough" crackle through the loudspeakers, and a happy sob bursts from my throat. It's just like in Bridget Jones, when she runs through the snow in nothing but her knickers and a camisole to prove her love to Darcy.

And now...

Now, Oliver Featherswallow, my solar eclipse unicorn, is doing the same for me.

And it's terrifying. And wonderful. And terrifying, and I'm pretty sure my extremities are going numb as I stumble forward, ducking under the ribbon of fabric keeping our line contained.

Almost instantly, Oliver spots me, his eyes flashing with relief as he changes direction, aiming himself my way.

I try to aim myself his way, too, only to find my legs petrified by fear.

What if I screw this up? What if I crash and burn in front of God and the people of London and the press who are always lurking nearby? Again?

Or, even worse, what if big romantic gestures aren't enough to make this work? What if I end up getting on that plane this afternoon and flying away? What if this is the last time I'll ever see Olly in person?

The thought is so horrible, it turns my stomach.

As I stand there, fighting the urge to be sick, Oliver closes the last of the distance between us without hesitation, clearly ready to fight for our future.

And if he can put it all on the line, so can I.

"I didn't have time to write anything down," he says, slightly breathless from his dash through the terminal. He lifts his piece of cardboard. "I barely had time to grab this, but if I'd had time to write a deck of posters to hold up outside your door, this is what they would say."

I blink faster, my hand flying to cover my lips as I realize what this is.

Dear God, it's a Love Actually and Bridget Jones *hybrid* romantic gesture, and my heart will officially never be the same.

Never.

Not even if I live to be a hundred and ten.

"Emily Darling, I'm not sure why you're leaving, but you shouldn't," he begins, his blue-gray eyes pleading his case. "You should stay because I know we can work through anything, as long as we put our heads together. And you should stay, because...I adore you. Have adored you from the moment you crashed through that nativity play and into my life."

I suck in a breath, fighting tears.

"I love how quick you were to call me out for being a shite," he continues. "And how equally quick you were to forgive. I loved dancing with you in that pub and kissing you in the snow, and every second I've been lucky enough to spend with you since."

The crowd presses closer.

Security gives up trying to intervene.

"Ain't no Mountain" swells higher, lifting us all up on its wings...

"I love your passion for lists and your passion for passion and the way you only laugh at my jokes when they're actually funny." His voice breaks a little as he continues, "I love your smile and your kindness and your bravery in the face of the British tabloids, my grandmother, and small boys, who are alarmingly fast on skates."

I let out a liquid laugh as a tear slips down my cheek.

Oliver's eyes fill with the same hope and fear swirling inside me as he adds, "I just love you, Em. I know the timing is all off, and you'll probably think I'm crazy, but I do. I love you." He shrugs, attempting to play it cool, "And if you think about it, Bridget and Darcy didn't spend that much time together before they started throwing the L word around, and they worked out just fine."

"No, they didn't," a woman calls out from somewhere in the crowd. "In one of the later movies, Darcy actually—"

She's instantly hushed by other members of the crowd, several of whom hiss something about spoilers.

I would normally be right there with them.

It is a fact, universally acknowledged, that women who enjoy making lists as much as I do, do *not* like spoilers.

But I do like this man.

I love him, in fact, and it's high time I showed him I'm half as brave as he is. So, I reach into my briefcase and pull out my emergency Sharpie, the fat one I can use to write big enough to be seen at the back of a boardroom, if necessary.

Then, I reach out, taking the cardboard from Oliver's slightly trembling hand.

I love that he's trembling, and I love that every cell in my body knows he's right—we *can* get through this, together—and I love that for once in my life there's no doubt about what I should do next.

I simply scrawl what's in my heart on the cardboard and turn it, holding it up for everyone to see—**I Love You, Too. Love IS all around.**

The crowd goes wild.

The line applauds, the guards applaud, the lover in charge of the sound system shouts, "Congratulations," through the speakers before starting our victory song all over again. People are hugging and kissing and crying, and for once it feels like there's nothing ugly left in the world.

There's just this amazing man in his underwear, who pulls me closer, kissing me with devastating sweetness as he murmurs, "Thank God."

A few minutes later, after Edward appears with pants for Oliver, congratulations for both of us, and an offer to drive us home, we head for the exit, arm-in-arm.

Oliver explains what happened with his grandmother, and I instantly feel like a complete asshole.

"No, I'm the worst," I insist when Oliver refuses to accept my apology. "I mean, yes, they said 'Featherswallow' not Lady Plimpton, but—"

"Exactly," he cuts in. "I don't know why people always lump Grandmother in with my father's side of the family. It is literally impossible for her to have birthed him. She was only eleven years old when he was born, to my paternal grandmother. Who has been dead for quite some time."

"Still," I insist. "I should have known you would never do something like that."

"How?" he asks, making me blink in surprise. "Those people said the wrong name, Em. Naturally, you were upset and confused. And I mean, yes, we've come a long way in a short amount of time, but we're still strangers in a lot of ways."

"You don't feel like a stranger," I murmur, huddling closer to him in the backseat as Edward pretends that he can't hear us.

"You don't either," he assures me softly. "I'm just saying that I understand why you felt betrayed. And I can't promise we won't have misunderstandings in the future. But from now on, just...talk to me before you head for the airport?"

I nod fast. "Yes. I promise. I should have talked to you this time, I was just scared." I lean in, bringing my lips closer to his. "But I'm not scared anymore."

"I soothed your fears by dashing through the airport in my underwear?"

I grin. "You did. You're a genius romantic of the highest order."

"Only with you, darling Darling," he murmurs. "Only with you."

Then, he kisses me, and it's the best make-up kiss I've ever had.

I'm so happy, not even the terrible picture of me mid-sob posted by the first gossip site to report the story can bring me down.

And later that night, when Oliver pulls me aside at the holiday party for a panty-melting "girlfriend proposal" on the roof, with all the dazzling lights of London sparkling around us, I don't hesitate to say "yes."

I say "hell, yes," kiss him senseless, and spend the rest of the night dancing with the man of my dreams.

We have the best Christmas Eve dinner at his brother's and the best Christmas Day luncheon with the Feather-swallow clan. His grandmother apologizes profusely for her overreach—all while assuring *me* that James assured *her* that I was by far the best planner for the job and shouldn't hesitate to sign the contract.

Then, Oliver carries the hideous speedbump he bought his mother to the attic, and we head home to watch movies in our pajamas on the most magical night of the year.

And when Oliver gets me *out* of my pajamas, that's as magical as ever, too.

It's the best Christmas of my life, followed by the best New Year's, followed by a madcap spring in which Oliver moves to New York for a few months, and then Maya and I both sell everything, pull up stakes, and move to London.

We do!

We move to London, where we learn to work and play in equally reasonable amounts.

I move in with Oliver, we adopt Princess Fluffy Nugget, the sweetest, best girl in the whole world, and only end up embarrassed in the tabloids a handful of times before Oliver proposes.

By the time he gets down on one knee on a warm June night, in a field full of wildflowers by the sea, with his mother's ring and his family's enthusiastic blessing, there's no doubt in my mind that this is where I belong.

Where I will always belong, with my fake British boyfriend turned real British Husband and a hot mess happily ever after of our very own.

Epilogue

Princess Fluffy Nugget

A warm night in June...

It all began at Christmas, in my fourth year of being the most bullied Princess the world has ever known...

I was at Lady Plimpton's holiday pudding party, putting on a brave face while being relentlessly harassed by other dogs—a motley lot of hooligans and lugs, with more fur than capacity for feeling, and a cruel obsession with shoving smaller creatures into drifts and kicking yellow snow into their faces—when an angel walked into my life.

It was Emily, and I loved her instantly.

Truly, the devotion was immediate and profound.

Sometimes, you meet someone and just know your life—and heart—will never be the same. I knew right away with Em.

And here are four things *you* should know about my new mum:

Why my Mum is the Best Mum (and I love her SOOOOO much)

1. She is unfailingly kind, deeply loyal, and fantastically funny (And occasionally a tiny bit anxious, just like me.)

2. She makes the very best chicken and rice with vegetables and never makes me feel guilty for having a fussy tummy that requires homemade dog food. (Preferably served in the bone china or the good crystal my grand mum, Gretchen, brings for me when she visits us at our apartment.)

3. She throws fantastic parties.

4. Her bosom is the best bosom. Second to none.

My only complaint about Mum's bosom, in fact, is that Dad is so often "all up in it" as Emily's friends from America would say.

Which is ridiculous, really! He's much too large to fit neatly between her breasts for a cuddle, the way I do.

Nevertheless, he insists on trying.

Again and again.

Like now, for instance...

The sun is setting on a gorgeous lawn party, the

Midsummer bonfire is lit, and it's the perfect time to pull up a chair—and a corgi—and have an after-dinner snuggle in front of the fire.

And perhaps a few roasted marshmallows, which I do very much enjoy…

But no, Dad still has Mum clasped tight in his arms, her bosom pressed tight to his chest as they sway in the field of wildflowers at the edge of the Swallow House grounds. There's not even any music! But still, they're dancing.

And gazing into each other's eyes, the way they do before they disappear into their bedroom and close the door.

I half expect them to make a dash for Swallow House the way they did during the last lawn party, leaving me to fend for myself at the bonfire until they finally return, rumpled and flushed.

Instead, Dad suddenly drops down on one knee, Mum's hands fly to cover her mouth, and everyone at the party begins to gasp and murmur.

Vivian, Dad's mum, whispers, "Oh, look! How romantic, I'm so pleased," and Suze, Dad's grandmother, replies, "Took him long enough. He should have locked that fantastic girl down in January, if you ask me."

Then Auntie Izzie—who just broke off her engagement with a terrible rat-faced man Mum refers to as "That Nasty Shit Weasel," and is currently emotionally fragile—starts to sniffle as she agrees, "They're so perfect together. I know they'll always be so happy."

Maya, Mum's best friend, pulls Izzie in for a hug, murmuring, "They will, and so will you, sweetheart. There are great things ahead for you, I just know it."

Then, Mum nods "yes," and Dad slides a ring on her finger, while everyone at the party cheers and cheers.

And then, they're hugging again, and twirling and laughing, and I have a feeling I'm shut out of Mum's bosom for the rest of the night.

But that's all right, I decide, wagging my tail in fierce congratulations as Mum and Dad rejoin the party on the lawn. Because my favorite humans are getting married! And soon we'll be a proper family, the kind that stays together forever and ever.

And they will never get another dog.

Only a cat, maybe, because we all really like cats.

Especially Thomas, the barn cat who lives in the Swallow House garden, and helpfully licks my head clean after Uncle Peter spills champagne on me during the toast to Mum and Dad's engagement.

Thomas is a lovely friend, a fact he proves by giving Suze's dog, Jasper, a slap on the nose when he tries to steal the marshmallow treat Mum gives me.

Jasper has a very hard time respecting boundaries when food is involved, but he's working at it. Just like Jezebel, his sister, is working on not chasing the seagulls, and I'm working on sharing Mum's bosom with more generosity of spirit.

I'm making progress, I really am, but when Emily pulls me in for a cuddle later, wrapping my ears in a scarf to protect them from the big bangs as the fireworks explode over the sea, I do not complain. I just snuggle into her bosom and count my blessings.

Of which there are many.

🎄 *Did you love **All I Want for Christmas Is a Fake British Boyfriend**? Yay!* 🎄

Now imagine your favorite reality show had a baby with a steamy Hallmark holiday movie—then ran away to New York to find true love...

Welcome to New York, festive fools!
The Holiday Games is out now and free in Kindle Unlimited!

Grab it now if you love:
✅ Small-town girls with existential angst & big-city dreams
✅ Broody heroes & off-limits workplace romance
✅ Diabolical cats
✅ New York City at the most magical time of the year!

Get it now or keep reading for a sneak peek...

Sneak Peek

Enjoy this sneak peek of
THE HOLIDAY GAMES
by Lili Valente
Out now and Free in Kindle Unlimited!

CHAPTER ONE

Candace "Candy" Caroline Cane

A woman living the small town
holiday lover's dream in rural Vermont,
complete with hot cocoa, sleigh rides,
and...existential angst.

When you're born and raised in a town named Reindeer Corners, several things are taken for granted...

One: You will LOVE holidays and await the annual Tinsel Time festival with a rabid fervor usually reserved for grandparents awaiting the birth of their first grandchild. (Or a transplant candidate awaiting an organ donor...)

Two: You will develop an addiction to the peppermint cocoa from the country store and crave it fortnightly. (But that's fine. Everyone in town is addicted, and the store never runs out, not even in the endless twilight of midsummer.)

Three: You will keep the spirit of Christmas all year long and greet every stranger you meet with a cheery smile and a bright, "Welcome to Reindeer Corners, where it's *always* the most magical time of the year!"

This is especially true if you work in the tourist industry, which most of us do. There aren't a lot of job options in rural Vermont. You're either a farmer, a remote worker, a lumberjack, or one of the many locals catering to the leaf peepers and powder seekers. Two of my three best friends from high school are ski instructors and Kayla, my bestie and I, are innkeepers. Between the two of us, we keep The Reindeer Corners Inn running like a well-oiled, relentlessly festive machine.

And I'm proud of that.

I truly am.

I'm thankful for a fast-paced job that pays well-above minimum wage, my sweet, Christmas-tree-farming boyfriend, my friends, and my loving family.

Everything would be perfect...if it weren't for the existential dread and thoughts of impending doom.

Even as I'm showing Mr. and Mrs. Templeton a map of the county, circling various points of interest perfect for a crisp December day, inside, I'm spiraling.

My lips say, "Fat Horse Farm has an incredible maple latte and a museum where you can see how the syrup is made," but my thoughts whisper, *This is it. The rest of your life. Giving tourists directions to sugar shacks and snowshoeing trails. Is that okay with you? Does that feel like your purpose? Is it really enough?*

I smile and add, "Then you can take the loop through Cavender's Hollow on your way back to the inn for some amazing mountain views."

Meanwhile my soul mutters, *You could be dead in twenty years. Aunt Candace only made it to fifty-five. Uncle Carl was barely fifty. Heart disease runs in the family. Your one wild and precious life could be halfway over, and what do you have to show for it aside from two "employee of the year" plaques and an obscene number of Christmas sweaters?*

I silently remind the voice about my friends, especially Kayla, who is more like my sister, and always has my back. I also have a kick-ass grandmother, who makes me turkey and stuffing sandwiches year-round, and amazing parents. Mom and Dad have never left our small town for more than a long weekend, but when I moved to New York City to get my degree in hotel management, they supported me wholeheartedly.

Even if they were too scared of muggers, subways, and big city rat infestations to come visit...

The inner Voice of Doom makes a smug *harumphing* noise. *I notice Bobby Christmas Williams didn't make that list. Add being stuck in a lukewarm relationship to the warning signs that your life is going nowhere.*

I frown and counter, *I was getting around to Chris. Chris is a sweet man with a huge heart. I'm lucky to have someone like him in my life.*

The Doom Voice snorts. *Are we still pretending you aren't dying for a man to take you against a wall? Preferably with some hair pulling and dirty talk?*

My jaw drops. *Inappropriate. Very inappropriate. We're at work!*

Work shmerk. The voice sighs. *But sure, any excuse to keep reality at bay. Keep the denial going, and maybe you'll make it down the aisle before you jump off a cliff.*

I clench my jaw. *I'm not jumping off a cliff. And I'm not talking to you anymore. Go away, I'm busy.*

"Dear? Candy?" Mrs. Templeton says, something in her voice making me suspect this isn't the first time she's said my name.

Realizing I've been caught wrestling with the void—again—I laugh and adjust the big red bow holding my ponytail in place. "Sorry. I was up late last night helping my mother make fudge for the festival. Still a little spacy this morning. Can I answer any more questions for you? Or fetch a hot cocoa and cookie basket from the kitchen for you to take with you on your adventure?"

Mrs. Templeton smiles, her fears for my sanity apparently allayed. "Oh no, that's all right. We've already had pancakes *and* pie this morning!"

"Gotta watch the waistline," Mr. Templeton adds with a laugh, patting the ample belly straining the front of his Santa sweater. "At least a little bit."

"And we're saving up calories for the festival," Mrs. Templeton adds, clapping her hands. "We can't wait for it to start. It's one of our favorite events of the entire year."

"Oh, me, too. So much fun," I say automatically as the Templetons wave goodbye and head out to their car, though I'm honestly not sure how I feel about the festival anymore.

Back when I was a kid running wild through the booths, having snowball fights with my friends while my parents sold fudge, I adored Tinsel Time. I still love how much revenue the festival brings to town—it's our primary fundraiser for both the library and road repair—but in the past few years, my opinion of the cutesy small-town shtick has soured.

We present a merry, magical front, but behind the scenes, Reindeer Corners suffers from the same ills as any other aging mountain town.

Our Select Board is full of grouchy old people who refuse to approve permits to build affordable housing for young people and families, insisting on "preserving the historic nature" of the town, while housing grows so scarce and prices so inflated that most people born and raised here can't afford to stay unless they move in with their parents.

The housing crisis is further exacerbated by millionaires and investors snatching up smaller homes for cash and turning them into vacation rentals. Or, even worse, setting up a fake Christmas tree in the home's living room and leaving it up year-round, because they only visit their "holiday place" from December Twenty-Second to January Third. The rest of the year, the homes sit empty, taunting those of us shacking up in studio apartments above our grandmother's garage with visions of what could have been, if we'd been born somewhere else, where everything wasn't so damned cute and tourist friendly.

"Your inner Grinch is showing again," Kayla whispers inches from my ear, making me flinch and my heart leap into my throat.

"Peppermint sticks," I curse, laughing as I turn to face her. "You scared me."

She grins, her green eyes flashing as bright as the sequins on her blinged-out Frosty the Snowman earrings. "You didn't look scared. You looked grouchy."

I huff and flap my hand. "I'm not grouchy. I'm having a fantastic day spreading holiday cheer during the most magical time of the year."

"Right." Kayla crosses her arms over her ample chest and lifts her freckled nose. With her blond hair and permanently rosy cheeks, she looks like a young Mrs. Claus, even when she's not wearing the inn's signature red-and-white striped sweater and matching bow.

I have to work harder to look appropriately festive. I use blush to brighten my pale cheeks and add caramel highlights to my black-like-my-soul hair to brighten it up.

At least, I usually do.

This year, I dyed it all black for my Lydia Deetz, Beetlejuice-inspired Halloween costume and never got around to highlighting it again. That eighty dollars was better spent on a new space heater. My tiny apartment above Gran's garage gets chilly in the winter and my old heater fizzled out last April.

Yes, it's still freezing cold in Reindeer Corners in April. I didn't think much of that when I was a child and didn't know any better. But after living in New York City for four years and experiencing how lovely a milder spring can be, I lose my sense of humor about the cold by the end of March.

"Well, you don't look like you're feeling the magic," Kayla doubles down. "You look like a cat peed in your cocoa."

"Ew," I say, wrinkling my nose. "I take that to mean the litter box training isn't going so well?"

She sighs. "Smithers is still peeing in my snow boots. Every night. I had to wear my tennis shoes out to the car this morning and almost killed myself on the ice."

Clucking my tongue, I mutter, "I've already shared my solution."

She rolls her eyes. "I can't fill my old snow boots with litter and buy new snow boots. Boots aren't intended to be litter boxes." She props her hands on her hips with a huff. "And knowing Smithers, he'd decide he liked peeing in *both* pairs, and I'd be back where I started. He's a menace."

"But an adorable one," I add.

"So adorable," she coos, pulling out her phone. "Look at the shot I took of him last night by the fire in his reindeer antlers! Isn't he the most precious thing? I'm going to print this one out and hang it on the community bulletin board out front. Our guests will love it!"

As I make appropriately girly noises over the cuteness that is Smithers, Voice of Doom pipes up again, insisting, *You will never love anything as much as Kayla loves this cat. Your heart is turning into a lump of coal. By the time you're thirty-five, you'll be completely dead inside.*

"I will not," I hiss. "Now chill out, you're exhausting."

I don't realize I've spoken aloud until Kayla glances sharply my way, her brow furrowing. "What?"

"N-nothing," I stammer, my heart racing. Am I really losing it this time? Are the inside voices about to become *outside* voices?! Maybe I should have invested in therapy instead of that space heater... "I didn't sleep well last night. Sorry."

"Don't be sorry. I just want to be sure you're okay, C.C. You haven't been yourself this season."

I wasn't myself last season either, but I guess I did a better job of hiding it.

Forcing a smile and a festive wave for the Grangers as

they herd their family of six through the lobby toward the restaurant for a late breakfast, I whisper, "I'm okay. I promise. I'll pull it together. I won't let you down."

Kayla's gaze softens. "Honey, I know you wouldn't mean to, but I've caught you with resting Grinch face three times this week."

"Three times in an entire week isn't that bad."

"It's Wednesday," she says bluntly, making my shoulders slump. She smiles and pats my back. "But it's okay. I have a plan to help you get your Christmas groove back. I called the conference organizers, and they said it was no problem to change the name on the registration."

I straighten as my jaw drops. "What?"

"And I booked a business class train ticket for you and called The Empire to change the name on the hotel reservation, too," Kayla adds, looking increasingly pleased with herself. "Everything's all set for you to take my place. All you have to do is pack your bags and find someone to drop you off at the train station tomorrow. I would offer, but I'll be covering your shifts."

I shake my head. "No, Kayla. I can't. You've been looking forward to this trip all year. You were going to see the tree at Rockefeller Center and the Rockette holiday spectacular and ice skate in Central Park."

She shrugs. "I'm still going to do those things. I'll just do them on New Year's Eve instead. That way Harry can come with me, and I won't have to worry about work stuff. It'll be all holiday fun and romantic mistletoe kisses with my boyfriend." She sighs and her giddy grin stretches wider. "And if I'm lucky, he'll take one of the many hints I've been dropping since last Christmas, propose to me by that giant tree, and make all my romantic dreams come true."

Kayla is a Reindeer Corners true believer. Even after a lifetime of having holiday magic forced down her throat, she still loves this time of year above all others and can't imagine a better place to say "yes, I'll be your forever girl," than under a giant Christmas tree.

She's also an incredible friend.

"Thank you," I say, wrapping an arm around her waist and hugging her to my side. "You're the best."

"I know," she says, grinning as she returns the squeeze. "But honestly, I'm happy I won't have to miss the Tinsel Time festival. I thought I wouldn't mind, but the more I thought about leaving tomorrow, the sadder I got. I've never missed a festival, and I don't want to start now." She releases me with a final hug and reaches for the mouse to awaken our ancient desktop computer. "Besides, you'll do way better at a big hotel conference. I get overwhelmed by crowds." She glances up at the large clock above our equally massive lobby tree. "Speaking of crowds, the Baxter family reunion called for an early check-in and catered lunch. Could you run check and make sure the kitchen was able to get the banquet room set up for them?"

"On it." I move out from behind the desk but pause on the other side to tap a finger on the polished wood in front of my bestie. When she looks up from the screen, I say, "Thank you again, babes. I think a trip to the city will be the perfect thing to help me reset and get excited about the rest of the winter season."

"Me, too," she agrees with a smile. "And who knows? Maybe you'll learn some fabulous new innkeeper tricks we can incorporate into the business *and* the true meaning of Christmas while you're at it."

I laugh, too excited about my upcoming escape to my

SNEAK PEEK

favorite city to listen to the Voice of Doom as it softly assures me that some people—people like me—never learn the true meaning of Christmas.

That isn't true! I just need a break from all the pressure to perform holiday magic for our guests, a chance to simply experience the good vibes this time of year brings without forcing it. After a few days wandering the city holiday markets and food stalls in between conference lectures, I'll be feeling festive and fabulous. I'll be back to my old self, the woman who couldn't wait to graduate from hotel management school and return home to her sweet, small town.

I believe that. I truly do.

I go about the rest of my day, putting out fires at work and hurrying home to pack for the trip with no clue that my entire life is about to change.

Or that the Voice of Doom isn't finished with me yet.

Not even close.

THE HOLIDAY GAMES
is out now!

About the Author

Author of over sixty novels, *USA Today* Bestseller **Lili Valente** writes everything from steamy suspense to laugh-out-loud romantic comedies. A die-hard romantic, she can't resist a story where love wins big. Because love should always win. She lives in the world with her hopes, dreams, and an imaginary cat named Hambone.

She also writes paranormal romance as Bella Jacobs, dark romance as Everly Stone, and young adult books as Logan Riley.

Find Lili at...
www.lilivalente.com

Also by Lili Valente

Find all Lili's books, as well as author store exclusive releases at www.lilivalente.com

That Steamy Hockey Romance

The Fake Husband Play

The No-Touch Roommate Rule

The Penalty Box Affair

The McGuire Brothers

Boss Without Benefits

Not Today Bossman

Boss Me Around

When It Pours (novella)

Kind of a Sexy Jerk

When it Shines (novella)

Kind of a Hot Mess

Kind of a Dirty Talker

Kind of a Bad Idea

When it Sizzles (novella)

Forbidden Billionaires

Take Me, I'm Yours

Make Me Yours

Pretending I'm Yours

Baby I'm Yours

The Virgin Playbook

Scored

Screwed

Seduced

Sparked

Scooped

Hot Royal Romance

The Playboy Prince

The Grumpy Prince

The Bossy Prince

Laugh-out-Loud Rocker Rom Coms

The Bangover

Bang Theory

Banging The Enemy

The Rock Star's Baby Bargain

Holidays with Bang-ifits

The Bliss River Small Town Series

Falling for the Fling

Falling for the Ex

Falling for the Bad Boy

The Love Bug

Hometown Heat Firefighters

All Fired Up

Catching Fire
Playing with Fire
A Little Less Conversation

The Hunter Brothers

The Baby Maker
The Troublemaker
The Heartbreaker
The Panty Melter

Bad Motherpuckers Series

Hot as Puck
Sexy Motherpucker
Puck-Aholic
Puck me Baby
Pucked Up Love
Puck Buddies
Puck Sweat Love
Pucking the Grump

Fake Dating in the City

Fake Dating the Boss
How to Lose a Fake Boyfriend
Fake Dating on Thin Ice
Fake Dating the Ex

The Lonesome Point Cowboy Series

Leather and Lace
Saddles and Sin

Diamonds and Dust
12 Dates of Christmas
Glitter and Grit
Sunny with a Chance of True Love
Chaps and Chance
Ropes and Revenge
8 Second Angel

The Good Love Series

(co-written with Lauren Blakely)
The V Card
Good with His Hands
Good to be Bad

Made in the USA
Coppell, TX
20 November 2025